PENGUIN BOOKS

PIECE OF CAKE

Swati Kaushal is an MBA from IIM Calcutta, and has worked with Nestlé India Limited and Nokia Mobile Phones, India. She lives with her family in Minneapolis, USA. Besides her best-selling debut novel *Piece of Cake* she has also written *A Girl Like Me* (published by Penguin Books India).

PRAISE FOR *PIECE OF CAKE*

'There's much to be enjoyed in this breezy, devil-may-care first novel' —*Tehelka*

'It brings a whiff of fresh air into a literary landscape that was fast becoming jaded, academic and predictable...the narrative whizzes by, sweeping the reader along with its irrepressible *joie de vivre*'—*Tribune*

An interesting plot...enriched by a host of very real characters, and by the author's gift for humour, reflected in sparkling conversation and one-liners loaded with attitude'—*Deccan Herald*

'Truly a new age read...a naughty and delightful romantic comedy powered by the protagonist's mischievous and complex character' —*Sahara Times*

piece of cake

swati kaushal

PENGUIN BOOKS

PENGUIN BOOKS
Published by the Penguin Group
Penguin Books India Pvt. Ltd, 11 Community Centre, Panchsheel Park, New Delhi 110017, India
Penguin Group (USA) Inc., 375 Hudson Street, New York, New York 10014, USA
Penguin Group (Canada), 90 Eglinton Avenue East, Suite 700, Toronto, Ontario, M4P 2Y3, Canada (a division of Pearson Penguin Canada Inc.)
Penguin Books Ltd, 80 Strand, London WC2R 0RL, England
Penguin Ireland, 25 St Stephen's Green, Dublin 2, Ireland (a division of Penguin Books Ltd)
Penguin Group (Australia), 250 Camberwell Road, Camberwell, Victoria 3124, Australia (a division of Pearson Australia Group Pty Ltd)
Penguin Group (NZ), 67 Apollo Drive, Rosedale, North Shore 0632, New Zealand (a division of Pearson New Zealand Ltd)
Penguin Group (South Africa) (Pty) Ltd, 24 Sturdee Avenue, Rosebank, Johannesburg 2196, South Africa

Penguin Books Ltd, Registered Offices: 80 Strand, London WC2R 0RL, England

First published by Penguin Books India 2004
This edition published 2008

10 9 8 7 6 5 4 3 2 1

ISBN 9780143065081

Typeset in Perpetua by InoSoft Systems, Noida
Printed at Gopsons Papers Ltd, Noida

To Vivek and Neel,
my loves, my strengths, my reasons to write

Official recipe for *Piece of Cake*

Take 635 Minnesota mornings and evenings (mostly frozen);
thaw with 1635 cups of coffee;
sweeten with 11,635 cakes, pastries, doughnuts, cookies and other sugar fixes;
blend with inspiration, encouragement, help and wishes from Sandhya and Vijay Gupta—my lovely mom and dad; Satya Govil (Ammaji), S.S. Gupta (Babaji), Indu and Ajit Kaushal, Rashmi Gupta, Sanjay and Poonam Govil; Namita M. Anand, Vikram Achanta, Shruti Bajpai, David Housewright, Juhi Prasad, Sanjeev Sharma, Bhavna Shivpuri;
sprinkle with fond memories of friends and colleagues;
whip to smooth consistency under the expert supervision of Diya Kar Hazra, Radhika Rao Gupta and Poulomi Chatterjee.

Bake, decorate and ***enjoy*** hot off the press!

one

Ten days after my twenty-ninth birthday Mom sent me a letter. It was waiting for me with the bills and credit card solicitations in the mailbox in the foyer when I got home from work. Fool that I am I opened it first.

My dear Minal,

I have been waiting patiently for some good news from you on the matrimonial front, but it is beginning to take on an unfortunate resemblance to our country's great freedom struggle. I have therefore taken the initiative and placed an advertisement for you in the newspaper, a cutting of which is attached . . .

:-O!? She must be kidding. This was happening to someone else. MTV Bakra, ha, ha, ha. Except that no one popped out with cameras and silly grins, and a mouldy grey newspaper cutting stuck sideways out the envelope.

I slunk miserably up the two flights of steps and carefully reviewed the vast body of my life's embarrassments to see if anything matched up. Actually, crushingly, yes.

- Age 13: Shopping for shoes at Bata men's section
- Age 15: Being dumped by four-eyed guy with green braces
- Age 26: Acquiring Spineless Jaggu for a boss

And now,

- Age 29: A debut in HT Matrimonials under 'Miscellaneous'

Interesting pattern; not to mention the kind of numerical possibilities and circumstantial progression to give any mathematician or social psychologist an instant hard-on.

I tossed my briefcase on the table, marched to the fridge for a beer, kicked off my shoes and plopped down on the sofa. Half a bottle down, I figured I couldn't put it off forever and pulled the cutting out for a quick read.

. . . Honourable match invited for great granddaughter of legendary freedom fighter and daughter of professor and social worker. Bride is 29 yrs/175 cm/ wheatish complexion/ MBA working in MNC. Family remains devoted in the service of the nation and the great ideals of the great Mahatma. Prospective groom must be well educated, idealistic and high-minded. Please respond with . . .

That was it? Sixty words of specious shorthand, and not one mention of any key attributes (sunny personality, keen sense of fashion, killer legs to name a few) or even of stuff like strong leadership potential (as verified by last performance appraisal) or 'highly creative and innovative in approach' (as aspired to in objectives for the year)? What we had instead was ancestry, height, make, colour, date of manufacture. I could have been a car or the Qutab Minar.

Tchhh, Mom! If you had to do it, couldn't you have done it right? Ask yourself: Does it get the message across? Does it capture the essence? Does it hook the 17.5 lakh claimed readership base (all editions) of the HT? Go back to the drawing board, give it another shot.

I gave up. Sarcasm is so totally wasted on beer and blotchy old newsprint.

An hour later I washed down the last of the resentment with the rest of the beer and lay back on the sofa to contemplate my size-ten feet and plan my future strategy. This was a wake-up call; I had no illusions about it. My uneventful flight across the twenties was coming to an end, my plane was bearing inexorably in towards the torpid arrivals terminal of the thirties, time to do something and quick or contend with the dubious line-up of haphazard hopefuls at the gates (courtesy well-intentioned but pesky parent).

I wished she'd waited, though. It's not like I hadn't been trying (and it isn't easy when you're four inches taller than the average guy). Five violent crushes, four non-starter relationships, a handful of kisses and a month of secret meetings in the playground (though perhaps that didn't qualify on account of being pre-puberty) were nothing to scoff at, even if none of them had translated into the real deal. God knows good investments are hard to come by, especially in these troubled times. Even Aman . . . I picked the letter up again.

The ad has had a very encouraging response from people wanting to learn more about the work of your great grandfather, and to contribute to the continuing works in his name. This reaffirms my faith that the righteous are not dead. There were fewer eligible boys, but I am attaching particulars of two, whom I think you should meet.

1. *Kishore Kumar, 32 yrs/173 cm/dentist with small independent practice in Meerut. Deceased father was college professor of dentistry. Unassuming, homely personality with simple interests: philosophy/poetry/pets/wildlife preservation (active member of WWF).*
2. *Naveen Singh, 29 yrs/190 cm/tenured physical education faculty and cricket coach in Rajasthan University. Family is related to royal family of Jodhpur and owns property in neighbouring areas. Mother is active member of the Rajasthan ethnic crafts foundation.*

Additionally, Rani Auntie was mentioning her nephew Yudhishter, who is based in London and is actively involved with organizing tours to

Sewagram and Bodh Gaya. He is currently visiting India and plans to settle here to promote tourism to the many sacred and holy places that our country is so richly endowed with. I have given him your number; you can expect him to call.

Rest is fine. My work continues in its small way as ever. (I got a very nice letter of appreciation from the Army Widows Fund last week and 'Outlook' magazine has expressed interest in our Women's Pickling Society; it may even result in an interview.) Your father is busy with his gardening; he has plans for double chrysanthemums in the front lawn next year.

I am sending my love and blessings, as always. God bless, and may you be ever guided by the enlightened spirit of your great-grandfather.

Affly yours,

Ma

'Go away! Leave me alone! Stop messing around with Mom's head!' I yelled at the far wall with the GGF's self-righteous portrait, and sent the crumpled ball of paper flying into the waste bin.

It's not really mom's fault; her conscience is just too screwed up by the guilt she's inherited. I guess she's never completely recovered from the blow of my choosing an MBA over a Masters in Human Services, or a multinational company over her numerous pickling and spinning societies. That must be it; this whole arranged marriage thing was probably a renewed attempt to salvage my soul. Probably inspired by Sangeeta from three houses away who got married to that guy from UNICEF last month, gave up on her law degree and was now hanging out in brown saris and no make-up at SOS villages.

Sorry Mom, no deal. Sure I want to get married, but a dentist? *Yudhishter*? I think I'll find my own man, thank you. A Rahul, or a Rohan, or at the very least a Ravi. Someone who'll bring me flowers and buy me diamonds and laugh and flirt and throw parties and take happy pictures on our overseas vacations with a six-mega-pixel digital camera. No postcolonial hangover, no quixotic desire to reform the world, just a healthy, wholesome twenty-first century pursuit of wealth and prosperity. And a really classy car.

The phone jerked me out of my daydream. It was Aman.

'Hi, how's it going?' I asked, cheerful, engaging.

'Great! Can you believe the markets closed two hundred points higher today! I'm glad I held on to Infosys. Thanks for the tip.'

'Not at all. It's sweet of you to call to say thanks.'

'Actually, that's not really why I called. I just wanted to ask you . . .'

'Hmmm?' *Go ahead, ask. Ask me out.*

'If you don't mind . . .'

You can do it bashful boy.

'I was wondering what the impact of the VSNL privatization will be? I'm thinking of holding till it hits 200 and then getting out. What do you think?'

'Of course, VSNL. Good plan. Though there was this analysts' report that predicts it tanking at around 185.'

'Really? Gosh, thanks.'

'No problem.'

'Say, would you like to catch that Round Table Conference on exports tomorrow evening? We could have dinner afterwards.'

'Sounds lovely.'

Hey, don't knock it.

So what if it's mindlessly boring, reading all kinds of business dailies cover to cover just to form an opinion on the long-term impact of a petrol price reduction and merits of screen-based trading. And big deal if companies like Paradip Phosphates and Eternit Everest take on grotesque shapes in my dreams, or ugly mugs of business magnates zip past my mind whenever I flip through the pages of a *Cosmopolitan*. Aman, at least, is normal.

And loaded.

two

Very little has changed in the world of showbiz in the past two thousand years. Reality shows have been big ever since the Romans built the Colosseum. Through the ages, the genre has only matured and evolved; the French enjoyed a brief honeymoon with their guillotine, the Spaniards institutionalized their bullfights, and in modern times ABC has come up with the highly . . . well, 'Survivor' *was* in its fourth season. And International Foods (that hallowed multinational where I work as Associate Product Manager, Cookies) has perfected its own version of 'the public spectacle', also referred to internally as 'Advertising Meeting in the Fourth Floor Conference Room'.

Built less than a year ago, the Fourth Floor Conference Room is IF's pride and glory; a James Bond affair with wireless, digital and laser, miles of mahogany table top, acres of grey carpeting and thousands of leather chairs. Most afternoons it plays to indifferent audiences of VPs, Directors and Managing Directors, but Tuesday afternoon, the day of the ad agency meeting, we had an entire ecosystem in there.

What is it about an ad presentation that pulls in the entire office? Every single seat in the room was occupied. Tan suits, grey suits, black and brown; they were all there, with coffees and moods to match. And the entire ad agency that had come along to cheer. (Or mourn, depending on how things went.) In that non-smoking room Yogi's voice droned, the suits thrust out their chins, the agencywallahs sucked in their cheeks. And five chairs from the left exit I inhaled lungfuls of anticipation and blew rings of fright. Yogi was spewing jargon again.

I watched Lolita, the 'creative' head at the agency, warily. She was new; she'd joined two months ago, right after the previous incumbent left without notice 'to find his inner self' in Hollywood. The agency claims Lolita is from their UK office; I maintain she's from La-La-Land. You can see it in the pink gloves and orange scarves she wears (in June) and in the hundreds of beads that hang about her person. They claim she speaks English, French, German, Italian, Hindi, Bangla and Oriya, but Yogi was droning jargon and she was meditating and it made me nervous.

And the big boss had a cold. Not just a few adventurous early-adopter-type viruses; he'd captured the whole mature virus market. He sat propped on his elbows at the far end of the table, amidst tissues, and his red-rimmed eyes rolled from time to time.

We were on slide 15 of 103. 'The strategic imperative of this challenging market scenario . . .' Yogi's voice droned on and I buried my head in my hands.

Yogi is the Account Director at the agency and my cross to bear. Short hair, long face, big hands. Some brains, some attitude and a severe substance abuse problem. (Assuming you can call jargon a substance; it does have the same life-threatening consequences.) I have killed Yogi in my dreams a thousand times. Sometimes I use a gun, sometimes a knife and sometimes my bare fists, but the end is always a happy one. There was no such escape today.

'The purchase and usage patterns of the core consumer group . . .'

I closed my eyes and sent up a desperate prayer. 'Dear merciful God in heaven, just because our Curly Cookies are a lot better than those rip-off Creamy Delights by Gourmet International, just in the interests of all of consumer-kind, *just for today*, please stop his gibberish and let him make a great presentation.'

It worked.

Vik, head of Marketing, and my hero, stepped in. 'Yogi, let's get on with the ad, we're all familiar with the context.' The big boss honked in agreement and Yogi sat down to skip slides. He stopped at 52 of 103. We all gazed at the screen, which now displayed a larger-than-life close-up of a Curly Cookie, oozing cream, titled PEARLY TWIRLY CURLY COOKIES.

:-O!? My heart backed all the way up to my lungs.

'Our creative team has tried an entirely new approach,' Yogi began, without looking at me. 'We believe it will be a very powerful one. Lolita, over to you.'

Lolita tossed back her mane of thick black hair, adjusted her scarf and stood up with a jangling of beads and a swishing of skirt.

I went frantic trying to catch Spineless Jaggu's eye.

'Everyone close your eyes and clear your minds,' Lolita commanded. Everyone, including Spineless Jaggu, meekly obeyed.

'Now imagine green meadows, blue skies, puffy clouds, gentle breeze, background music. A delightful, cherubic boy of four is playing with his little puppy. Two words: Joy, Innocence.'

Kid? Puppy?

Lolita continued, 'The boy is tossing a stick, twirling it in the air. He laughs as the puppy grabs it in his mouth and brings it back. One more word: Fun.'

I started as she began to prance and twirl about the room, a stuffed dog with a missing eye clasped tight to her bosom. She stopped two chairs away from me and whipped out a Curly Cookie.

'The boy pulls out a Curly Cookie from his pocket. His eyes light up as they travel over its golden, creamy flakiness. The puppy bounds up and playfully knocks the cookie into the air. The boy laughs and then catches it in his mouth.'

She threw the Curly Cookie in the air and caught it in her mouth.

'They collapse, laughing, onto the thick lush grass. The camera freezes on a close-up of the two. We end with the line "Pearly Twirly Curly Cookies; have some wholesome fun".' She stopped and waited, arms outstretched and embracing the room. 'You can all open your eyes now.'

Everyone opened their eyes. The right-hand side of the room (agency team) burst into applause, the left-hand side (everyone else) blinked. Lolita smiled graciously, hugged the one-eyed dog to her chest and sashayed back to her seat.

Yogi got up again. 'That's our TV idea. Of course, we'll have the works: magazine ads, posters, hoardings, web banners, radio spots, you name it. Everywhere a kid looks, there'll be a Curly Cookie.'

I gazed horrified at Spineless Jaggu. *Say something, boss, do something, anything!* He smiled nervously, jiggled his ankles and traced patterns on the mahogany table with his little finger. 'Hmmm, nice, nice. It focuses on the child and yet speaks to the mother. We'll need to have long, appetizing shots of the cookies, though. And maybe we should say Pearly Curly Cookies a few more times?'

The pain blinded my eyes.

The new research guy with the crooked canines stirred to life four chairs away. 'Yes, I think it will go down well with audiences. Today's parents are looking for wholesome foods. Pearly captures the purity and goodness of cream, which is important.'

Goodness of cream? Wasn't it just fat and cholesterol? Oh goodie, Aman looked ready to say something. Come on dearest; kill it, kill it!

'Good point, the health angle is important. It will be a good way to link up with our Bountiful Breakfast bars. We could even consider a cross-promotion between the two products.'

Did Aman just say that?

Max the Axe (Sales Head, much feared in company) barged in:

'Let's cut the crap. It all sounds terribly sissy, and what do we need a dog for? (*Yeah, rah rah Max!*) We need to get kids excited about this, so they can bug their folks to buy it. I'm thinking, an ad with jammin' music and X-treme sports, that'll do it!'

Aaauuughh!

Vik looked slowly round the room at the nodding, smiling faces and fixed intent eyes on me. 'Minal, what do you think?'

The room fell silent, awaiting my pronouncement.

Say it, say it, it doesn't matter if it's good or bad, we just need the goddamn ad to launch the goddamn product, they prompted, and rushed at me with their wide, hopeful, spiteful, sneering, questioning, threatening pair after pair after pair of eyes.

'I think this is a good concept,' I said. Spineless Jaggu and Aman and Sales and Marketing and Production and Research and Finance all let out a collective sigh of relief. It was like watching the air leak slowly out of a thousand balloons.

It was horrible. It changed my mind.

'It's a great concept for breakfast bars,' I said. 'But it's totally off for Curly Cookies. Curlies are expensive, indulgent, "pamper yourself" cookies. They're meant for adults, not kids. A Curly Cookie is something I'd treat myself with, curl up with; something I'd want to bite into at the end of a long day, for pure pleasure. Not something I'd toss to a puppy.'

The room grew quieter and scarier than a snake about to strike. The big boss sniffed, Yogi swallowed, Spineless Jaggu hissed and the rest of the ranks stared. Any moment they'd lunge at me with their fangs and venom and scaly coils, but for now they just sat there stunned and unblinking. A creative-type in a red T-shirt finally got up with a glazed look in his eyes.

'Way cool, man. Picture it: a leggy, tanned babe in a pink bathtub. White bubbles, scented candles, soft music. A silver platter of Curly Cookies. Total self-indulgence. I like it.'

'Bu-a-we-the-uh-we're not talking about you or Minal here, are we?' Spineless Jaggu said.

Yogi nodded. 'Let's not miss the woods for the trees. Research indicates that ninety per cent of heavy users are in the four-to-fourteen demographic, so that's our core consumer segment.'

Lolita was sulking. 'Gourmet International targets kids too, and our ad is much better than theirs. We'll use British producers; we'll shoot the ad in South Africa. We'll use a Chihuahua; that's a very sophisticated dog. Let me present the rest of the drawings; you'll love the hoardings!'

'But man, imagine the babe in the bathtub on hoardings,' Red T-shirt breathed.

The big boss sneezed, fumbled, and found he was out of tissues. He held a hand to his nose and heaved himself up out of his chair.

'Vik,' he dribbled, 'it's your call; I'll leave you to it. Personally I can't stand dogs or kids.' With that and one last, fruitful honk, he ran out of the room.

This unleashed twenty minutes of free-for-all between suits and jeans, kind of like a ping-pong game with eight balls and fourteen players.

'Girl.'

'Boy.'

'Let's change the ad.'

'We need the ad.'

'Let's change the product.'

'Just a moment.'

'There are more adult consumers than children in Goa.'

'Let's have two ads.'

'One moment, please.'

'Let's change the product manager.'

'Puppy instead of girl.'

'Can you all settle down?'

'We could put in a mom.'

'We're launching in four weeks.'

'Four is too young.'

'Quiet please.'

'Fourteen then.'

'Eighteen-year-old in bathtub.'

'We could use Aishwarya. On the hoardings.'

'Quiet please.'

'How big are hoardings?'

'Huge.'

'Cool.'

'SHUT UP EVERYONE!'

Vik was glaring round the room and thumping the table. The commotion died down; everyone waited.

Vik rounded on Spineless Jaggu. 'Jaggu, this meeting has been a complete waste of my time. I can't believe we have four weeks to launch and you still don't know who your consumer is. Minal is right. The product is expensive, child consumption will be limited. I think it's time you took a long, hard look at the product and figured it the hell out.'

'But the ad . . .' began Lolita.

'The ad STINKS,' Vik roared. 'I can't think of a worse slogan than Pearly Twirly Curly; it sounds like some cheerleader in heaven. I want the ad totally reworked and I want it yesterday. This meeting is over.'

He grabbed his papers and strode out of the room without a backward glance. I took one look around the silently screaming suits and jeans and bolted out behind him.

The long drive back home is my oasis, my quiet time for reflection.

The exhaust and the exhaustion go wonderfully together, creating the perfect atmosphere for self-recrimination. And there was enough to recriminate about.

Thank goodness I'd had enough sense to leave the meeting; they'd have lynched me sure as I was alive. I knew they'd get around to it sooner or later but at least for today I was safe and free in my second-hand Maruti, sweet sweat in my face and smoke in my hair.

At the next stop light though, I kicked myself roundly. Three years and five months it had taken me to make Associate Product Manager, and it had been a long, hard climb up the IF rope; past the knots and the kinks, the slips and the slides, the rough patches and the sharp edges. And even before my feet had fully left the ground I'd managed to get the damn thing twisted round my neck. It was a free fall now; no ad→delayed product launch→missed targets→fewer sales and profits→no increments, sub-zero chance of promotion . . . and my confounded conscience still insisted I'd done the right thing.

It was entirely the GGF's fault of course; it always was.

The saddest part of the whole business, though, was Aman. *Health angle is important*, he'd said, and with a straight face too, and avoided me for the rest of the afternoon, regretting via e-mail his cancellation of the Round Table rendezvous, and '*by the way, was I sure VSNL wouldn't make it to 200?*'

I supposed I'd have to fall back on Mom's list after all. Either that, or wait out the slump and pray that good men, like good cream (or fat and cholesterol), would eventually rise to the surface.

At least I could get rid of that infernal stock ticker at the bottom of my computer screen and renew my *Stardust* subscription. And *Cosmo*. And I could cancel *Investors Guide* and *Financial Times*, and it could rain on the moon before I went to another Round Table or productivity workshop, and that would be fine. Come to think of it, I could even go back to high heels and extra-cheese pizzas and *Friends* reruns and . . . *this was great!*

My elation begged expression. I rolled down the window at the next stop light and bought all the glossies the old man had to offer. He threw in the evening newspaper as a freebie in acknowledgement, so I handed him a free sample pack of Curlies, so he handed me a free car wipe and the light changed to green and we both moved on, two happy ships passing contentedly in the dusk. I sailed smoothly into the apartment parking lot, humming softly, and drew up short in front of my allotted spot.

The violently ugly Jeep was still there, still parked too close to my spot, still offensively dirty. Third time this week. I pulled out a Post-it and wrote in my politest manner:

Dear owner of DL3G 4232,
Could you please park your vehicle nearer the wall to your right? There is not enough room for me to park comfortably.
Thanks,
Owner of DL2C 2225

I lifted the wiper and stuck the note underneath. Some caked mud dislodged and fell on my shoe.

P.S. You could also consider cleaning it once in a while.

three

I considered cleaning the cow crap off my shoe with the duster in my bag.

Would it really matter? Spit, snot, drains, mongrels, soggy newsprint; steaming kettles, burning milk, sweaty armpits, noisy flies; everything around me was just as nasty anyway. I decided against; at least this way I blended in. I stepped up to the tea–coffee shop to my right and put a smile on for the man behind the counter. He was swatting flies off jars of home-made candy and *beedis*.

'Hello, I'm from International Foods, how are you?'

'Huh?'

'I'm from the food company, IF. We make cookies and other baked products. How are you today?'

'Okay.'

'I notice you don't stock any of our products. Why is that?'

'Huh?'

'Why don't you sell our cookies?'

'Why should I?'

I wiped the sweat from my brow, took the weight off my right foot by leaning against the counter, and persevered.

'The margins on our products are very good. And I could put together a special scheme for you as an added incentive. What would be the daily sale of cookies at your store?'

'A hundred, a thousand,' he shrugged. 'What's the scheme?'

'If you sell one carton every week—that means thirty-six packs of twenty cookies each—it would entitle you to a special discount of two per cent in addition to the regular margin. How does that sound?'

'How much money is that?'

'You'd make thirty rupees on one hundred and seventy rupees; that's seventeen and a half per cent!'

'I don't have that kind of money. Leave the carton in the corner and I'll pay next month.'

I controlled my middle finger with an effort, smiled with calm regret, and stepped back out into the blazing sun. I should have guessed; this was a tough neighbourhood.

And this was no ordinary assignment either—this was retribution. Since the beginning of civilization, the Spineless Jaggus of the world have been getting back at the insubordinates in a variety of spiteful and grisly ways. We've been crucified, burnt at the stake, banished to solitary confinement and, in modern times, sent on sudden, highly urgent, week-long surveys of tea–coffee shops in outer Delhi constituency, with nothing but the June sun and the desert dust for company.

Well, no amount of heat and dust and sullen shopkeepers would get me down; I'd win this war. I'd go back to the office laden with enough consumer and trade insights to bury Jaggu in, so help me God. I hitched up my salwar and stepped into the next shop with fierce determination.

Business was brisk, and I sat down at a table with the careless disinterest of a customer.

'Hello, how are you?' I smiled at the waiter who materialized at my table.

'Hot tea, ice tea, black tea, milk tea, cream tea, masala tea, super-deluxe morning special for two rupees only. What will you have?'

'Iced tea please, and some cream cookies.'

'No cream cookies, only sugar ones.'

He whipped a duster off his shoulder and dabbed half-heartedly at the sticky stains on the table.

'Oh, you don't have cream cookies? What a pity, those are terrific, especially the IF ones.'

'We don't have. You want sugar cookies?' He was scratching his stubbly jaw.

'Actually, I'd like to talk about cookie consumption at your store. How many cookies do you sell in a day?'

This brought the fat guy who'd been totting up numbers behind the counter to rumbling life.

'Chhotu, why are you dawdling by that table? Hurry up!' he roared.

'Sir, this person wants to know how much we sell.'

The fat guy emerged from behind the counter, slow and suspicious, as Chhotu sauntered off in a huff.

'Are you from the income tax department? We don't sell any cookies, hardly any tea. No profit, all loss, loss.'

'Oh, no, I work for a food company. I just wanted to . . .'

'Food inspector, tax inspector, what difference does it make? Please, Madam; we are honest people trying to do honest work. Don't take away our livelihood. I have five children, all girls. What more tax can I pay?' He threw up his hands in despair.

'Anyway . . .' he conjured the waiter with a snap of his fingers. 'Chhotu, get some super-deluxe special tea for Madam, with extra milk and elaichi. No charge, Madam, have with my compliments and please go away. God will bless you.'

'No, but . . .'

But he had already sauntered off and I was left to await my deluxe-special tea with burning ears and mouthful of feet.

Ten minutes later I was back on the street.

The man behind the counter in the next shop looked pleasant and helpful.

'Hello, I work at International Foods, the food company. How is business?'

'Hello, Madam. I am Prem, BA pass. What business, Madam, *dhanda* is totally *manda*. Economy is bad, you know, what with all the slowdown in the US and software boys coming back home. Madam, you are lucky, working in a good company like International Foods. Must be growing, no . . . everyone eating out of depression? Do you think you could get me a job at IF? I am very intelligent and hard-working, I got distinction in Inter and first class in college. If you come back later in the afternoon, I can show you my degree.'

I bought twenty rupees worth of things I didn't need and bolted into the shop next door.

The balding guy at the entrance looked me over with interest. I decided to give the student approach a shot; it usually worked with middle-aged men.

'Hello, I'm Minal. I'm a student, trying to do a survey about the tea–coffee and cookies business. How are you?'

'Hello! How are you?' he smiled.

'Are you the owner of this shop?'

'Yes. I'm the owner, Kishori Lal. See the sign up there, K.L. Enterprises? That's me. Actually, I have two more stores in east Delhi, and one more opening in Khirki village next week, God willing.'

'I was wondering if you had a few minutes. I'd like to speak with you . . .'

'More than welcome. Please, have a seat. Heh, heh. Bahadur, bring out some coffee, double espresso. And some sweets and cashews. So, Minalji, what can I do for you? I can call you Minal, can't I? Such a pretty name. It suits you.'

He smiled an intimate little smile and looked caressingly into my eyes.

I put my glasses back on before I entered the next shop and said in my sternest, 'Hello, I'm from International Foods, here to ask you something about cookie sales at your outlet.'

'Sorry, Madam,' came the stinging reply, 'no time, no money, no interest. Next please!'

There was just one more shop on this road, a small distance away from the others. It emanated a chilling aura of danger as I got closer; the flies were thicker, the smell stronger and the walls crumblier than anything that had gone before. For one weak moment I considered skipping it, but my ever-vigilant conscience sprang immediately to action and told me it wouldn't let me sleep all night if I left out this shop; it would have me back here the next day at the crack of dawn.

I held a hankie to my nose and smiled at the guy in the grey vest behind the food-stained counter.

'Hello, I'm Minal from International Foods . . .'

'International Foods!' he spat. 'You company people think you are bigshots; you only care about the big stores. No one ever visits my shop. And your products are useless. Three months ago I bought some of your breakfast bars, and now they are lying ruined and useless in the storage. Thirty whole packs, not a single one of them sold. I'm never going to buy anything from your company unless you replace them.'

'Bring them out, let's have a look.'

'They're all rat-eaten. Your company should come up with better packaging, rat resistant.'

'Don't you think it might be easier to get rid of the rats?'

'Why should I? They don't bother me. Besides, rats are auspicious. So will you replace them?'

'We don't usually replace rat-eaten products, but I'll make a special case just for you. Now how about trying out our cookies? They . . .'

He shook his head. 'I keep only Gourmet International cookies. The Gourmet International officer visits every week and straightens out the stocks himself. Maybe if someone from IF were to put the packs properly . . .'

I got the drift.

'No problem, can I borrow your duster?'

Twenty minutes later I stepped back into the street, looking and smelling just about as wholesome as the rest of the shop.

Ten down, a few hundred more to go. I squinted up at the cloudless sky, licked the sweat that had trickled down from my brow and looked down the next narrow row of tinplate/ waterproofing shops. It was as fertile a hunting ground for consumer insights as the Sahara.

And then, all of a sudden the digitized strains of '*Kambakth ishq*' poured out of my bag, dispersed the flies and startled the dog that had sauntered up to sniff my ankles. I pulled out my cellphone, grabbing at the chance of renewed contact with humanity. Radha, the caller ID showed.

This couldn't be good; why was Vik's secretary calling me?

'Hi Radha, what's up?'

'Minal, where are you? I've been trying to track you down all morning. You need to come back to the office right away; Vik wants to speak with you.'

I walked back to my car with deep misgivings. All week I'd been having this recurring dream of Vik transferring me to the wilds of Tripura, where I tried to sell Curly Cookies to the tribal chief's wife, kid and puppy. The dream had ended every time with the tribal chief getting angry and chopping my head off. I was uneasy.

Radha looked up at the wall clock as I limped into the office.

'There you are! You'd better hurry, Vik has a meeting that's supposed to start in five minutes and then he's off to Mumbai for the rest of the week.'

I started towards Vik's door.

'Wait a moment.'

She walked up, and looked me over.

'What in the world have you been up to?'

'Am I being transferred?'

'How did you know?'

'Premonition. When do I have to start?

'Right away, but I'll let Vik tell you all about it.'

'But where to, how long, what . . .'

'Later,' she said, holding up her hand. 'Right now, I suggest you get cleaned up. Here, take this. I keep it for emergencies.' She slipped a bright green overnight kit into my hands and pushed me towards the door.

Would a wash make the news any better? Wasn't I better prepared for my new role in my current state?

Three minutes later, rinsed, dried and deodorized, I stood knocking on Vik's door with trembling heart and pounding fingers. 'Come in,' I heard and turned the knob.

Vik's office is the stuff my dreams are made of. Thick pile carpeting, wood on the floor and walls, leather on the chairs. A towering map of India, three easy chairs around a small coffee table and, straight up, a mahogany and glass case full of IF packs from around the world, a vase full of fresh flowers and a wide desk that gleamed with dignity and was polished twice daily.

Maybe, someday, I'd be arranging my family pictures in a discreet corner of that desk, putting my feet up to watch the sun set over the shiny green grass in the park next door, its dipping rays converting it to a bed of jewels. Emeralds on fire. Like Oz.

Maybe . . . if I survived Tripura.

Vik looked up as I walked in. 'Minal, there you are! Jaggu tells me you've been working in the market this week. That's good; though a bit sudden, isn't it?'

He was smiling. Maybe it wasn't Tripura after all.

'Good morning, Vik.'

'Afternoon, actually! I was hoping we'd have more time to discuss this, but . . .' he looked at his watch and pulled a face. 'Anyway, to put it to you without the frills, I think you've been doing a good job in cookies. You're enthusiastic, you've got a good grasp of the business and you're not afraid to stand up for your convictions. I like that.'

Huh? Vik wasn't supposed to compliment lowly associate product managers; he was supposed to eat us for breakfast! I tried a weak, cautious smile.

'I'm planning some reorganization in the team,' Vik continued. 'You probably know how we've been struggling with the Cakes business all this year. What I need is a really creative and aggressive team to pull Cakes through; in fact, I'm planning to head the group myself. I've recruited a new manager from one of the big consulting firms, and I want you in too. You'll both report in to me of course. It's a big challenge, but I think both you and the product will benefit from it. What do you say?'

What does a house-elf say on being presented with the master's clothes?

I spluttered and choked and managed to communicate that the idea wasn't exactly abhorrent to me.

'Yes? Good then, I'd like you to start Monday. I'll let Jaggu know you need to start winding up at the cookies job right away.'

He wasn't kidding; Spineless Jaggu was already waiting when I got back to my desk.

'Congrats, Minal. Vik just called to tell me he's moving you to a new assignment. I must say I'm surprised. There's a lot of unfinished work on Curly Cookies, especially on the advertising front.'

His voice was a rich cocktail of scorn and disbelief, topped off with a twist of mild envy. I shuffled my feet and willed him to go away. He didn't.

'Of course, the cake business is much smaller than the cookies one,' he continued.

The thought seemed to please him; his voice became friendly and patronizing again. 'Actually, Minal, this is probably for the best. Not everyone is cut out for the really tough jobs. My only word of advice is that you start taking things seriously now, and maybe get a bit more organized?'

He was eyeing my desk. I tried to sweep the unruly tangle of pencils, pens and erasers into the drawer and yanked it off its hinges instead. It crashed down, spewing forth two years of accumulated odds and ends and unfiled papers and dislodging the delicately balanced tower of unread memos on the far edge of my desk. The latter tipped over and landed in a mocking heap around my feet.

Jaggu smiled as I sprawled on all fours. 'Well, I'll leave you to it, Minal. You can start by filing those papers, and don't forget to prepare a handover list. Oh, and I'll need your detailed market visit report by the end of the day.'

The friendly neighbourhood Jeep was there again when I got home, still filthy, still hogging my spot. I backed and forthed my weary Maruti a couple of times, squeezed into the narrow space and walked sideways out the passenger side. A Post-it stuck on the Jeep's side view mirror caught my eye.

Dear owner of car DL2C 2225,
Who are you?
AI

????? Who was he, Aristotle? I pulled out another Post-it.

Dear AI,
How does it matter who I am? You're still parking too close to my car.
MS

four

TGIwasF.

I'm not really your manicure-pedicure-facial kind of girl, but the past few days of sun and sand had been rather hard on the epidermis, and my face was ready to give up on me.

God bless the folks at *Femina* and their compulsive sampling; the 'Mud spa treatment five-minute masque' (with natural papaya, grapefruit and cucumber) that came with last month's issue seemed just the thing. I smothered the pistachio green paste all over my face and neck and waited for 'new and improved' ancient science to work its wonders. An encouraging coolness spread across my features, followed by a promising firmness. No wonder women swore by the stuff; it sure beat sticking your head in the fridge and pulling at your cheeks, besides being a lot cheaper than a visit to a spa too! (I remember going to one of those beauty boutiques a couple of months ago with Radha; she'd paid five hundred rupees for one hour with the 'special thermal pack'; a lava-like substance that had solidified in many crusty layers on her face and had come off whole, like a hollow Egyptian mummy.)

I studied my face in the mirror as I waited for the masque to do its stuff. A guy in Class 11 had once told me I was beautiful. I'm assuming it was hormones, or my Chemistry notes.

It's not that I'm *ugly*; in fact I like *most* of the way I look. It's just that I wish I didn't have a big forehead, long nose and extra-wide lips in that slightly non-Julia Roberts kind of way. And also my sideburns. I could definitely do without them. I turned my head sideways to check their current length, winced, and turned my head back around again.

At least I had good eyes. On the bigger side like everything else, but intelligent; and they looked especially arresting popping out from the green icing around them. And my eyebrows, and the way they never need threading; I especially like that. In fact not bad, all told, if only there were something I could do with the ears. I squeezed out the last of the green paste from the sample sachet and quickly covered them with it.

My ears are a social embarrassment and cause for deep personal anguish. I have no lobes.

I remember a visit to an ear-piercing salon, many years ago, when the entire staff had buzzed excitedly about my ears, in the manner of scientists around a rare specimen measuring and marking with special finely calibrated rulers to find a spot to pierce. In the end they'd recommended I forget the whole idea.

I'm assuming God used up so much material super-sizing the rest of me that he ran out of stuff to throw on the ears, so he just sort of wrapped up the job with comical miniatures, tucked them behind manly sideburns and hoped no one would notice. Of course, it didn't work. People notice all the time; my ears are bigger draws than cleavage.

It wouldn't be so bad if it were just a case of size and appearance. What really distresses me is that I am also tone-deaf. I love music, but my ears just don't get it. Ever noticed how musicians tend to have nice, big ears with extra-large ear lobes that hang and quiver delicately at the ends, like they were specially designed to pick up variations on even a hundredth of a note? Well, mine have yet to acknowledge the differences between a *do, re* and *mi* and I have watched *The Sound of Music* a thousand times. And I'm sure things would have worked out with Rajiv, back in Class 12, if it hadn't been for the time I got carried away and tried to sing *'With a little help from my friends'* in his ear.

He did stand up and walk out on me.

The digitized strains of *'Kambakht ishq'* sliced through my ruminations and I ran to retrieve my phone.

'Hello?' I gritted, careful not to move a facial muscle. The pack was hard and brittle.

'Hello, could I talk to Minal Sharma?'

'Yes.'

'Is this Minal?'

'Yes.'

'You sound a bit strange. Anyway, this is Yudhishter Pandey. I'm Mrs Rani Pandey's nephew. Your mother may have mentioned I'd be in touch?'

'Yes.' *Oh, no!*

'Well, how are you?'

'Okay.' Damn, the pack was cracking up.

'That's great. Are you at home?'

'Mmm.'

'That's good. I was wondering if I could come by this evening.'

'Mmmm?'

'I said, "could we meet up this evening?".'

'Mmmm.'

'Great, I'll be by in ten minutes then.'

'Uhnnnn?'

'I said ten minutes. Actually, I was in the neighbourhood, just outside your building in fact. My work finished early, so I thought I'd take a chance. Hope you don't mind?'

'Uhnnnnn.'

'Okay, so I'll see you then!'

NNNNNNNNN!

So it had begun. Friday evening, and without notice; like a headache or a period. Damn this Yudhishter guy, condescending to drop by, like he knew I'd be home without a date. Probably a freeloader too, looking for a free meal. Well, he could think again. I raced through the shower, threw on the most repulsive outfit I could find (my baggiest jeans with missing pockets and crushed brown T-shirt from five summers ago), put my hair up in two schoolgirl ponytails and pulled out my spare glasses with the tiger-stripe frames and extra-thick lenses that magnified my eyes to the stuff optometrists' nightmares are made of. I waited for the doorbell to ring, stuck my stomach out, and remembered to slouch as I opened the door.

He was gorgeous. He was the man I wouldn't mind spending the rest of my life with. He looked repulsed. He was taking a step back and checking the apartment number. This couldn't be happening.

'Oh, I'm sorry, I thought . . .' he began.

'Yudhishter?'

'Er . . . *Minal*?'

I ripped off the glasses and tossed them far, far away. 'Heh, heh, these aren't mine, heh heh, just a silly toy some kids left behind.'

He swallowed. 'Er, maybe this isn't a good time . . .'

'Oh, come in, come in; don't be shy.' I grabbed his arm, yanked him over the threshold and locked the door for good measure. 'Sit down, won't you?'

He followed me at ten paces and hesitated in the middle of the room. 'Really, I could come back some other time.'

'No, this is fine.' I thumped the cushions on the sofa and racked my brains for an excuse to jump into my room and emerge in a little black number. 'There. Now, you just make yourself comfortable, and I'll be . . . '

'You know, I just remembered I left something in the car . . .'

'Forget it! I mean, never mind. So what can I . . . .'

'Actually . . .'

'Sit!'

He perched miserably on the edge of the sofa.

'So, Yudhishter . . .' I stalled as I cast around for a brilliant conversational ice-breaker.

'Why is your name *Yudhishter*?'

'Yudi.'

'Pardon?'

'Yudi. That's what everyone calls me.'

'Ah,' I said relieved. 'So, how are you, Yudi?'

'Fine, thank you.'

'That's good.'

He coughed and looked glumly round the room. 'Nice place,' he said finally.

'Ha, ha, sorry, the maid didn't show up last weekend, and I've been a bit busy and . . .'

'Oh, no, I meant nice, um . . . nice, er . . . . nice layout.'

'Thanks.'

'You're welcome.'

He drummed his fingers on the armrest and looked out the window. Suddenly, he brightened. 'Wow, what a view! That structure must be at least two hundred years old!'

He was smiling. There was still hope. I tugged at the rubber bands in my hair.

'That old well? Yes, I believe it's from the eighteenth century. I call it my wishing well. I wish it would go away, and then I'd have a great view of the park, har, har!'

'Actually, I love ancient architecture. Delhi is such a marvellous city. Did you know it's been destroyed and built again seven times in the two thousand years of its documented history? It has an indestructible spirit, gritty and proud. I'd love to have an old well in my backyard.'

'Of course, of course. Me too.'

I worked away at the rubber bands. If I could just get him to suggest dinner, it would be the perfect excuse to change and reappear as the woman of his dreams.

'So, ancient architecture, wow,' I said. 'You know, there's this new Afghan restaurant that's opened up nearby, Jewel of Persia, or something. I've heard they've got some really authentic eighteenth-century decor.'

'Yes, I've been there. Awful food.'

'Of course. So would you like a drink; glass of wine, maybe?'

He sighed. 'Okay.'

'Oops, I forgot, there's no corkscrew. I guess we'll just have to step out and . . .'

'A glass of water would be fine.'

It would have to do. I poured it out, flawless and just a centimetre short of the rim, and not a single splash. I held it out with a flourish and a gracious smile. He stared at my ears.

'Mom told me you were into promoting tourism, and that you organize tours to Sewagram and Bodh Gaya?'

'Yes, those were the assignments I worked on in my final year project. Before I knew it, almost a hundred people had signed up for a tour. It's a great business opportunity. I'm already in touch with the Lonely Planet and the Archaeological Survey. Next week I plan to contact the local tour operators.'

'How about the restaurants? Food is a very important part of a holiday, you know. My, it's already eight, almost time for dinner!'

'Maybe I should get moving.'

He began to get up. I pushed him back down.

'Oh no, I never eat before nine anyway. Say, isn't it really warm in here? I'll just change into something . . .'

'Yes, well, it was nice meeting . . .'

'Or not. So, do you plan to settle in Delhi?'

'I'm not really sure. Jaipur is a nice place too. It has a lot of potential for tourism . . .'

'I love Jaipur. I've always wanted to live there.'

'But not on the same scale as Agra, of course.'

'You know, the Taj is one of my favourite spots. So romantic, and it's so close to Delhi too!'

'My idea of heaven is Kerala, though. Anyway, I haven't decided yet, it's all up in the air.'

'Yes. And I expect it would depend on other things. Like marriage and stuff?'

'Marriage?' He stared at my ears and got up. 'Actually, I'm not planning to get married for a while.'

I slumped back in my chair. What was the point?

'Why are you here?' I asked.

'Excuse me?'

'No really. It's Friday night. Why *are* you here?'

'I, just . . . just thought I'd say hello.'

'Okay then. Hello.'

'Ha, ha. Funny.' He grinned briefly. It put two dimples in his cheeks and a huge cleft in his chin. I looked away and walked him to the door.

'Well, all the best,' I said. 'Goodbye.'

Suddenly, strangely, he hesitated.

'Minal?'

'Yes?'

'Actually, if you don't mind, I needed a favour. I have this friend in London; she's . . . actually, she's my girlfriend . . . she works in advertising.' He pulled a picture of a toothy blonde from his wallet and pushed it under my nose. 'Her name's Marianne. We haven't made up our minds about anything yet, but in case things work out—and she's looking for a job here . . . I was wondering if she could get in touch with you?'

Ten minutes later, after waving goodbye to the most eligible guy to have ever crossed my threshold, I caught sight of myself in the mirror. For once I could see my ears. They were a vivid pistachio green.

Well, there was always the psycho with the Jeep. I pulled out his last Post-it, which I'd preserved.

Hey MS,
You're right. It doesn't matter who you are. It doesn't matter who I am. We are all invisible points in infinite time and space. So are parking spots.
Ali

Just my type, wouldn't you say? I was glad I had resisted temptation and had responded with dignity.

Dear Ali,
Let's try this again. I'm Minal Sharma. I live in this building and would appreciate it if . . .

five

Something strange happened to me over the weekend.

I didn't notice it till I got to the office and the starchy guard at the entrance saluted smartly. I looked over my shoulder, but there was no one there. *He'd saluted me?* And then a couple of vice-presidents getting out of their Hondas almost knocked me down with their cheery 'Good morning!' The Mona Lisa print in the corridor winked two thumbs up as I scurried past and people in the corridors smiled and nodded as though they'd all just put on their glasses and could finally see me. 'Congrats!' the receptionist boomed as I swung past her, and that's when the realization hit me: the office had discovered my new assignment.

I had arrived; people knew me. And somewhere between Friday evening and Monday morning, *I had sprouted an identity*!

So I was a new person. This called for serious and immediate adjustment of attitude and projected image. I slowed down my nervous quickstep to a confident long stride, hoisted my chin a couple of notches and swung my legs out from the hips as I walked, the way I'd seen models do on Fashion TV.

'Hi Minal!' the Senior Operations Manager called from his cabin, and I wagged two jaunty fingers back at him.

Man, this was great! More warmth, better illumination, higher visibility—like I'd jumped orbits and landed a couple of spots closer to the sun. I aimed a careless wave at the Juices manager as

I sailed past his office, and wondered how long it would be before I got my own cabin. Maybe they'd give me the one at the end of the corridor. That way I'd have the same sweeping view as Vik.

Too bad I forgot to duck as I walked past Sam's cabin. He hailed me in with a hearty smile.

Sam is this really powerful, slimy, Gollum-type in the office. Officially, he's our Internal Communications Director, with the major responsibility of publishing a quarterly newsletter. Unofficially, he's the big boss' wife's cousin and everyone on my floor bows and scrapes to him. *Two minutes,* I promised myself and walked in.

Aman, I noticed, had got off to an early start; he was already there, sipping his coffee, paying his daily respects.

'Hi, Minal!' Sam boomed. 'Where have you been hiding yourself? One hardly sees you around!'

'I was out on a market visit last week. Hi, Aman, hope you got rid of VSNL in time?'

'Hi, Minal.'

I guessed he hadn't.

'So, what's up?' I asked.

'Oh, nothing much,' Sam said. 'It's that time of the year again; I'm working on next year's calendar.'

A new editorial challenge! I wondered how he'd make time for it with all his hectic social and political responsibilities.

'What's the theme?' I asked.

'It's a new one; IF products in sporty, outdoorsy lifestyles,' Aman chipped in.

'Good theme.'

It *would* be a welcome change from the close-up cows, udders, oranges and beehives that adorned this year's calendar (the management had gone overboard with the 'fresh ingredients' theme).

'What are you planning?' I asked Sam.

'I'm planning to put fruit juices on the May/June page,' Sam said. 'Help me choose some models.'

He held out some photos of sultry women in swimsuits.

'I'm thinking of summer and beaches, three, maybe four women. Bursting with health.'

Aman grinned.

'Aman feels we should have a close-up of just one,' Sam winked. 'What do you think, Minal?'

'Beach is good, but I think you should show a whole family. Mom, Dad, kids. We do target the entire family for juice consumption, don't we?'

'That doesn't mean we have to show them all!' Sam sounded horrified. 'Come on, Minal, you know advertising is meant to be inspiring. In fact, I'm wondering if I should put swimsuits on all the pages.'

'It'll be very good for worker morale,' Aman agreed.

'Yep; swimsuits and breakfast bars. You could even do a cross-promotion,' I said and started to leave.

'Hey, wait up.' Sam lowered his voice and leaned in. 'I hear you're moving to a new assignment?'

'I'm moving to the Cakes team.'

Aman was all ears.

Sam nodded shrewdly. 'Really hush-hush, huh? Even I didn't find out till this morning.'

'It's not a big deal,' I shrugged. 'There's another manager too.'

'Still, you'll be working directly for Vik!' Aman blurted.

'Uh-huh.'

'Quite an achievement, I'd say,' Sam said. 'How did you swing it?'

So *that's* what was bothering them! I could see the question in both sets of eyes. They were Tarzan, I was Jane. How did *I* swing it?

'Without a swimsuit,' I confirmed, and walked out.

Suicide? I didn't think so, as I strode up the stairs and down the management wing. I stood up for my convictions, isn't that what Vik had said? I didn't need a bunch of losers like Sam and Aman to make it; I could do it all on my own. Yessir, *Competitive Advantage*, *Building Strong Brands*, *Why We Buy*, I knew it all. *Self-awareness*, *self-management*, *motivation*, *empathy*, *social skills*, I had it all. I was five feet ten inches of marketing strategy, sixty-eight kilos of emotional intelligence. I was a corporate miracle just waiting to happen. IF was my oyster . . .

I stopped; I'd reached Vik's office. I knocked twice, twisted the knob and opened the door.

'Minal? Come on in,' Vik called.

I shut the door behind me. There was a thin guy in a black suit in the chair opposite Vik, his back to me. The new manager? I put on my best 'good team player' smile and walked up.

'Rana, this is Minal Sharma, she'll be your team member on the project,' Vik introduced. 'Minal has been with us for three years, and she's a real asset. Minal, I think I've already mentioned Rana Bhatia to you. He comes to IF with a lot of experience, and hopefully a fresh perspective. Between the two of you, I think we should see some real action now.'

Rana and I pulled back our outstretched hands and recoiled in synchronized horror.

Rana Bhatia was back in town!

Vik hadn't noticed; he was busy pulling papers out from his desk. 'Sit down, guys, let me give you some background on the cakes market,' he said.

It must be over fifteen years!

'It's still very nascent; there aren't too many players.'

He hadn't changed one bit.

'That's because it's a very tough market.'

Same pinched nose, same sneer.

'The only real players as of today are Gourmet International and International Foods.'

Same gap in teeth where I'd knocked out the front left one.

'GI is bigger and has been around longer; but we're leaner and we'll work harder.'

Why was he here?

'Guys? Minal? Sit down please?'

I sank faintly into a chair. Rana shifted his as far away from mine as he could.

Vik was frowning. 'Is something the matter?' he asked.

Yes!

'No, no, carry on, Vik . . .' I leaned forward. It would take all my concentration to focus on the cakes market with Mr Nemesis in the next chair.

Vik sat back and pushed his papers aside. 'Look guys, I'll warn you straight off, this is going to be a hard market to crack. Let me run a word association game past you. What's the first thing that comes to mind when I say "cake"?'

'Profit,' Rana said.

'Fruitcake,' I said, genuinely shocked.

Vik raised his brows. 'In a study done recently, ninety-nine per cent of the consumers responded "birthday" to the word "cake". Surprisingly, the only other association that was as close was between mothers and pickles.'

If Rana was back, his mother couldn't be far behind.

'It seems Indian consumers think cakes are meant solely for birthdays; just something to stick candles in and clap and sing around. Moreover, the only birthdays that ever get celebrated are kids' birthdays. In a typical family of two kids, that means two cakes in one whole, long year.'

Unless you were Rana and had a birthday party every month.

'There's obviously huge potential for growth. How do we get

consumers to buy more, consume more frequently? How do we grow the market? How do we make more money? How do we get there before GI?'

'Lower prices, better distribution,' Rana said.

'Better quality, more variety,' I said.

We glared at each other. We were back at it again.

Vik looked happy. 'I'm glad you both have different points of view. They both have merit, and we'll have to figure out which is the stronger one. I can see this is going to work.'

I bit my lip to stop the bitter laughter.

'So guys, I'm going to leave you with the following: GI vs. IF. The leader and the challenger. The battle's been going on for too long; it's time to fight it out and settle who the leader is once and for all. Who's going to win this war?'

Who, indeed?

six

'There, I think I have everything,' Radha said, striding back to the car for the third time. She joined me in the back seat of her Ford Ikon, where I'd been waiting for the past several minutes.

'Take us to South Extension,' she told the driver.

The driver fiddled around with the controls and looked across at the imposing double doors of the bungalow. As if on cue, a servant dashed out and panted up to the car.

'Memsaab, Mataji sent me to remind you about the fifty silver coins for the evening's puja. Also, a dozen *paans*, and four banana leaves.'

'Yes, yes, I know! Will I ever be allowed to leave?' Radha exclaimed. 'If anyone else remembers anything, tell them I have my cellphone.'

She rolled up the window, pulled out her cellphone and firmly switched it off. 'South Extension?' she reminded the driver in a dangerous voice. The driver eased into gear and the car lurched forward respectfully.

I never cease marvelling at Radha and her joint family of thirty. A traditional family, a profitable business, a rambling bungalow in GK I that houses four generations of Mehtas of diverse ages, voices and political opinions. The four-storeyed mansion always seems like a huge pile of dried wood and kindling to me; the only thing that keeps it from erupting in a red-hot explosion of domestic discontent is Mataji, the eighty-year-old matriarch, and her steely, arthritic fingers that have steered the Mehta clan through five decades of bickering, petty grouses, financial uncertainty and hazardous social obligations. Everyone under that huge arched roof dances to Mataji's tune. Everyone except Radha, who just happens to be married to Mataji's favourite grandson, Vinod.

'So how do you feel about that new guy Rana?' she asked.

'Same way I felt about the old guy Rana.'

'You know him?'

'We used to be together in school. Same class, in fact.'

'Really? What was he like?'

'High achiever. First in class, lead role in plays.'

'And?'

'His servant used to carry his school bag. His lunch used to arrive hot and fresh at noon.'

She wrinkled her nose. 'That type, huh?'

'Worse. And don't even get me started on his mother.'

She nodded sympathetically.

'Any redeeming qualities?'

'None. That gap in his teeth? I did it.'

'What did he do?'

'His dog bit me.'

'His dog?'

'Same difference.'

She grinned and shook her head.

I looked out the window as the driver rounded a turn.

'Where are we going?' I asked.

'Sari shopping. Vinod's brother is getting married next month. I have to organize a bunch of things, buy some new clothes, the usual wedding stuff.'

'What are you planning to wear?'

'When? There are six functions—the engagement, the cocktails, our sangeet, their sangeet, the wedding, and then the reception. I'll need something new for each ceremony and, of course, jewellery to match.'

I hid a smile. 'Of course.'

A few minutes later, the driver pulled into a narrow, crowded by-lane and slowed to a halt in the middle of the road. The cars behind honked half-heartedly, and the cow who'd been blocking our way got huffily up and ambled off to another spot where she hoped she wouldn't be disturbed. I followed Radha into the unassuming shop entrance and stood a moment on the threshold, breathing in the sandalwood perfume, drawn almost irresistibly to the brilliance and bustle within.

There has to be a cosmic link between an Indian woman and a sari, a certain something about that cumbersome, six-yard length of material that gets under your skin and turns you into a lifelong hoarder and collector. I could imagine owning almost everything in the shop even though I'm sure I'd never end up wearing any of it. And even though it was the middle of June and the lean season, the shop was full to overflowing with bulging purses and salivating matrons. If ever things didn't work out for me at IF, I'd open a sari shop.

A middle-aged salesman came over and led us to a nearby counter, smiling and bowing deferentially. 'The latest, madam?' he asked Radha, and pulled a huge stack of saris towards him.

The counter started to pile up with yards and yards of brocaded silks in vivid pinks, oranges, peacock blues. I watched, mesmerized by the dazzling web, spun with a sharp twist of agile, skilful wrists. It was a shimmering rainbow, a kaleidoscope of colour that intensified with each successive layer, till I had to almost shield my eyes when the salesman whirled out a particularly bright creation, the approximate colour of hot chillies drying in the sun. The sari billowed up and was descending softly when a fleshy wrist grabbed one end and yanked it off.

'Pinky, look isn't this perfect? Exactly the same shade as our new Honda, what do you think?'

'Mom!' the young girl accompanying her winced, 'I think those people were looking at that sari.'

'What?' The mother turned around and glared. 'Oh, I didn't see you. Were you interested in this sari?'

Radha smiled sweetly. 'Not at all, that red really is you, and so car-like!'

'You really think so?' The woman's huge bosom jiggled as she held it up against her.

'Absolutely,' beamed Radha. 'And you know, there's an accessory shop right around the corner with a handbag and sandals in the same shade.'

'Really? I've been looking for red sandals for a very long time, thanks so much!'

I gaped in disbelief as she sped off.

Radha smiled wickedly at me and turned back to the salesman, 'Could you show us some Kanjeevarams? And this time in more subdued colours, please.'

Forty minutes later, we'd traversed miles of silks; from Pochampallis to Patolas and Kanthas to Kanjeevarams and everything in between, and Radha was still going strong. My head swam.

I stumbled over to the cotton corner to the left and was admiring a moss green creation with a simple bandhini print when a salesman came over, smiling.

'Why don't you try it on?' he encouraged.

Why not?

I ducked into the small changing room, did my best to drape the six-yard length of fabric, and emerged holding up the various folds that kept getting tangled in my feet. I looked around for

Radha and froze as a familiar, high-pitched voice pierced through the store and bounced off the walls.

'Rana, stop complaining. You promised to take me shopping today!'

I looked around quickly. My worst fears were confirmed. It *was* her. There was no mistaking the pencilled eyebrows and pinched nose, even after all these years. I thought fast and hid behind the potted palm.

'And show me your hands, I hope they are clean, I don't want you to get the saris dirty!'

A few women glanced up as the imperious voice drifted their way.

'Mom!' Rana hissed as he pulled his hands away.

'Well, those antiques in the previous shop were really dusty. Which reminds me, I hope you told the shopkeeper to leave the price tag in before he gift-wrapped that lamp. Don't want to spend five thousand rupees on an old lamp for Simi Aunty and not have her know how much it costs.'

'But wasn't that statue she gave you last year worth nine thousand rupees?' Rana asked.

'That's impossible. It's so ugly, and chipped at the base besides.'

I realized with horror that they were headed straight in my direction. I made a quick attempt at camouflage, got hopelessly entangled in the sari pallu, and was gasping for air when she stopped short in front of me.

'You, girl, what's the matter, is something wrong?'

I smiled out from behind the strangling folds.

'You look familiar. Do I know you?'

'I don't know. Maybe you're mistaken?'

'No, wait a minute, you look just like . . . *Minnoo*! Aren't you Prabha Sharma's daughter? Say namaste, dear? It's me, Vimi Aunty!'

I was enveloped in a leathery embrace.

'Heh, heh, hello Vimi Aunty. Yes, I'm *Minal.* How are you?'

'Rana look, it's *Minnoo* Sharma from Meerut. Remember those ugly brown flats just down the road from our bungalow? You two were in the same class!'

Where was Radha?

'So where are your parents these days; how is your mother? Still making pickles?' Vimi Aunty asked.

'They're in Meerut. Dad retired, and Mom is quite busy with her women's cooperatives.'

'Yes, I'll never forget, she asked me to join once. Just imagine, and no air-conditioning too! So what are you doing in Delhi?' she asked.

'I work at International Foods.'

'International Foods! But Rana just joined that company. As a senior manager, you know.'

'Fancy that.'

'What?'

'I meant that's great, it'll be just like old times, huh Rana?'

'I assume our paths will cross.'

Vimi Aunty performed a quick visual check on my forehead, fingers, neck and toes for any signs of matrimony. 'Are you married? Children?' she asked.

'I don't think so.'

'You don't *think* so? What kind of answer is that?'

'I mean, not really.'

'Ah.' She nodded, satisfied. 'And you must be what, thirty?'

'Twenty-nine.'

'Yes, whatever.' She patted my arm 'Well don't worry, things may still work out. Though with your height I really don't think you should wear heels. And try 'Fair and Lovely' cream; it's really good for dark complexions, I'm told.'

Where was the salesman?

'Rana got engaged last month, you know.'

'*What?*' This was news. 'Who?'

'Kunika.'

'Not Kunika *Malik*?'

I gaped at him speechless. To his credit, he turned bright red.

Vimi Aunty looked smug. 'Her father's in shipping, you know. What a pity you missed the engagement. It was at the Meridian.'

Kunika Malik. Skin like cream, hair like velvet, brains like snow in July. I wondered if she'd finally found out where it was that baby bunnies came from.

Rana seemed to read my mind. 'She's a very nice girl,' he scowled. 'And she's changed a lot.'

I sure hoped so.

'Mom, we should go; we're getting late,' Rana said.

Thank God.

Vimi Aunty pulled me in for another teeth-rattling embrace. 'Bye then, *Minnoo* dear. Come by sometime. Rana, why don't we have her over for dinner next weekend?'

Dinner?

I winced.

Rana shuddered.

It was good to see we still had that old chemistry going.

seven

Rana had his nose stuck in a pile of papers when I walked into his office the following morning. He waited till I took five steps in, and then pretended to just notice me. 'Oh, there you are,' he drawled. 'Just give me a minute, will you?'

He bent his head down once again and studied the thick file with a concentration most men reserve for *Playboy*. I was sure he wasn't registering a single word. I sat down and began silently counting off the seconds.

Exactly sixty-five seconds later he pushed the pile aside, leaned back in his chair and began to smile affably.

'So, Minal, how are you? Would you like some coffee?' he said.

'Sure.'

So we were to play at charades to start with.

'I've been studying the market information and the research available, in fact I was up quite late last night. It's not very encouraging, is it?'

Ma'am, I've read the next chapter, even though you didn't tell us to!

'Two hundred tonnes annually, that's chicken feed!'

Show-off.

'And most of that is from the north and west. In fact, Delhi and Bombay alone account for fifty per cent of the current market.'

Go ahead, Mr Geography Topper.

'So what do you think?'

'I think you're up to something.'

'I beg your pardon?'

'I think you've got something up your sleeve.'

'Well, I do have some ideas up my *sleeve,* as you put it, but I understand we're to work on this together. So tell me, what do you make of all this market data?'

'I haven't been through it yet.'

He knew I hadn't read any market data. Vik had just handed one set out.

'Really? Well, that has to change. You'd better get a move on and go through the material. Today. We don't have any time to waste; I want to have a game plan ready before the next meeting with Vik.'

'Look, we may have to work together on this by some bizarre twist of . . .'

'Minal,' he interrupted, 'I hope you're not going to rake up the past. Let's not forget, we're both here for one reason only, and that is to sell cakes. Let's keep it that way, shall we?'

'Weren't you going to order coffee?'

He picked up the phone and dialled Radha's extension.

'Radha? This is Rana Bhatia. Can we have two coffees in my room please?'

What was he, crazy? I watched fascinated. There was a long silence.

'Oh. Well, would you call the cafeteria then?'

Silence.

'Hmm. So what's the cafeteria number?'

Silence.

'I see. Thank you.'

He scowled at the phone and looked up at me.

'You wouldn't know the cafeteria number, would you?'

I took the phone.

'Let me. Incidentally, Radha is *Vik's* secretary. Also, he gets his own coffee.'

'See, that's what I can't understand. He really shouldn't mollycoddle the staff. They're here to boost our productivity, not the other way around. If this Radha had any brains, she'd be a manager not a secretary.'

Mom, this Ramu is very ill-mannered; refuses to untie my shoelaces. I think you should sack him.

His face was back in the research papers when I put the phone down. I sighed and wondered how I'd survive the next several weeks. I looked at the gleaming desk, the razor-sharp pencils, the patent leather diary and planner, the Mont Blanc pen lying at right angles to the new, ruled notepad.

Ma'am, Minal took my new pen.

I looked away and up at the bare walls. How long would it be before they too were filled with rows of medals and certificates in gilded frames?

And this, my dear Minnoo, is Rana's medal for the Class IV science quiz.

Suddenly, Rana pushed back his chair and got up. 'Well, let's get right down to business, shall we?' he said.

I quickly stopped my mental doodling and sharpened my mind. If business was what he wanted, business was what he'd get.

'The part that interests me most is Gourmet International,' he said. 'We don't seem to have much competitive intelligence, do we?'

'They're very secretive.'

'We need to get hold of some inside information; someone willing to spill the beans. Meanwhile, what *do* we know about them?'

'Besides secretive? They're very competitive. They have deep pockets.'

'And what about their cakes?'

'They sell more than we do.'

'Yes, but why?'

'They've been around longer.'

'Yes, and . . .?'

'They're always giving freebies and price-offs.'

There had to be a point he was leading up to, except that I couldn't see it.

'Price!' he emphasized. '*That's* where we need to attack them.'

'No, I don't think so. Their quality is pretty bad, and there's very little variety, just plain vanilla, pineapple and chocolate. I'm sure a lot of consumers are waiting for a whole new product.'

'How do you know what consumers want?'

I didn't. 'Let's research it,' I said.

'Exactly.' He strutted to a nearby flip chart and turned a page. 'Step 1: Research.'

I groaned as the full extent of his intentions (and number of pages on his flip chart) dawned on me.

'Let's find out what consumers want,' he said, 'and fast. We need to map out the potential, explore the options, determine the long-term viability and profitability. I suggest we follow this PERT chart that I've put together. I'll run you through it; pay close attention.'

I programmed my eyes and ears to 'open yet shut' mode and sent my mind on a rambling tour of the galaxy. Rana was the only kid who'd continue to recite his project report after everyone else, including the teacher, had left the room.

This would take a while.

eight

Much, much later that evening, I yawned, pulled myself up over the steering wheel and congratulated myself on making it out of the office. There had come a time during the day when I'd wondered if I'd ever see home again. What had started as a strategy meeting in the morning had erupted in a volcano of work in the afternoon, and by the evening I'd been buried under layer upon layer of folders and files that had been pulled out by Rana from the deepest corners of the office. And as the night had come down around me, I'd felt like a fossil, caught between a desk and a chair in the deep belly of the office, and time and memory had all but evaporated. It had felt like the longest day of my life.

I stretched as I turned into the parking lot. What time was it anyway? My back hurt, my neck protested, I was shrink-wrapped in a film of exhaustion. Shower, bed, sleep, sweet sleep . . . the evil shape of the confounded jeep was blocking my way again. This time it had crossed the thin yellow line of decency and was squatting exactly midway between its spot and mine like a Sumo wrestler. I got out and kicked its big fat tyres.

There was only so much crap I could take in one day. Aristotle upstairs would have to rearrange his approach to parking, or I'd have to rearrange his features for him. I located 'Ali Imran B-406' on the row of mailboxes in the dim foyer light, marched four winding flights up the echoing stairs and jabbed the doorbell till it bleated for mercy.

I rang and rang.

Good, he was asleep.

I rang and rang harder.

Where was he? Not dead, I hoped; not before he moved the Jeep.

My thumb turned red and came off pale when I took it off the ringer. Crafty, but I knew he was home; there were ugly shadows in the light that shone through the curtains. Waiting, hoping, pleading with me to leave. *Well, tough luck, you grey ghouls; Judgement Day is here.* I walked round the landing to the other side, located a windowsill and tugged at the panes till they swung open. It was quiet inside, but the shadows on the curtains began to dance up a frenzy.

I lifted a corner of the curtain and peered in curiously.

The room had no furniture!

Bare white walls, swathes of white marble floor, dim yellow lights. An impressive orchestra that played vigorously and soundlessly on a TV screen at the far end. The only real colour came from the middle of the room, where a brilliant rug in all the shades of the earth radiated warmth and energy right up to the window where I stood. It was the kind of rug I would have stopped and coveted a while if it weren't for the figure that stood, proud and nude, in the middle of the rug.

No, wait up.

He wasn't nude; he *was* wearing something. Tan jeans and a back to match. A strong, gleaming back, the colour of polished teak, with wide shoulders at the top, a corded belt at the bottom, and a deep ridge that cut through the shoulder blades, deepened, darkened, and then disappeared inside the low-rise jeans. A hint of muscle rippled in the arms that rose and fell; the fingers, waving a baton, were a sinuous, elongated blur. A head of dark hair bracketed between sound reduction headphones swayed gently with the soundless music.

I felt weak in the knees as I let go the curtains and stepped back into the passageway. *This* was Ali? Twenty-nine years of rummaging around in the scrap pile and hanging out with the likes of Rajiv and Aman, and suddenly—Brad Pitt and Zubin Mehta all rolled up in one?

It didn't make sense.

It called for a drastic change of tactics.

It meant I'd have to abandon my opening line. 'Your Jeep is blocking my way, you asshole' hardly seemed appropriate anymore—and of course the karate chop ending I'd been planning would be wholly out of line. This was opportunity's door (or window sill, rather).

Sometimes in life you have to take matters into your own hands.

I took a deep breath, grabbed the windowsill and hoisted myself up.

'Hey,' I yelled.

The eyes stayed shut; the arms kept conducting the music.

'Helloooo!'

He responded with a flourish of the baton.

I pulled myself over the ledge and landed with a resounding thud on the marble floor.

He swayed to the soundless music like a reed by the riverside.

I walked across the room and tapped him on the shoulder.

Big brown eyes snapped open, blinked and widened in horror. Nice eyes; a little muddy with fear, but potentially sharp and clever, and exactly level with mine.

'Hello,' I smiled.

'Oh my God!' He lunged for a shirt that was lying on the settee. 'Wha-who-how did you get in here?'

I pointed to the window.

'You're kidding.'

'I kept ringing, but you didn't answer.'

'God, I'm going to have to do something about that window.'

'Absolutely. You should get a grill put in or something; you never know who'll climb in next.'

I noticed he was doing up the shirt buttons quick and wrong.

'You missed one there,' I pointed.

He bounded across the room and turned off the TV.

'Who are you?' he demanded.

'Your neighbour.'

'And why are you here?'

This continuing hostility thing was getting to be a drag.

'Your Jeep is blocking my way again,' I said.

Recognition dawned. And disbelief.

'*You're* the Post-it girl?'

'Minal Sharma, B-206,' I confirmed. 'That's just two floors below you. Want to see my driver's license?'

He gaped for a few seconds and then began to laugh.

'No, that's okay. Do you make a habit of breaking into people's homes, though?'

'Only when I really need to.'

He stared at me some more.

I looked round the room in search of conversation. 'So, nice place. Of course there's no furniture.'

He shrugged.

'Did you just move in?'

'A couple of weeks ago.'

'No wonder it's so nice and clean. You should see my room.'

'Really?'

I realized that that last bit could be misconstrued.

'Figuratively speaking, that is.'

'Of course,' he smiled. 'Why don't you sit down? I wasn't

expecting company, but now that you're here . . .'

The clock on the wall chimed 11:00.

Eleven p.m.?

'No thanks, it's getting late. If you could just move your Jeep? There's no way I can park; it's too much on my side.'

'Sorry,' he said, without the slightest trace of contrition. And for some reason he was beginning to look extremely amused. 'I still can't believe that *you* are Ms Post-It,' he said. 'And to think I had you written down as some . . .'

'Some?'

'Some very nice, well-mannered person, of course.' He was grinning now; and very attractively too. 'You have to admit, that parking spot is really tiny,' he said. 'I should probably ask for a bigger spot.'

'Oh, you don't have to move to a *different* spot,' I said quickly. 'This one is pretty good, it's near the steps, and so convenient. It's not that hard to park there, it's just a question of perfecting the technique.'

Too eager?

He didn't seem to notice.

'Well, let's get my Jeep out of your way,' he said.

He picked a bunch of keys off the table, thrust his feet into a pair of Timberlands and opened the door.

'You gave me quite a scare, you know,' he smiled, 'sneaking up on me like that. What if I were a psycho or a murderer?'

'Don't worry, I watched you for a bit before I jumped in.'

'You what? Well thanks; that's reassuring! I probably looked like a complete nerd.'

I followed him down the steps, admiring the way the jeans creased and smoothed and clung as he walked.

Far from it, I thought.

'Well, here we are,' he said as we neared the two cars. 'How about you back yours up a bit, and then I can move mine closer to the wall?'

I got behind the wheel of my Maruti and reversed, and watched him back and forth into the narrow space that was his spot. He was rummaging around in the Jeep when I got out.

'Looking for something?'

'Nope, just haven't cleaned this out in a while.'

He scooped up a pile of assorted clutter and dived in for more.

'I'll help,' I offered.

There was a lot of it. I removed various pieces of crumpled sheets, newspapers, cartons, plastic, tangled tapes and broken CDs and carried them over to the dumpster in the corner. He emerged from the depths of the back seat with an armload of empty cans, bottles, and bags of potato chips as I returned. I stared hypnotized at the lacy pink strap that hung out at one end.

'What?' He looked down. 'Oh, that!' He pulled the bra out of the pile, stuffed it into his jeans pocket and dumped the rest of the stuff in the dumpster.

'Well, that's the lot,' he said and dusted his hands on the seat of his jeans. 'Thanks for helping.'

We started up the stairs.

'So, would you like to come up for a cup of coffee or something?" he asked.

'No.'

It came out more frigid than I'd intended. He glanced at my face, then grinned. 'What, never seen a bra before?'

'Not on a guy.'

'Touché.' He laughed, but didn't elaborate.

We reached the second floor and I stopped outside my doorway.

'Is this your apartment?'

'Yes.'

'The one you wanted me to see.'

'Maybe not.'

'Hey, just kidding.' He shook my hand. 'Anyway, good night. I'm not home that much, but you're welcome to drop by anytime.'

I watched him make for the steps.

'Oh, and Minal?'

I waited.

'Try the door next time.'

I sighed and pushed the door open. He was delicious. He had a girlfriend.

I should have guessed; it stuck out a mile. A guy that hot could not be unattached. Who was she? Some well-endowed, Barbie-type who hung about his empty flat in satiny pink negligees, no doubt. I dragged myself to my room, pulled on a pair of gloriously faded and thinned-from-several-washes pyjamas, padded over to the bathroom on my elephant feet and squeezed some pink toothpaste onto my pink toothbrush.

He'd offered coffee though.

It could be nice. The empty living room, the warm rug, some soft music, steaming cups of coffee.

What if I had it all wrong? What if that bra belonged to his mother or sister or cross-dressing uncle or was just a free gift he found inside one of those bags of potato chips? (God knows those guys were desperate enough to put anything in their chips to move the stock.) Maybe I ought to take him up on the offer after all. He'd mentioned coffee and winked; and if that wasn't flirting, I wasn't twenty-nine.

I rinsed twice, washed my face and looked back up in the mirror. The tube light flung dark saucer-shaped shadows beneath my eyes and bounced off the limp hair around my ears. Without the pretence of even my customary mocha lipstick, I looked about as distinguished and striking as a streetlight on the blink.

Who was I kidding. That guy was probably going out with some drop-dead gorgeous sex goddess, and loving every minute of it. Twice a day, seven days a week. And I looked like the 'before' part of a 'before and after' ad.

Be realistic, Minal, my reflection sighed, *you'll be better off focusing on Mom's matrimonial ad varieties. And if you don't mind my saying so, it may be time for another face pack.*

nine

The fresh bunch of papers that made its way up from Rana's office the next morning took up the last few available inches of real estate on my desk and, like all the others that had preceded it, had 'URGENT!!' scribbled across the top in bold red marker, crying out for instant attention like some highly inconsiderate baby.

RESEARCH QUESTIONNAIRE, PROJECT: SWEET TOOTH (DRAFT 1A), the title read. I could see instantly that something was hideously wrong.

Q1.a Do you like desserts?

- Yes
- No

(Hello?)

Q1.b How much do you like desserts?

- Like them very much
- Like them
- Like them somewhat
- Indifferent
- Dislike them

(. . . *??*)

Q1.c What kind of desserts do you like?

- Cookies
- Cakes
- Puddings
- Ice cream
- Flavoured yoghurt
- Chocolates
- Any other

Please rank in order of preference. (*How?*)

Q2.a Approx. what quantity of cakes is consumed by each member of your family in:

- A day
- A week
- A month
- A year

Please mention separately for each member of your family. (*Good grief!*)

And for the next twenty-six pages, a relentless stream of:

Q3.a What are the ideal characteristics you look for in desserts? Please rank in order of preference.

Q3.b What is the primary occasion for consumption?

Q3.c What is the primary time of day for consumption?

Q4.a What . . .

I sat back, reeling. How was anyone ever supposed to fill out all this information and stay awake at the same time? Were we really planning to interview five hundred respondents for answers to these philosophical questions of questionable merit? What would we discover: that eighty-two per cent of the population preferred ice cream to chocolate and twenty-one per cent of all cakes were consumed by uninvited guests on Saturday after 10 p.m.?

I called Rana. 'Hi, it's Minal,' I said.

'What is it? I'm busy.'

'I'm not comfortable with the draft questionnaire that the research agency sent in this morning.'

'It's just a draft. You're supposed to flesh it out.'

'I think we need a totally new draft.'

'Why would we need to redo all that work?'

'Well, for one, we seem to be asking too many extremely obvious questions. We'll put the respondents to sleep before we get around to any of the real questions.'

'Your view is that we should use our research money to provide respondents with a rollicking read?'

'No, but we could definitely . . .'

'Look, I really don't have time for this. I have a meeting with Finance in an hour. Why don't you figure it out by yourself? And while you're about it, see if you can bring down the cost. Do we really need five hundred interviews?'

'But . . .'

'And can you have it finished today? We need to debrief Suresh first thing tomorrow morning.'

The picture of Rana debriefing the lead researcher on the team was diverting. Briefs? Boxers? What would it be beneath those skinny pants? There was a loud click, and the phone went dead. *Swine! He'd hung up on me.*

Well, I had to get this right, with or without Rana.

It all began with consumer research. One misstep and it was downhill all the way. One could never forget the chilling lesson, now a classic case study, of the company that had once brought out a chocolate-flavoured lice-repellent for kids. Fantastic response in research; mayhem in the market. All because the marketing team had made the mistake of conducting the research on kids instead of on moms. *What did the cake customer want? Why? What would make them want more?* What *I* wanted were some consumers to answer my questions. I picked up the questionnaire again and wondered where to start.

IF employees!

I looked around for someone to test the questionnaire on. No one from Marketing, they'd be too biased. Ditto for Sales. In the end, I decided to emulate the research agencies and take a random sample. I pulled out the office phone list, closed my eyes, and stuck my finger in the middle of the sheet. I opened my eyes and saw that I'd picked the big boss. Better skip this one; there was no point in getting fired for random behaviour.

For my next choice I twirled my finger and spun the paper around a few times too. I landed on M.S. Swamy.

Now who was this? Of course, the new HR Head, the one nobody had ever seen.

With a newfound resourcefulness I called and set up a meeting for later that afternoon, and feeling extremely pleased with the morning's work, stood tapping on his cabin door at precisely 2 p.m.

A well-dressed, pleasant-looking man got up from behind the desk and smiled wide as I approached.

'Mr Swamy? I'm Minal Sharma, from . . .'

He grabbed my hand and shook it vigorously. 'Yes, yes, I know. So nice to meet you. Would you like some coffee?'

'Yes, thanks!'

'So, you're here to discuss the desserts, are you? Do sit down.'

'I hope this won't take too much of your time?'

'Oh, no, don't worry about it. Just doing my job.'

I blinked. He was the HR manager. He knew who I was. He seemed nice. *He was the HR manager?*

'So, shall we start?' he said. 'I like cakes, cookies, soufflé, pudding, and how about tiramisu? I really like tiramisu.'

'I see. Now, do you think you could rank those in order of preference?'

'Rank them? Why? So that we can decide which ones to leave out?'

'Oh, no, you can keep them all in; it's really up to you.'

'No, I think five is too much. Maybe we should leave out the cookies; they don't go well with the rest.'

'They do fall into a different category of desserts.'

'Actually, I think we should really picture it in terms of the entire meal. Appetizers, main course, dessert. Which dessert would go best with which entrée and so on.'

Really, the man was brilliant. I'd never thought of it that way before. I scribbled away in my notepad.

'You know, this is great feedback,' I said, 'but would you mind if I asked a few basic questions first, start at the beginning, you know?'

'Okay.'

'So, Question 1. Do you like desserts?

'Yes.'

'Question 1b. How much do you like desserts? Choose one: Like them very much, like them, like them somewhat, indifferent, or dislike them?

'I don't know. I guess it depends on the dessert.' He shifted a little in his chair and shot a glance at his watch. 'I don't see where we are heading with this.'

'You see, that's exactly it, neither do I!'

We regarded each other for a few seconds.

'Can we start over, *my* way?' he said finally. 'Now, as I was saying, let's choose the desserts to go with the entrées. What do you suggest would go well with grilled fish?'

'I'm sorry?'

'Well, we've got three entrées; let's pick desserts to go with each.'

'I think matching the cakes with different savouries is something we'll need to do at a much later stage. Right now, I'd just like to explore your current usage and attitude towards them.'

'But how would that help? Besides, the dinner's not too far away, I was hoping to finalize the menu today.'

He looked put out. Not crazy, just put out.

'Are we talking about my research questionnaire here?' I ventured. 'The one I mentioned on the phone?'

'What questionnaire? We're supposed to be putting together the menu for Dan Avery's dinner next Friday!'

'Dan Avery's coming to India?' I exclaimed. 'When? How long will he be here?' This was big. The big boss was probably having fits. Dan was the CEO of International Foods Worldwide.

M.S. Swamy, meanwhile, was holding his head.

'Who *are* you?' he pleaded.

'I'm Minal Sharma, from Marketing. Upstairs, on the third floor, you know?'

'You mean you *work* here? Oh no! I thought you were from the event management agency. What a waste of time.'

Paradox solved. He *was* the HR manager.

ten

It was a rare summer evening, quiet and cool. A dust storm in the afternoon had swept away the heat, leaving behind a lazy breeze that fluttered amongst the leaves of the trees that lined the high walls of the apartment complex. Some young boys were engaged in a serious game of marbles under the shade of the old banyan tree. To their right, a squirrel scurried about, gathering fallen nuts.

We sat out on my balcony and watched the evening sky turn pink, peach, apricot and orange. The overhead fan circulated gentle eddies of air that played with the ends of his crisp shirt collar and lifted the flounces of my cotton skirt from time to time. I crossed my legs to help it along.

Naveen approved.

His eyes flitted over my legs every time I moved, and then looked hastily away. I didn't mind; he was supposed to be well-bred, not dead.

He recounted some basketball anecdote and I nodded and smiled and watched the way his lips moved. What an air of distinction! I imagined good breeding flowed effortlessly in his veins after generations of royalty. It was part of him, in the way he sat straight up in his chair, and crossed his legs and laced his fingers, and had his head turned courteously in my direction. His features weren't perfect, as Yudhishter's had been, and he didn't scream sex appeal like my neighbour upstairs, but something in his bearing reminded me of those maharajas whose pictures hung in gilded frames in the lobbies of the hotels in Jaipur.

And I liked his face. It was a clean, open face, untroubled and unlined. A face that smiled easily, a face that saw a good night's sleep, a face that dreamed pleasant dreams.

He reminded me of the Ents of Entwood; he looked like he'd live to be a hundred.

'What did you think of *The Lord of the Rings*?' I asked on a whim.

'Nice movie.'

'Yes, but I meant the book.'

'Nice book. The scenes were nicely written.'

'You know what you remind me of? An Ent. I love the part about the Ents; I've always wanted to meet one.'

'Yes, the characters are very nice.'

So he wasn't big on adjectives. Big deal. And really, wasn't intellectual snobbery every bit as deplorable as vanity about one's looks or wealth? At least he was cultured and well-mannered and we had tonnes in common. Cats, not dogs; rock, not pop; coffee, not tea; popcorn, not chips . . .

I could picture our lives together quite easily. Leisurely strolls down the paved paths of his bungalow (or palace); long vacations on golden beaches watching the waves roll gently off the sand; drinks and dinner Friday evenings at the local club for royals. Life with Naveen would be one long ride in a shiny chariot; finely balanced, impossibly full. I'd whiz off to my high-profile job in my chauffeur-driven car in the mornings; he'd go shoot a round of golf, chase it up with basketball practice and cricket; and late in the evening, we'd get together to head out for a nice late-night movie.

'Do you like movies?' I asked.

'Oh, sure. Do you know what my favourite movie of all time is?'

'Let me guess. *Chariots of Fire? The Godfather? Lagaan?*'

'*There's Something about Mary*,' he chuckled. 'Isn't that the funniest movie ever made? I've seen it a dozen times!'

'Ha, ha, ha,' I laughed.

Hey, it *was* a funny movie.

'So you like comedies?' I asked.

'I love a good laugh. There are so many sad things in real life; a funny movie can really make you forget it all.'

'Come now,' I teased, 'what do *you* need to forget?'

'Well, I may be lucky, but there's so much poverty and misery all around. Can you imagine, some kids never even get to hold a cricket bat? That's why I teach at the university. I don't really need to, but there are such few good sports facilities in our country! Sometimes I really feel I'm making a big difference.'

Yup, the country needed more guys like him. High time we won an Olympic gold or two. High time I moved things along.

'What's Jodhpur like?' I asked, 'I've never been there; it must be very romantic.'

He looked up at the sky and sighed. 'Yes it is. Though out here, right now, Delhi is very beautiful too.'

Slam dunk and two points! I tried to achieve a modest, attractive blush.

'Er, if you don't mind,' he said, clearing his throat, 'could I have a glass of water please?'

'I'm so sorry!' I jumped up, instantly contrite. 'I completely forgot to ask. What would you like to drink? I've got juice, wine, beer . . .'

'Oh, I don't drink alcohol. Just some water or juice, whatever is more convenient.'

Health drinks. From now on that's all I'd ever have too.

I tried to imagine his parents' charming little haveli. We'd visit on weekends; a game of tennis in the morning, *nimbu pani* and yoga class in the afternoon, five-course healthy dinner at night. He'd teach me how to ride his beautiful horses and we'd gallop home together like that couple in the Siyaram ad.

On an impulse, I put some ice in glasses, squeezed some lemons, and mixed in Nani's special syrup.

Naveen put down the sheet he'd been writing on and rose to take the tray as I walked back from the kitchen. Now what had he been writing so surreptitiously in the fading light? A poem, a tribute to the lovely summer evening, an ode to my eyes?

He was fond of poetry; it had said so in the ad. Or was that the dentist guy?

'Did you need to write something?' I asked. 'We could go inside; the light's much better there.'

'Oh, no that's okay. This lemonade looks nice.'

'Try it,' I smiled.

And that's when it happened.

I picked up a glass with a flourish, tripped over his foot, and a generous five ounces of Nani's special lemonade went sloshing into the fine fabric of his understated yet expensive trousers.

'Oops!' I cried.

'Oh, no!' he said.

Clumsy, clumsy, and now he'd think I'd done it on purpose.

'We could catch it before it stains,' I said. 'Just rinse those pants out right away.'

'But . . .'

'You could use that bathroom,' I said, pointing. 'Just hand them to me when you're done, and I'll iron them for you.'

'But . . .'

'Go ahead; you'll be fine.'

I settled him in the loo with a towel and a magazine, and went back out to clean up the mess.

I happened to see the sheet he'd been writing on as I dabbed away at the chair. I wouldn't have noticed it, but it had my name on top. I picked it up.

MINAL SHARMA

	Score/10	Weights	Adjusted Score
Beauty	4	30	120
Family	5	30	150
Hostess skills	2	20	40
Values	4	10	40
Personality	6	10	60
		100	410
Mean score: 4.1			

I was still working out the mathematics of my barely passing score when I heard him call out to me from the bathroom. 'Minal?' he called, in his nice voice.

I walked up slowly.

Now be calm, my conscience said.

'Here you are,' he said, and a nice, muscled arm held out the pants. 'A light iron, without steam, should do the trick.'

Minal, pleeease . . .? my old conscience pleaded.

I took the nice pants, spread them out and put the iron on the seat.

Good girl, the good voice breathed, relieved.

I cranked up the heat on the iron, and walked to the kitchen looking for ammo.

'Minal?' Naveen called from the bathroom.

Minal! the virtuous one yelped, horrified, as I pulled a tall plastic bag from the cupboard.

'Aw, shaddup!' I whispered, and began to fill my bag.

A few minutes later I hoisted the bag on my shoulder, walked back to the drawing room and noted with satisfaction the wisps of smoke that were starting to rise from the pants.

This wouldn't take long; the smoke alarm was directly above. I waited for the wisps to turn into big puffy clouds; then went quietly out the door and up the stairs to wait on the third floor landing, directly above.

Fifty seconds later, the sirens started screeching and the sprinklers went off. Naveen Singh, royal scion of Jodhpur, came sprinting out the doorway in shirt tails and faded brown briefs as fast as his long legs could carry him. I hoisted my bag, took aim and whistled in awe at my own marksmanship as five days of accumulated garbage rained down with precision on the regal head below.

'How's that for hostess skills,' I called, as I walked past him into the drawing room. 'Oh, and don't forget your pants.'

The alarm kept screeching and the sprinklers spraying, and I took a moment to stand in the middle of the living room, exulting. It had been perfect—a sweeping Broadway finale, a breathtaking extravaganza of sound, light and smoke. I felt I deserved a Tony or something.

And then the alarms fell silent, the sprinklers trickled to a drip-drop, the smoky haze settled at a comfortable eye level and I surveyed my trophy—the soaking-wet living room, the garbage in the doorway, the many hours of scrubbing and sponging that lay ahead.

I went to the fridge for a beer.

Half an hour later I stood squeezing a wet mop over the sink and mulling over the evening's events for the twentieth time.

Faded brown briefs! I shuddered, remembering. *Who'd have thought with all that money and royalty and all?* Sometimes you can never tell.

In fact this whole dating and mating thing was getting to be pretty discouraging. Sagging briefs, towering egos, garlic breath, hidden girlfriends, sweaty armpits, nasal whines, dandruff collars, missing spines . . . the dangers were infinite. I'd probably be better off playing Russian roulette; at least the odds of surviving were one in two.

Or was it five in six? Or one in six? (I'd have to check with Akshay next door; he always got 100 on 100 in maths, or so his mom claimed). Anyhow, they couldn't be worse than the odds of finding a regular, inoffensive guy. And to think he'd seemed so nice!

I winced at the adjective.

Come to think of it, it had been a pretty narrow escape. *What if I'd never seen that score sheet; what if we'd really gotten married?* We'd have had a nice wedding on a nice day with a lot of nice guests and after it was all nicely over we'd have gone on our nice honeymoon and come back with a nice Minal-in-bed scorecard which may have looked something like: ardour 8/10, naked body 4/10, left hook to right jaw 10/10.

I pulled out a dry mop from the cupboard and headed for the soaking sofa.

The evening star winked in the window as I scrubbed away at the armrest.

Do you really work? I asked.

It winked again, a little playfully, I thought.

I clasped my hands, linked my fingers, closed my eyes.

So send me someone, I dared it. *Anyone, as long as he's halfway decent. And soon; I don't have that much time.*

In mocking but quick response, I heard the doorbell ring.

The evening star had a strange sense of humour, I found. I opened the door and leaning against the frame stood none other than the dashing neighbour, all freshly showered and shaved and primped and primed, radiating enticing wisps of some hard-to-place cologne, eyes travelling over my wet blouse and damp skirt with interest.

'Ali, what a surprise!'

'I guess you weren't kidding when you said your home was a mess,' he said, his attention shifting to the mound of garbage on the floor. 'What happened?'

'Oh, just one of those things,' I shrugged. 'I had a little spill, and the smoke alarm went off and then the sprinklers . . . nothing much, really.'

'Are you okay?'

'Oh, sure. I'll have it all cleaned up in a trice.'

'I could help.'

'Weren't you on your way somewhere?'

I eyed his crisp shirt, remembering the skin and muscle that lay beneath.

'Not for a while,' he said.

'Are you sure? What about your clothes?'

'I'd worry more about yours.'

I looked down at my soaked skirt. 'I look a fright.'

'I wouldn't say that,' he grinned. 'Wet and clingy has its merits.'

'Ha, ha.'

Now why did that come out all self-conscious and breathless? And why was I smoothing my skirt back down around my knees?

He smiled and held out a hand. 'Come, give me that mop. Why don't you go and change.'

'Thanks,' I said, stepping back. 'I'll be back in a minute.'

The vote was divided on what to wear; two factions battling bitterly as I stood surveying my wardrobe.

The red skirt with the deep slit, the left brain was exhorting, its judgement jammed by a thick block of adolescent excitement. *Did you see the way he kept looking at your legs!*

The faded jeans, you moron, the right brain was scoffing through its suit of invincible armour. *You're supposed to be mopping the floor.*

The sheer black wrap-around blouse, insisted the democrats.

The grey T-shirt; it needs washing anyway, pointed out the republicans.

In the end I managed to forge a consensus and pulled on stretch jeans and a white blouse that revealed a hint of cleavage.

He was patting the wet patches on the TV when I returned.

'Do you do this often?' he smiled as I joined him.

'Ask a neighbour to help clean up? No, usually I wait for the maid.'

'I meant set-off-your-fire-alarm-by-mistake kind of thing.'

'It wasn't by mistake.'

He raised his brows.

'There was this guy who'd come over,' I explained.

'That hot, huh?'

I couldn't help laughing. 'That *weird*! I couldn't stand him.'

'So you decided to smoke him out?'

'Something like that.'

'And the garbage?'

'That too.'

He whistled. 'I sure hope you can stand me. Or should I leave while I still have the chance?'

'Don't be silly,' I laughed. 'I wish I'd omitted the garbage though; this is disgusting.'

'Here, let me.'

I passed him the broom and went to the kitchen for a plastic bag to fill it in.

'So, this guy; what did he do, make a pass at you or something?' Ali called.

'No, he was just someone my mom wanted me to meet. She's trying to help me get married.'

'Arranged marriage?' He watched in surprise as I returned. 'You don't strike me as the type.'

Type?

'What type do I strike you as?' I challenged.

'Let's see now,' he said, sitting back on his haunches. 'The first time we met you broke into my apartment. The second time you tell me you dumped your garbage on someone you didn't like. What do you do for a living; hold up banks, crash-test cars?'

'Nothing quite as exciting,' I laughed, feeling a bit like Lara Croft the Tomb Raider. 'I sell cakes.'

'Yeah, right.'

'It's true. I work in Marketing at International Foods. In the Cakes division.'

'International Foods!'

'Why, is there something wrong with that?'

'No. Except what's a bad girl like you doing with a good company like that?'

He dodged as I threw the bag at him.

'No, seriously. IF is such a proper company! Everyone wears a suit and tie, don't they? I met a guy called Aman a couple of months ago, when your breakfast bars sponsored our show. Real weirdo and I swear he was wearing gold cufflinks!'

'Your show?' I asked, intrigued.

'The Lara and Ali Show, 107.4 FM.'

'FM? As in *radio*?'

He nodded.

'You mean you're a *radio jockey*?'

'Yep.'

'Oh.'

'You don't sound too impressed.'

'No, really, that's . . . that's great.'

Really, it wasn't.

Now don't get me wrong here. It's not that there's anything wrong with being a radio jockey or hosting a radio show; in fact the Lara and Ali Show was pretty hot I'd heard, good ratings and reviews and all, but . . . just picture it! I'm at work, crunching numbers, talking strategy, impressing the pants off Vik and the big boss, and suddenly I go, 'Guess what folks, I'm going out with a radio jockey!

Still, there was that back . . . and that skin . . . and that smile . . .

'Something the matter?' he asked.

'No. So, what's it like, working in radio?'

'It's a blast,' he grinned. 'I just wish it paid more.'

Me too.

'You know, the way you were conducting that orchestra the other day, I thought you were a musician or something,' I said.

'In my next life!' he laughed. 'I hope. I love music; really, really love it. I tinkered around with all kinds of things, even a guitar and a college band, but . . .'

'So what were you doing that day; rehearsing for your *radio show*?'

It didn't make sense.

'No, just relaxing after a long day. You know how sometimes you just need to *feel* the music, to reach out and touch it, wrap it around yourself, fill yourself with it?'

I didn't.

'Anyway, that piece is my favourite,' he smiled.

'Really?'

'I know it backwards. I even have my own little flourishes and improvisations.'

'What is it?'

'Beethoven's Fifth Symphony, with Karajan conducting the Berlin Philharmonic Orchestra.'

'Uh-huh.'

'It's the best version there is!'

'I'm afraid I don't know much about classical music.'

'Really? I've got a pretty good CD collection; you're welcome to check it out any time.'

An invitation?

'Actually, I'm pretty clueless when it comes to music in general. Just never got any exposure to it,' I smiled.

'That's a pity.'

'Yes. I've always wanted to learn, but . . .'

'I have a keyboard upstairs,' he said, after a second. 'I could teach you some basics if you want.'

An invitation.

I held it close for a moment, like a precious, precious gift. And then, almost perversely, 'Oh, thanks, but I really don't know . . .'

'Maybe one of these days,' Ali said, with a casual shrug of the shoulder.

'Maybe one of these days,' I nodded, with a glum biting of the lip.

And the moment was tossed aside and we both went back to cleaning up the mess.

A half hour later we stood rinsing the last of the mops out over the kitchen sink. Ali stretched and leaned back against the counter.

'Thanks for helping out,' I said, washing my hands. 'It would have taken me ages on my own.'

'No problem.'

'So, um, would you like some coffee or something? Actually, it's almost dinnertime. I have some pizza leftover from . . .'

'Dinnertime?' He shot up suddenly. 'God, it's past eight! I'd better run; I have a meeting ten minutes ago!'

'A meeting at eight? For your radio show?'

'No, for my website,' he said quickly. 'Look, sorry to rush out like this, but I really need to vanish. See you!'

I stood in the kitchen for a minute, bewildered. Then I went to the computer and spent the next hour looking for a 'Lara and Ali' website.

There was none.

eleven

Wednesday next week, I was counting the leaves on the moneyplant behind Vik's head. Then I'd count the leaves on all the other plants in the room, then all the leaves on all the branches of all the trees outside the window. Hopefully, by the time I finished, Rana would be done.

I suppose I should have been paying attention. He made a forceful presentation; offering up the mundane and the commonplace with an artistry known only to exotic dancers and consultants. His voice rose and fell, underlined and italicized, and I watched with grudging admiration as he pranced expertly through the slides, stripping away fact after cumbersome fact to reveal in a small square spot of light, the final tantalizing titbits he'd been building up to:

- Eighty-five per cent of people like cakes
- Price is the most important attribute influencing purchase

Rocket science?

Vik certainly thought so; he leaned forward to stare hypnotically at the slide.

And then, just when I was about to despair, Rana made a strategic error. Like someone chopping off his own head, he turned on the lights, turned off the projector, and stopped presenting.

'To summarize: The research findings indicate . . . primitive market . . . need for basic sponge . . . common man's cake . . .

inexpensive . . . deep cost cuts . . .' he explained, and without the golden halo of the projector he was once again his usual nasty and pompous self. My hopes lifted—perhaps all was not yet lost.

I watched Vik, who was sitting back with a little furrow deepening between his brows. 'How do we compare with Gourmet International?' he asked.

'We're still neck-to-neck on brand preference,' Rana said promptly, 'but they score better on price.'

'We come out higher on quality,' I added.

'Yes, but of all the attributes, price is the most important factor,' Rana scowled.

'I know that. But price is the most important factor for everything.'

'We're higher on quality?' Vik asked.

'Yes, and on taste too.'

'But GI's selling more overall,' Rana was quick to point out.

'Tell me something I don't know,' Vik grimaced.

Rana straightened, triumphant. 'I think pricing is the key, Vik,' he continued. 'If you look closely at the responses from . . .'

'I think we should also consider the findings from the group discussion,' I interrupted.

'Those weren't statistically significant.'

'They were very insightful!'

'They were just the opinions of a handful of housewives.'

Vik raised his brows at that.

'Let's hear them; every consumer is important,' he said.

Rana glared at me. 'The group discussions were just an input for the actual research, Vik; more to generate variables than anything else. We really didn't find anything new, just a bunch of women getting together to trade recipes and oven sale prices.'

He gave Vik one of those 'you-know-how-it-is' smiles.

The SOB He hadn't even been there.

'On the contrary, Vik,' I said, 'you'd be surprised by how much interest and enthusiasm there was about cakes. Almost everyone at that GD had an interesting cake story. I could sense the pent-up demand for a quality product. In fact, once the group got going, there was no stopping the flow of ideas!'

'Each of them more fanciful than the other.'

'Oh yeah? And what about that woman who said cakes were like cards and flowers? That really got the group excited; even the moderator took that down as an important insight.'

'Mere fluff.'

'I don't get it. Cards and flowers?' Vik said.

'You know, like Anniversaries, Valentine's Day, New Year's, Best of Luck, Thank You, Sorry, Miss You, Get Well Soon? The point was that any occasion can call for a cake.'

'But there's no comparison!' Rana scowled. 'Cards are non-perishable and low cost. Plus you can mail them to someone thousands of miles away without having to worry about diabetes or cholesterol.'

'It's the basic "reason why" that's similar. The women felt that cakes fulfilled the same need as cards and flowers; the need to feel good, to celebrate, to show you care.'

'Occasion-led marketing. That *is* an interesting line of thought,' Vik mused.

'I really think that if there were good-quality cakes available for every occasion and mood, more consumers would lean towards us, irrespective of the price.'

'I disagree,' Rana sulked, in a voice reminiscent of the Class V school debate.

'It would be a big risk, though,' Vik continued. 'And it would call for totally different industry dynamics. New supply chains, alternate distribution channels—in fact very complex distribution, which would mean less direct control . . . we'd even need new production processes. We're talking about a totally new approach to marketing here. I'm sorry, Minal, we'd need a lot more information before we could go ahead.'

'Can't we at least try with any one occasion, just a test market?'

'Well . . .'

'I agree with Vik,' Rana said quickly. 'This is not the time to try any fancy experiments; we need to capture market share quickly.'

'But . . .'

But he'd turned on the projector, put in another impressive-looking slide and begun his hypnotic act once again.

'To get back to the research findings and the *hard data* that is available,' he was saying, 'this chart indicates that if we decrease the price by twenty-five per cent, we can expect sales to go up by hundred per cent!'

'Reduce price by twenty-five per cent! How do we do that?' Vik asked.

'Cost optimize,' Rana announced. 'Play around with the recipe a little; increase the sugar; reduce the cocoa; review the quality standards, that kind of stuff.'

'He's talking about cheapening the product!' I gasped.

'I'm talking about increasing our profits,' he said dismissively.

I marched over to Vik's seat, shaking with fury.

'This is ridiculous,' I said. 'We need to improve the quality, provide more variety, create some excitement, upgrade the product!'

Vik passed me some water. Rana skipped hurriedly to his next slide.

I gulped down the entire glass, wiped my lips with the back of my hand, set down the glass and declared war.

Rana launched a series of pie charts, trend lines and bar graphs onto the white screen. I countered by thrusting handwritten notes under Vik's nose.

Rana fired some time scales and logarithmic functions.

I played a tape recorded during the group discussions.

Rana unleashed a fury of PowerPoint tubes, cones, bubbles and doughnuts in a fireworks-like explosion of colours and shapes.

I talked circles round Vik's head.

Fifteen minutes later, Vik blew the whistle and called halftime.

Who won?

Well, it had been David vs. Goliath, Ram vs. Ravan, and myth and history never lie.

twelve

Two days later, there was a cryptic message stuck to the notice board in the lobby.

Private music lessons at B-406. Land up any time after 9 p.m.; coffee and cakes are on the house.
Ali

So he was back.

Eight days of distracted wondering and confused regret, of imagining he'd fled his apartment or moved in with Pink Bra or worse, and now this invite.

I re-read the Post-it; the familiar scrawl, the implied intimacy. *Private lessons,* the message promised. *After* nine, when it would be too late for dinner and too early for . . .

A tremor of excitement ran through me and left my knees weaker than Aman's telecom portfolio. *What was it about this guy?* What with the music and the mystery and the pink bra and the sex appeal, reading that one-line invite was like flipping breathlessly through the pages of some glossy travel magazine; a promise of vivid lands and sumptuous delights that I neither needed nor could afford, and yet were so tantalizingly within reach.

No, the wise inner sage whispered.

Yet at a quarter past nine, after changing my mind and my

clothes about a hundred times, I shocked myself by walking up the two flights of steps, ringing the doorbell and fiddling with the top button of my shirt as I waited.

Should I leave it open? Closed? Too low? Prudishly high? Would he gaze as interestedly at modest cleavage as he did at clingy skirt?

I was still fiddling undecided when the door swung open.

'Thank goodness it's you!' Ali exclaimed looking harassed, and extremely non-flirtatious.

'Hi?' I said.

'Come in, come in. Now that you're here, I can turn off the lights.'

'Huh?'

'I should never have put that note in the foyer,' he said, disgusted. 'I've already had three inquiries from mothers of precocious children.'

'For music lessons?'

'What else?'

'That's nice.'

'Are you crazy? Anyway, with the lights off, they'll think no one's home, I hope.'

He pulled me in, shut the door and turned off the lights.

'Ali?'

'Shhh, follow me, the music room is at the back.'

He grabbed my arm and steered me past the living room, down a dimly lit hall. I followed, trying to ignore the tingling where his fingers pressed lightly above my elbow. We turned a corner past what looked like a bedroom, with a cane lamp that sprinkled tiny diamonds of light all round the beige carpet, the ivory walls, the dull gold bedspread that was pushed carelessly back, half falling to the floor, like someone had just tumbled out of bed, like two could just as easily climb right back in.

Minal! my conscience squeaked.

Past the bedroom was a door to the right of the hallway. Ali pushed it open and turned on the lights and a whole new world came to life.

The room was tiny; probably just a study, and teeming, virtually frothing over with geeky-looking music stuff. The shelves were crammed full, and bowed in the middle with the weight of tapes and CDs and albums; old-fashioned amplifiers and spool tapes stood up wearily against the far wall, and masses of wires lay tangled in variegated red, green, grey and black between the speakers and the players and all the other equipment that cluttered the room.

I could have been standing inside a music curio shop, or the hard disk of a computer. I stared wide-eyed at the assortment of instruments; the only ones I could correctly identify were a guitar, a sitar, the keyboard by the window, and some kind of flute.

'Do you play *all* of these?' I asked.

'I used to, but I never seem to get the time these days. Mostly it's just the flute.'

'You must have a fortune in here.'

'Hardly! Most of the stuff is obsolete.'

'They seem to be in great condition.'

'They're old friends,' he smiled. 'I look after them. And they make the apartment seem a lot friendlier when I get back.'

'And is that a real gramophone?'

It was lovely; gleaming and polished and obviously well looked after.

'I'm a bit of a hoarder when it comes to music,' he said, grinning wryly. 'That used to belong to my grandfather. I'm keeping it for my grandson; it might actually be worth something then, don't you think?'

'After five generations? I sure hope so!'

'So here's the keyboard I was telling you about.' He walked up to the keyboard and flipped the cover open. 'Come on over.'

I sat down at the bench.

'Now this keyboard here is a very basic one, it has five octaves; we can start with that.'

'Octaves?'

'The basic notes. They're the building blocks for music. Here, this is *do* . . . the white key just to the left of the two black keys.'

He pushed my right thumb down on the key. It trembled involuntarily.

'No, no, don't lift your hand up,' he said, pressing it down again. 'Now that's *re*, the next one is *mi* . . . . look, why don't you just close your eyes and let me guide you for a bit? It's very intuitive; you'll get it in a trice.'

A half hour later, I could finally tell the difference between C sharp and F. It was a brilliant moment, way up there with the first time I tied my shoelaces.

'I got it, I got it!' I said, turning triumphantly on the bench. Ali straightened up above my shoulder and sighed.

'I could be playing this real soon, don't you think?'

'Maybe you should start by just listening first, to train the ear.'

He was rubbing the base of his spine, looking exhausted.

'I'm hopeless, aren't I?'

'No, no, it just takes longer for some people.'

'Thanks for trying anyway,' I smiled.

'My pleasure. Shall we head back?'

He led the way back down the hall. We drew level with the bedroom once again and for a heart-stopping moment he seemed to pause. Or perhaps it was just my imagination. The next instant he was walking on ahead to the living room, whistling softly, a dark silhouette in the feeble light that streamed in through the windows. I stood, watching.

Go home Minal, my conscience piped up. *It's late.What do you think you're doing outside a strange man's bedroom anyway?*

There was a soft click as Ali switched on the floor lamp by the TV, and a soft glow descended like stardust on the walls and the earthy rug nearby, turning Ali the colour of polished teak once again. 'I guess nobody will be coming by at this time,' he smiled, his eyes deep and dark in the lamplight.

'Well, thanks for the lesson . . .' I began.

'You're welcome.'

'I guess it's time for bed now,' I said and could have swallowed my tongue. 'I mean . . . .'

'I don't sleep till much later,' he grinned. 'Why, are you sleepy?'

'Oh, no! But . . .'

'Besides we're not done yet!'

'We're not?'

'Coffee and cake, remember?'

'Oh, right.'

'The kitchen's this way. Want to join me?'

'Sure.'

I followed him to the kitchen and hoisted myself up on the countertop next to the fridge. I watched as he put water on the stove and spooned coffee into two mugs.

'Milk?' he asked.

'Just a little.'

'Could you pass it, please? It's in the fridge.'

He walked past me to the china plate that sat at the far end of the counter, and lifted off the cover to reveal a dark chocolate cake.

'That looks good!' I said.

He grinned. 'Plates, and a napkin, and then it's all yours.'

He reached behind my shoulder to open the cupboard. 'Excuse me,' he said. I ducked to give him more room and my head came up against his shoulder. The hair stood up all along the nape of my neck as he strained forward, his shirt brushing my cheek.

'There we are,' he said, as he shut the cupboard and moved away. 'Should I cut you a nice big piece?'

I watched him slice through the cake, his long, slender fingers curling around the knife.

'So, how's it been at work?' I asked, striving for breezy nonchalance. 'Haven't seen your Jeep around.'

'Don't ask! I've been getting back really late. And then there's the show in the morning. Sometimes it seems like I'd be better off sleeping down at the radio station!'

'I know what you mean; I've been really busy with this new project of mine.'

'Well, I'm glad you could make it tonight.'

He passed me the coffee and the cake and his fingers brushed mine again, the way they'd done all evening. *Do-me-so, do-me-so* . . . we'd gone on and on, all through the music lesson, his fingers light and firm on mine, pushing the keys down and rest, down and rest, piano and forte, soft and loud.

I took a big, determined bite of the cake.

'Mmm, this is good!' I said, licking the chocolatey streaks that clung to my fingers. 'Where did you get it?'

'It's a secret,' he said, watching intently.

I stopped licking. 'You can tell me. I'm on Cakes you know.'

'I know.'

'Oh, come on, I'm looking at making some big changes, hopefully bringing out some new products. I need all the help I can get. You have to tell me, this is a really good recipe.'

'Thanks,' is all I got.

I shook my head. 'You're mighty secretive. And what's this website you were talking about the other day?'

'That's a secret too.'

'In that case I might as well head home.'

'In that case, I might as well tell you,' he said swiftly and moved to bar my way. 'It's a website for the radio station.'

'And you're working on it?'

'It's *my* site! I came up with the idea a few months ago and the management loved it. They're backing it up with a generous budget, enough for a big burst of publicity and advertising when we launch, and then we'll continue to promote it on radio.'

'Sounds like fun! What's the site about?'

'Music, of course. Not the run-of-the-mill gossip and review thing, but more serious stuff. Online lessons, instrument buyer's guide, concert listings, auditions and talent searches, biographies, downloads, exclusive interviews, the works. We're due to launch in a few weeks.'

'You must be working like a madman!'

'I don't get much sleep,' he grinned, 'but it's fun. And you should meet the guys I work with!'

'I wish I could say that about the guys I work with.'

'No good? You could always move in with us.'

His voice had a teasing, flirtatious edge to it. With that and the look in his eyes, my cheeks seemed to self-ignite.

'I'll think about it,' I said, and jumped off the counter. 'Anyway, I'll get going. See you around.'

'You're not leaving?' he said. *Chicken*, his eyes added.

'I have a long day tomorrow.'

'You still haven't seen my classical music collection. I keep that in my room. It's just down the hall . . .'

'I'd love to check it out,' I said, 'but I really ought to get going now. I'm—I'm waiting for a call from my mom.'

I made for the living room.

'Hey, wait up.'

He caught up with me at the door.

'Well, thanks for everything; I had a great time,' I said and held out my hand.

He took it in both his.

'Right then,' I tugged.

He bent his head and kissed the corner of my mouth.

'Minal,' he said, pulling back just a little. 'There's this party tomorrow night, one of those usual radio affairs. It'll be loud and noisy and terribly boring. Come with me?'

thirteen

Ali whistled soft and low when I opened the door. And he looked good enough to inhale, whole. The black jeans fit like a second skin, the shirt was sharper than a knife, the eyes sparkled party fun. And when he put together those soft, gleaming lips and blew a low, weightless, musical note of a whistle, I nearly floated away. I could have been a rare symphony, a Renaissance painting, a Beatles' classic.

And if there was anything on earth to justify those eight thousand and six hundred rupees (dress: Rs 4,166, shoes: Rs 899, salon: Rs 765, handbag: Rs 755, new perfume: Rs 2,015) and sixteen mindless hours (shopping: 10, makeover: 2, shower-dress-change-dress-change-panic-dress: approximately 4) that I'd spent, that whistle was it.

'You look nice,' he said, with a look that made a ridiculous understatement of the words, and kissed my cheek. It was an innocuous, momentary contact that would have seemed perfectly innocent to a bystander. Yet his lips caressed softly, and a thrill sparked to life in my toes and shot straight up to my scalp. I strangled the panicked warblings of my stuffy old conscience and kissed him back.

'Care for a drink?' I said, stepping back.

'I'd love to, but we're already kind of late. Maybe after?'

Maybe after.

Amazing how all it took was two soft words to morph the ramshackle room into a cosy love nest. The comfy couch that used to be something to park my behind on now beckoned coyly, the old lamp that I read draft memos by was a sensuous glow of light, the standby emergency candles shimmered with romantic promise, the dusty sound system screamed 'play me, play me'.

Maybe after, I promised the Sony speakers, and pulled the door softly shut.

Where would tonight lead—back to my couch, up to his rug, down through the corridor to the music room with all the stuff? Or that little room with the diamond lights on the bedspread?

Be good, Minal, my conscience tried one last time as we bobbed down the steps, black sleeve brushing bare arm, crackling with electricity. BSES could have considered using us the next time there was a power shortage. The evening felt almost magical.

We reached the parking lot and I stopped short and stared.

The evening *was* magical. Like the pumpkin in the fairy tale, my old friend the Jeep had cast off its customary cloak of mud and grime and stood washed and gleaming in the yellow streetlights like a sexy beast.

'Just had it serviced,' Ali laughed as I rubbed my eyes. 'I've been neglecting it these past few weeks; thought it could use some pampering.'

It was even more surprising on the inside. I sat back in the passenger seat to admire the luxurious upholstery, the stylized stick shift, the snazzy gauges and the Bose sound system.

'What *is* this thing?' I asked as he climbed in behind the wheel. 'It's an import, isn't it?'

He grinned; shifting gears to reverse and edging out of the spot.

'It's a 1997 Jeep Wrangler; special edition. *And* it's been spruced up. Better fasten your seat belts; it tends to grow wings on empty roads.'

'You're one modest owner.'

'Hey, I worked hard to get it. It's always more precious when you have to work at it, isn't it?'

'Tell me more.'

'It used to belong to my uncle. I was going through this phase at college—long hair, wild parties, experimenting . . . you know?' He turned to me, a wicked smile curving his lips.

'Long hair?'

'Those were the days,' he chuckled. 'Anyway, everyone was worried; they thought I'd flunk out and worse. Then my uncle put his Jeep on the table.'

'So you passed?'

'Sure.' He moved into fourth gear as the traffic thinned out and the Jeep thundered forward. 'I love this Jeep; we've had some good times together.'

I could just imagine.

'Where are you from?' I asked, as we zipped through mostly empty streets.

'My folks live in Bombay, if that's what you mean. My dad grew up in Lahore.'

'Really? My dad's from Lahore too. We could be related!'

'Thank goodness, not!' he grinned.

'So, do you have any brothers or sisters?'

'Nope, I'm an only child. Spoiled silly, as you can see. What about you?'

'No siblings. Though with my folks, that's probably for the best.'

'Traumatic childhood, huh?'

'More like *principled* childhood.'

'Well, that can't be too bad.'

'Oh yeah?'

I told him some of my best anecdotes, including 'Independence Day at the Sharma Household' and 'One Year at NCC'.

He laughed out loud as I wound up with the story of the 2001 Toddler Parade. 'I'd really like to meet your mom, you know. She sounds like someone I'd get along with,' he said.

'As long as you're planning to promote the music of the villages and include free music lessons for the poor on your website.'

And marry her daughter.

I noticed we were off the main road and bumping along a dark, shadowy side street.

'Where are we going?' I asked.

'It's the last building down this road. Don't worry; the ravishing isn't until after dinner.'

Who said I was worried?

'There it is, those blue lights you see at the end,' he pointed. 'Not too many people know about this place yet; it just opened up. But it's very radio-funky; you'll see.'

Radio-funky?

I looked out as we neared the building. It seemed to be some kind of pub; small and undistinguished, save for the small blue neon sign above heavy dark doors. Hard to make out anything in the dark and the building ended abruptly in a dense patch of trees. Ali drove past what seemed like an endless row of cars and finally found a parking spot a few hundred metres ahead.

We made our way back hand in hand. I could distinguish a few blue shapes and silhouettes as we neared the entrance, then someone opened the door and a momentary splash of bright light from within illuminated the tangle of motorcycles around which they stood. Up close I could see that there was a fair crowd. Largely male, though with some it was hard to tell. Some had long hair, some were smoking and some were pierced in surprising places, but for the most part they were just lounging about with harmless swaggers and loud opinions, like guys without dates at college rock shows.

Someone called out to Ali as we got within marking distance, and I ignored the low laughs and mumbled comments that accompanied it. A thick cloud of noise and revelry enveloped us as we pushed through the dark doors, and moments later I was inside the house that radio rocked.

I looked around, searching for signs of celebrity and glamour. The place was like any of its kind; packed, smoky, and roof-rattling loud. The women were skinny and still hadn't learned to put their make-up on right, the men seemed awkward and silly, the drinks were large and straight up.

'Quite a young crowd!' I said to Ali.

'A lot of the people in radio are temps and students,' he explained, close in my ear. 'The experience looks good on their Mass Comm. resumes. Guys like me are considered old-timers!'

We pushed our way to the buzzing constellation around the bar. Like everything else, it was terribly crowded. Men with glazed eyes pressed in multiple layers around the bar stools, trying to attract the attention of the harassed bartender, while the women congregated like satellites around them. TV screens suspended above played multiple channels; a montage of soundless cricket, MTV and what looked like some teen horror movie in split screen. I grimaced as a red-eyed guy lurched past me towards the bar. Ali squeezed my hand as I recoiled. 'Don't worry, I'll get the . . .' he began.

'Ali!' A hefty guy with a square jaw and round earrings was slapping Ali hard on the back.

'Monty!' Ali said, and they did the hearty guy-hug thing.

I marvelled silently at Hefty's leather jacket. It had to be at least a hundred and fifty degrees, and humid, in there.

'What's up, dude?' Hefty asked.

'The usual, man,' Ali said.

I looked at him, amazed; he seemed to have acquired a newfound drawl and shed many, many years and grey cells right before my eyes. Very disconcerting, but maybe that's the way you were expected to talk in radio.

'Meet Minal, my neighbour,' Ali was introducing. 'Minal, this is Monty, from the 9 a.m. MRT Timeless Classics show.'

'Hi, sweetheart.'

'How do you do.'

'Monty is the host of the new 'Date-Mate' show on Vee TV,' Ali explained. 'You've probably seen his picture in *Delhi Times*; he's all over the media these days.'

Monty smiled star-type and waited for me to gush, scream or faint. I watched instead the trickle of sweat that ran down the side of his neck into the leather collar.

'Aren't you really hot in that?' I asked.

Seconds later Hefty was sauntering off to join a group of streaky-haired, spaghetti-strapped young 'uns who had been giggling and waving and trying to catch his attention.

'You certainly deflated him,' Ali laughed. 'He's quite a celebrity; I thought you'd be impressed.'

'By a sweaty teen idol in a ridiculous leather jacket? Sorry, but I prefer my men black and without sugar.'

'What'll you have to drink?' Ali grinned.

I looked at the stampede round the bar. 'Just some beer; draft if they have any. But how?'

'Don't worry; the bartender's a friend of mine. Be right back.'

'I'll find us somewhere to sit,' I called.

I spotted an empty table at the far end of the pub, walked over quickly and settled back in a chair, watching the gyrating mass of people on the dance floor as I waited for Ali. Kids, all of them; and the terrible noise that emanated from the dance floor was presumably some form of music. I could see what he'd meant by terribly boring; I suppressed an urge to stuff my fingers in my ears and bolt. I looked up as a group of five at the table to my right laughed loudly at something.

'Don't worry, they're harmless,' a tinny voice said at my elbow. It belonged to a squat, kurta-clad, middle-aged gentleman who was standing right beside me.

'I beg your pardon?' I said.

'Those guys at the table. Don't mind them.'

'Of course not; they look like they're barely out of college.'

He smiled and sat down opposite me. 'I'm Roshan Tyagi, the "Voice", he said, and held out a podgy stump of a hand, with massive rings on each finger. 'I haven't seen you around; are you new?'

'The "Voice"?'

'That's what everyone calls me. I do voices in radio commercials. Shah Rukh Khan, Preity Zinta, Johnny Lever, I can do them all. In fact most of the ads you hear these days are done by me. Lux, Halo, Rupa banian; even I lose track of them sometimes.'

'Really? I always thought Rupa banian was done by that guy, Amit somebody.'

'Oh, no! All those guys are going out of business now. They're just too expensive. Take that new cough lozenge ad; the one with six voices? It would have cost the company thirty thousand rupees for the voices alone. I gave them a package deal; fifteen thousand for all six.'

'So you can do any voice?'

'Sure, any voice. Any sound, in fact. Animal sounds, bird cries, even mechanical sounds. That new toilet bowl cleaner ad that's all over the air these days? That's me.'

I looked at him alarmed, and hoped he wouldn't start flushing from across the table. Where the hell was Ali?

'It's a God-gift.'

'Huh?'

'My voice. From Maa Saraswati.'

'Oh, right.'

'Can I buy you a drink?'

'No, thanks.'

'Oh don't be shy.'

'Actually, I'm here with a friend.'

'Really? So where is your friend? Is she as pretty as you?'

'*He's* probably at the bar getting me a drink.'

I looked around, trying to locate Ali's dark head in the crowd at the bar.

'Don't worry, I'll keep you company till "he" gets back,' the Voice said, leaning across the table. His podgy fingers stroked the back of my hand. 'So tell me about yourself. What's your name?'

I pulled my hand away. Where *was* Ali?

'Ali? You mean you're here with Ali Imran?'

I wasn't aware I'd spoken out loud. 'Yes,' I said. 'Have you seen him?'

'Oh, yeah,' he sneered, looking at a point behind my right shoulder. 'I see him. It's a good thing I came along.'

I turned to see why and spotted Ali sitting at a table a few feet away, flanked on both sides by skimpy female forms, apparently having a grand old time. Someone seemed to be telling some kind of joke; Ali threw back his head and laughed.

'He seems to have lost his way, don't you think?' the Voice drawled.

'Ali,' I called.

'You know, I really like your perfume.'

'Ali!'

'Bring your wrist closer, give us a whiff.'

'ALI!'

Finally, he looked up. He frowned as he noticed my companion and strode over immediately.

'Tyagi, you're back?' he said.

'You know how it is,' the Voice said, 'they just can't do without me.'

'So it seems. Well, goodbye.'

'I was just keeping your friend company.'

'Goodbye, Tyagi.'

There was an unmistakable threat in his voice. Tyagi sighed and heaved himself up. 'Well, see you around, my lovely,' he said, leaning over and depositing a wet kiss on my cheek.

'What the . . .'

He was already waddling away.

'What were you doing with that leper?' Ali frowned as I wiped my cheek. 'He got suspended from the station after he came on to one of the technicians. Don't know why he's back.'

This was my fault? 'He saw me alone and came over. I was waiting for you.'

'Sorry; I got caught up with a few friends. Come on over; I'll introduce you. It's much livelier over there.'

'Is that your website team?' I whispered as I followed him to the weird assortment.

'Just some of the regulars at the station,' he grinned. 'Guys, this is Minal. Minal, this is . . . well, this is most of 107.4 FM!'

Everyone nodded and smiled and Ali listed many names, all of which sounded unusual and exotic and none of which registered.

'Thanks,' I smiled, as a girl with an enormous nose ring scooted over to make room for me. 'What *is* this awful racket?'

'You mean the music? That's Nelly's latest hit; it's been playing at all the discos for the past two months!'

'That figures. I haven't been to a disco for almost a year.'

She gaped at me for a moment; then fortified herself with a long swig from a drink the colour of a swimming pool.

'I'll go have a word with the DJ,' Ali grinned.

I watched him disappear into the mass of people swaying on the dance floor.

'Did you hear that Suhasini babe from Doordarshan is trying out for the evening 6 p.m. slot?' a guy with scraggly stubble and long sideburns asked the group.

'That Vividh Bharati didi?' whispered a shocked voice.

'You're kidding,' a third tittered.

'Oh, no! Now she'll be reading requests from Sita, Gita and Mita from Saharanpur on 104.5 FM too,' the girl to my right groaned. I peered down at her flat pierced belly, and the several inches of bare skin below. A red thong rose up over her behind like an angry welt as she leaned forward.

'That show probably means a lot to people in Saharanpur,' I said.

'Yes, but she's so sugary-sweet and boring! And those requests they send in!'

'I'm willing to bet that show and those songs get more listeners than all your shows put together. You'll be lucky to get Suhasini,' I said.

Someone coughed into the awkward silence.

'Minal works in consumer marketing,' Ali explained, materializing at my elbow. 'You know how these marketing types are!'

'Oh, just like Lara!' Peeping Thong exclaimed.

'Lara as in your co-host?' I asked.

'Come on, let's dance,' Ali said instead, pulling me up as Bruce Springsteen's raspy voice rose up from the sound system. 'They're finally playing some real music!'

We joined the mad crush on the strobe-lit floor and 'danced in the dark' and 'shalalalala'-ed to the music. I laughed as Ali swung me round and round with long flourishes. He was a great dancer, moving with the grace and rhythm of a native African. I gave up trying to imitate his steps and concentrated on having the time of my life. Then the DJ cued the opening notes of *'I'm on fire'* and a collective sigh went round the floor as couples pulled close together.

I stopped, gasping, holding my sides.

'I hope you weren't planning to leave?' Ali said and suddenly I found myself pulled up hard against a solid chest.

I gasped as his arms circled my waist, moulding my body to his, and my heart raced to match the heavy freight-train beat of the song. We could have been the only people on that crowded dance floor; we were that close. No self-conscious line in between, no awkward fumbles; just his hands drawing me in, his eyes holding mine, his lips mouthing the words of the soulful, erotic song.

'I have a bad desire,' Bruce and Ali confided caressingly, and I struggled to bring the GGF's virtuous portrait into focus.

I needn't have bothered.

A white hand with red nails cut through the smoky darkness, tapped Ali on the shoulder and pulled him away.

'Ali! There you are. I've been looking for you all over!' the intruder breathed.

I stepped back and tried not to count the number of times Ali and Rude Person hugged and kissed.

'Minal, I'd like you to meet Lara, my co-host and very special friend. Lara, this is Minal, my neighbour.'

I smiled brightly. Why did he keep calling me his neighbour like I were Mrs Sahni from the fifth floor or something?

Lara of course was beautiful, and delighted to see me. Her red lips kissed the air round my ears and her pale arms hugged me close.

'Wow, you're *tall!*' she exclaimed in a way that made me want to slouch. 'I wish I weren't so petite!'

'You love being treated like some precious little bird,' Ali teased.

'You're terrible,' she tinkled, and slapped his sleeve. 'Come, let's go get something to drink, I'm so *thirsty*!'

Ali laughed a big protective laugh and led the way. I followed slowly behind.

There was nothing to worry about, of course. She was his co-host and they were friends. People in showbiz were always hugging and kissing anyway. Besides, Ali hadn't been singing 'I'm on fire' to her, had he?

I was so busy watching the short back swaying next to the black shirt that I nearly tripped over something hard and lumpy on the floor. I picked it up; it was a wallet.

I looked around and saw Ali's dark head bobbing away in the distance; and then a couple danced past and he disappeared completely behind them. I shrugged, walked up to the bar and better light, and opened the wallet.

Ali Imran, the driver's license proclaimed, and a sweet boyish picture smiled across at me. I smiled back and sneaked a look at the date of birth. 10.6.1978. Gemini! That explained it, all the hugging and kissing and hordes of girls. He just had a naturally flirty, extroverted nature.

Wait a minute. 1978?

Had to be a 1973 that looked like a 1978. I rubbed the plastic card and peered closely once more.

The 8 stayed an 8.

I sank down on a barstool and ordered a stiff drink. My friendly, neighbourhood sex-God was all of twenty-four years and five weeks old.

fourteen

The young punk who picked me up off the barstool and dropped me home on his motorcycle was really pretty sweet. He accepted my story without question, waited patiently while I threw up by the roadside, and went so far as to locate a bottle of mineral water and airline crackers in his gym bag.

'You shouldn't be doing late nights or booze in this state,' he said as he helped me up the steps.

'I'll keep that in mind.'

'Is it a girl or a boy?'

'Too soon to say.'

'So where's your husband?'

'Don't have one.'

'The bastard.'

He unlocked the door and helped me in.

'I could come round in the morning with some fruit and milk,' he offered.

'I have enough, thanks.'

He checked the fridge just to make sure.

'Here, lie down,' he said, propping up pillows on the couch.

I sank down and shut my eyes. The room started spinning even faster than before.

'Thanks for all your help,' I groaned.

'Just try to sleep it off; you'll feel much better in a few weeks.'

I swallowed as another bout of sickness welled up in my alcohol-drenched system.

'I'll get a bucket,' he said quickly.

'No, I'm fine.'

'Listen, my aunt's a gynaecologist. I could . . .'

'No thanks.'

'She's really very good.'

'No! I mean thanks, but I think I'll be fine now. You can go.'

He walked to the door reluctantly.

'Well, goodnight then.'

'Goodnight.'

'And good luck with the baby and all.'

'Sure, thanks. Goodbye . . .'

He stopped; a flash of an idea lighting up his pierced brow.

'You know; if you have a boy . . .'

'Please, for the love of God . . . GO!'

I woke up the next morning with a punishing hangover and a hysterical conscience. *How embarrassing*, it wailed. *A guy half your age,* it yelled. *Just how hard up are you?* it shrieked.

I tried to clobber it into silence by banging my head on the kitchen counter.

The truth was inescapable. I'd spent the last two weeks and most of this month's salary coming on to a radio jockey who just happened to be half my age. Writing Post-its, learning music, even crawling through his window to get his attention!

If only there were some way to crawl back out, back through that window, back past the last couple of weeks, back out that first damning Post-it.

He must have been all of fourteen when I started college. Softcheeked, girly-voiced, muddy-kneed, social-studies-and-algebra fourteen. Flying kites and paper planes, blissfully unaware of the perils of calculus, quantum mechanics and dirty old women who lurked around the corners of his future. A horrific picture of me in heels, lipstick and little black dress; he in sneakers, school bag and water bottle flashed through my head. I went to the bathroom and shoved my head under the shower.

The doorbell rang at 10 a.m.

I spilled my cup of bracing black coffee (my third since morning). I couldn't face him. Not now. Not ever.

The doorbell rang again, this time insistently.

I covered my ears. Go away! Go back to Lara and your bubblegum friends!

He started banging on the door.

Why didn't he get the message?

Tap tap-a-tap tap. Tap tap-a-tap tap. Tap tap-a—

I yanked open the door.

Mom stood on the threshold, complete in khadi sari, Bata sandals, heavy jhola and missionary zeal. She strode in briskly as I stood frozen.

'Minal, why didn't you open the door? You look awful! Are you sick? And why are you still in your nightclothes?

'Hi Mom, sorry Mom, how are you, Mom?' I mumbled, and picked up her battered old suitcase. 'How did you get here?'

And why?

'I took the six o'clock bus. It's very convenient.'

She looked round my nice, cosy, lived-in living-dining room. 'What's this awful clutter? And what a terribly musty smell!'

She marched to the windows and threw open the curtains. I recoiled as daylight streamed in and highlighted the dust on the window sill and table tops.

'I can't believe you live like this!' she clucked, shaking her head.

'My daughter! Go, go and bathe right now; I'll fix things up a bit.' She pushed me firmly out of the way. 'And hurry up; we have a hundred things to do today.'

No right. She had no right to descend on me without any notice, especially not when things were so screwed up. I wanted to spend my weekend sipping herbal tea and feeling sorry for myself; not traipsing all over town with Mom. I was not up to the 'hundred things to do' or the listing of my various shortcomings; I was decidedly not up to the imminent half-hour Naveen lecture and the blow-by-blow Yudhishter review. I shampooed my hair viciously and ended up getting soap in my eyes.

A half hour later I walked out to sunny dining room, rearranged furniture and a breakfast that involved lots of milk and lots of fruit.

'You heated my milk!'

'Drink up. Cold milk is no good.'

'I don't want any breakfast.'

She made her Mom face and tapped one foot.

I picked up the fork.

'What about you?' I accused.

'I breakfasted in the morning before I left.'

She eyed my jeans and T-shirt with distaste.

'Don't you have any nice salwar kameezes?'

'No.'

I drank up the horrid, tepid milk, picked up the banana and marched to the door. 'All right, Mom; let's go.'

She followed me down the steps, tsking and harrumphing away happily.

'I didn't see any Chyawanprash in your kitchen. Don't tell me you've stopped taking Chyawanprash? And you're all out of vitamins. We'll need to stop by the grocery store on the way back home. And don't drive fast; you know how nervous Delhi traffic makes me. Or maybe we should take a bus?'

I noticed the Jeep was missing.

Where was he . . . out with Lara? Did they even get back last night?

Does it even matter? my conscience screamed.

I opened the door of my Maruti and promised Mom I'd drive carefully.

We chugged along in the left lane with the auto-rickshaws and cyclists at what felt like 10 kmph. A couple of guys zoomed past on a moped, 'Lady Driver' written all over their leering faces. I bit back a surge of frustration and chewed my fingernails.

'Stop doing that!' Mom chided instantly.

She waited a few moments and then began in a soft, unbearably sad voice, 'I heard what happened with Naveen.'

'He deserved it, Mom.'

An auto-rickshaw behind me honked loud and rude.

'They think I should take you for psychiatric help.'

'Is that why you're here?'

She smiled at the grin on my face.

'Is there someone else?' she asked.

Yes, he's a sexy radio jockey who flirts shamelessly and just happens to be five years younger than me.

'No,' I said.

'Then what is it? Don't you want to get married?'

'Of course I do, but to the right person.'

'And where is this right person?'

I groaned; we'd done this a thousand times.

'You can't have everything, Minal. You have to compromise somewhere.'

'Are good looks, good job and right wavelength too much to ask for?'

'In our time, it was enough to be good. Nowadays you youngsters want too much. All of you. Just look around, everywhere there's greed and misery. This was not Bapu's vision.'

She looked out at the charging buses, the imported cars, the ogling men at the bus stops.

'How do you live in this city, beta? Come home to Meerut. We really need bright and energetic youngsters like you at the societies.'

'Mom, not again. I've told you—I want to make it in the real world, the corporate world. That's where you have the power to make big things happen. And all this,' I pointed to the unrelenting traffic, 'all this is just part of city life. You have to take the good with the bad.'

'Well, that's how it is in marriage too. You have to take the good with the bad.'

I shut up. She always got the last word anyway.

I slowed down for the endless wait as we approached the AIIMS intersection. The flyover construction was in full swing. Hawkers and beggars flitted from car window to car window and passengers leaped from bus to bus. A ragged woman with a listless kid on her hip zigzagged down the rows of cars in front, begging and wailing. I started to roll up the window.

'No, wait Minal; she looks like she needs help.'

'They're all professional beggars, Mom.'

Too late; the woman was clutching the window.

'Madam, my son is very sick; please give me some money for medicine.'

'What's wrong with him?' Mom asked.

'He's burning up, madam, very high fever. Please give me fifty rupees for medicine.'

'Why don't you take him to the hospital?'

'They won't admit him. The guard will shoo me away.'

Mom got out of the car and touched the boy's forehead. The occupants of the neighbouring cars looked on interestedly.

'Get inside,' she commanded suddenly.

'Huh?' the woman and I asked in unison.

'This boy is really sick. Let's get him to the hospital quickly.' She hustled the dumbstruck woman and boy into the back seat. 'Minal, drive as fast as you can.'

Ten minutes later we were speeding through the hospital gates, horn honking, tires flying, adrenalin pumping. The woman in the back seat clutched her child and held on for dear life. I shook my head as I deposited them at Emergency and drove slowly to the parking lot to wait.

She may be crazy, my Mom, but sometimes you just have to love her.

fifteen

Three p.m. I stood wilting in the damp heat of the Blind School exhibition hall, and Mom raced across the chipped floor to hug and kiss a small woman in a pale blue salwar kameez. When she eventually let go I saw it was Aruna Pandey. A little rounder, visibly older, but still lovely.

I remember the first time I went to the Pandeys' house. They had just moved to the neighbourhood, the 'haves' in that lane of 'have-nots', and, unlike the Bhatias in their big bungalow across the street, they had thrown their doors and hearts open to their poor (but virtuous) neighbours. *He* was distinguished and charming and had travelled the world; *she* was lovely and wore her saris with a careless elegance. And their house had many rooms.

I remember playing hide-and-seek in the many rooms. There were a million places in which to hide. The narrow hall with the ornate wooden console and tall brass Ganesh. The covered sunroom with sliding glass doors. The kitchen with two fridges. The dining room with the chandelier and table for twelve. The *baithak* with Rajasthani furniture and dozens of cushions. The living room with crystal and dark wood and silver picture frames. The guest room with the antique chest of drawers and bedside lamp and extra pillows. The massive master bedroom with the deep blue satin bedspread and sofa and rug and TV. And the attached bathroom.

It was the bathroom that did it for me. Before then, a bathroom had always been a tight place in which you did your business and made way for the next person. *This* was a place I could have spent entire days and nights in. Rose tiles, pink bathtub, burgundy curtains, deep pink vanity, gold and ivory faucets. One for hot, one for cold. They both worked; I had checked. So did the shower.

And everything matched! The His 'n' Hers towels, the fluffy oval rug, the wastebasket lined with linen, the toothbrushes, the lotion, the knick-knacks, the goodies. I'd had no idea you could keep so many things in a bathroom. Scented candles, picture frames, tiny plants, shells, flowers, potpourri in crystal platters. Everything you could ever need, and some you never would. A hair dryer on the wall, a box of tissues, rows of perfume bottles, drawers full of lipsticks and mascara, nail polish and chocolate. Chocolate! Kit Kat, imported, lots of it. I'd gobbled down five the first time I hid there. And decided that a bit of money may not be a bad thing after all.

Aruna Aunty smiled and hugged me close.

'Minal! After all these years. How wonderful.'

It was.

'How are you, Aruna Aunty?'

'Aruna, I thought you were in Chandigarh; when did you move to Delhi?' Mom said accusingly.

'Oh, Kunal and I are still in Chandigarh. I'm just visiting Sunil; he works here.'

Sunil; that was his name. The fat son who was always studying. Naturally, Mom was deeply interested in his whereabouts.

'Sunil works in Delhi? So does Minal. What does he do?' she asked.

'He's a doctor, he specializes in cancer surgery. In fact he's here with me; he's just parking the car.'

'A surgeon!'

Mom was swelling with hope. *Don't ask, don't ask,* I prayed silently.

'Is he married?' she asked.

'No,' Aruna Aunty laughed, 'we couldn't do that without inviting all our friends, could we? We do keep hinting from time to time, like all good parents, but you know kids these days!'

'Yes, Minal too! I'm so worried, she's twenty-eight now. I don't know what will happen.'

'Twenty-nine.'

'Excuse me?'

'I'm twenty-nine, Mom.'

'That's even worse.'

I sighed heavily.

'Come, come, Prabha, you have nothing to worry about,' Aruna Aunty said with a smile. 'Look at Minal; she's so smart and confident. And doing so well! We should let these kids make up their own minds. I wish my parents had been a little less strict; I might have done something entirely different with my life.'

'Oh, but you are doing something, aren't you? I heard you were working with underprivileged children,' Mom protested.

'Oh, I still am and I love it, but there are times when I feel I could have done more. Anyway, here comes Sunil.'

Or Humpty-Dumpty. Or Peter Parker?

I stared, shocked, at the serious-looking man heading towards us.

Somewhere along the way, Mother Nature had taken the boy firmly in hand, stripping away the fat, clearing away the pimples, flattening the overlarge cheeks, and throwing smart rimless glasses round clear, intelligent eyes. The transformation was complete and staggering.

'Sunil, look who's here,' Aruna Aunty exclaimed. 'Prabha Aunty from Meerut, remember?'

'Of course, Ma.'

He bent to touch Mom's feet. 'Namaste, Aunty.'

Mom almost swooned. 'Jeete raho, beta,' she said. 'Minal, see it's your old friend Sunil!'

Old friend? Bit of a stretch, but what the heck.

'Hi, Sunil,' I said.

'Minal! How are you?'

'Not bad.'

We shook hands and Mom hopped around excitedly. Had there been a priest and a fire at hand, she'd have had us circling it in minutes.

'Aruna, there's a fantastic sale at Fabindia,' she said. 'Why don't we check it out and give these youngsters a chance to catch up?'

'Mom! They've probably got other plans.'

'I have the afternoon free,' Sunil shrugged.

'I've been meaning to go to Fabindia myself!' Aruna Aunty said.

'Well, great! Then lets go!' Mom beamed.

Within minutes we were outside and piling into Sunil's shiny black Opel Astra.

'I'm sorry about Mom,' I said to Sunil once we'd dropped them off outside the store. 'We've probably ruined your plans,'

'Not at all. I'm glad we met; it must be, what, nearly eighteen years since Meerut?'

'About that.'

'I didn't know you were in Delhi.'

'And I thought you were in London or something.'

'I moved to Delhi four years ago.'

'Really? And how do you like it?'

He shrugged. 'I spend most of my time at the hospital.'

Right.

I squinted round at the crowded parking lot and the dazed

shoppers who were staggering out of Fabindia buried beneath big brown packages. It looked like the entire store was on sale. I wondered if I'd see either Mom or Aruna Aunty before nightfall.

Sunil seemed to read my thoughts. 'Any idea when they'll be done?' he asked.

'Sometime today, I hope.'

He smiled and drummed his fingers on the steering wheel.

'Look, if you need to get back to the hospital or something . . .'

'No, today's my day off.'

'Oh.'

I stared out the window again.

'Er . . . would you like to go and get some ice cream in the meantime?'

'Ice cream?' I said, turning to look at him.

'It's a really warm day,' he said, reddening a little.

'Ice cream sounds great. But where?'

He grinned, wistful. 'If you ask me, I wish we could go right back to Baale, that ice-cream vendor who used to come round every evening in Meerut. Remember that Kwality cart with those Choco Bars?'

'And that rear wheel that always squeaked!'

'And that strange bicycle bell . . . trrreng, trrreng!'

I laughed. 'Yes, I remember. You had quite a sweet tooth, didn't you?'

'I still do. Unfortunately . . .'

'You know, I wouldn't have recognized you if it weren't for Aruna Aunty. How did you . . .'

I stopped abruptly. Too rude.

'Lose all that weight?' he finished for me. 'Don't remind me. They starved me for six months in medical school before they stopped ragging me.'

'And you've kept it off ever since? That's good.'

'I hardly have time to eat when I'm working.'

'So where do you work?'

'At Apollo. I work with Dr Dubey's team.'

'Uh huh.'

'You must have heard of Dr Dubey? He's the best oncologist in the country.'

'You must be good if you're on his team.'

'No, *he's* good. The rest of us just try.'

'Is it very hard work?'

'Yes, but I enjoy it. And it has its benefits.'

Like the new Opel Astra?

I watched as he swung it smoothly around in a U-turn at the next stop light and pulled up in front of a smart, brick building. A wealth of shiny big cars filled up most of the parking lot, and drivers sat playing cards in the shade. A valet and a doorman stood to attention as Sunil drove up to the imposing three-storey foyer. Not exactly a Kwality ice cream cart.

'I thought you said ice cream?'

'It's a coffee shop; they serve ice cream too,' he said.

I got out and waited as he handed the keys over to the valet.

'What will you have?' Sunil asked, as he led the way up the steps.

'I don't know, Choco Bar?'

He laughed, and pushed the door open for me.

The interior of the coffee shop lived up to its nouveau riche promise. It was intimate, cool, and abuzz with well-dressed, good-looking types. The women's clothes looked like they'd just come off the racks; the men looked like they shaved twice every day. The pictures on the wall were black and white and very European, and the Tiffany lamps caught tasteful highlights off the mosaic tables below.

I sat back and admired the menu. It was in a classy-looking font, Rage Italic or Gigi or something. There was even a grand piano in one corner that appeared to be playing by itself.

Do-me-so, do-me-so, do-me . . .

Stop it!

A pimply young waiter with a courteous manner and a bold smile came up to take our order..

How old are you? Stop smiling at me like that; don't you know I'm twenty-nine?

I scowled at him, looking for the most intimidating item on the menu.

'I'll have an iced cafe latte. With Bailey's Irish cream,' I said.

'I'll have some jasmine tea,' Sunil said.

'What about the Choco Bar?'

'We're not kids anymore, are we?' he smiled.

I figured not.

The waiter sped away and Sunil settled back, crossing long thin fingers on the table.

'You know, Minal, you've changed quite a bit yourself,' he said. 'I seem to remember scraped knees and pigtails.'

I laughed and fingered the hair that hung loose around my shoulders.

'Horrendous, weren't they? I got rid of them as soon as I could.'

He smiled. 'It's been a long time. How have you been all these years?'

'Can't complain,' I said. 'Just about managed to scrape through college and get past business school, and now here I am trying to make my mark in the big bad corporate world.'

'What do you do?'

'I'm in product marketing at a food company.'

'Interesting.'

'That's one way of describing it!'

'What exactly is product marketing?'

He sounded like he was genuinely interested. He'd always had that soft, attentive quality about him, I remembered. It probably made him a darned good doctor.

'It's the whole basis of a business,' I explained. 'Right from figuring out what people want, to delivering it to them the way they want it, when they want it, at a price they're willing to pay. It involves everything about a product; its recipe, its packaging, advertising, distribution . . .'

He held up a hand. 'I believe you.'

'You shouldn't ask open-ended questions,' I grinned.

He shook his head. 'No, it's great to see someone so committed to their work. I used to think that sort of thing only ran in doctors.'

'Well, you guys just look after people's bodies; we look after their souls too.'

He laughed.

'You still have that crazy sense of humour,' he laughed. 'So where exactly do you work?

'At International Foods. I'm on the Cakes team.'

'IF? I know someone there. Vik Bahl; his mother's a patient of mine.'

'Vik? But he's my boss! His mom has *cancer*?'

This was terrible.

'Yes, she does, but we detected it early. She'll be fine,' Sunil said. He looked calm and reassuring, and I believed him.

Of course Mom had to plan my wedding with Sunil and think up names for our children the whole ride home.

I put my fingers in my ears.

'So what's wrong with Sunil now?'

'Nothing. You're just getting totally carried away, that's all. Sunil is nice, but we just met.'

'How can you say that; we've known the Pandeys for years!'

'Mom!'

'He's got a great future, you know. And he's so devoted to his patients. Did you know he treats poor people for free?'

'Well, he should.'

'And he's single. Anyway, why do you think he offered to drive me back to Meerut?'

'He said he has a patient to visit there.'

'Still, he needn't have gone out of his way. I think he likes you.'

I sighed as we reached the second-floor landing. Mom bent to pick something up as she followed me in to the apartment.

'What's this?' she said, holding out an envelope and CD.

I froze.

The envelope was plain, but the CD sleeve announced Beethoven's Fifth Symphony by the Berlin Philharmonic Orchestra.

'Some promotional material, no doubt,' I said, and quickly relieved her of the items. 'Don't worry; I'll pass it off to someone in the office.'

'I don't know why they can't distribute Indian classical music instead,' she complained. 'This Western influence is just taking over our society.'

'Mom, do you mind if I go straight to bed? I'm really tired.'

'Sure, beta; I'll make you some hot milk.'

In my room I opened the envelope. There was a Post-it inside.

You looked lovely last night. Why did you leave? Was it something I said?

Call me,

Ali

P.S. Here's Beethoven's 5th; I can't listen to it now without thinking of you.

sixteen

Every fourth Monday at work is marked by an unsettling visit from our factory personnel. The MPRPM (Monthly Production Review and Planning Meeting, for those who just *have* to know) is considered important enough not only to have an acronym all its own, but also for each and every conference room, cabin, table top and even standing room at the head office to be given over to the serious business of creation.

For us marketing types, the meeting is a point of reckoning, where marketing grey must sort itself into manufacturing black and white; where gut feelings are forced onto weighing scales and crushed between slide rules; where each and every sales projection must be squeezed through the fine apertures of filling machines.

And as if that weren't daunting enough, the deep sense of doom is compounded by the fact that each and every person at the IF factory is crazy enough to make your skin crawl.

At first glance the average factory man may seem normal. Two eyes, one nose, two lips . . . But watch the line workers carefully and you will see them talking, coaxing, even singing to the machines with which they enjoy strange and intimate relationships. Notice the twitching nose of the supervisor; chances are he has sensed a sudden drop in mean worker productivity as someone got down on his knee to tie his shoelaces. And one look inside the glassy eyes of the engineers and you are blown away by the terrible power they wield with their heat and pressure gauges and row upon row of countless red and green buttons.

Anyway. The factory guys command my awed respect and lively fear, and so it was with real anxiety that I watched the solemn procession that filed into the small meeting room at 9.59 a.m. There were three of them, in hierarchical progression, careful, regimented. They had a printed agenda, they carried precise information. Everything about them—the walk, the talk, the handshake, the headshake—everything was measured and accurate and built into the plan.

Would it work, I wondered. *Would they agree? Or would they vapourize from the trauma of the unorthodox suggestion we were planning to make?*

I looked sideways at Rana. I hoped he wouldn't blow it. At exactly three minutes past the hour, the trio suspended pleasantries, snapped to attention and got down to business.

(I glanced at the printed agenda. 10.03–10.42: Line Manager's Update.)

Mathur, the line manager and head of the procession got up to speak. Badhwar, the emaciated assistant licked his thumb, flipped to a new page in his diary and started recording the minutes of the meeting at an efficient 50 wpm. Mukesh the programmer amused himself by multiplying and dividing strings of random numbers on his calculator.

Patience, I told myself. I could do it, there were ways. The past three years at IF had taught me basic survival skills through the prolonged Japanese tea ceremony of a production meeting. I fixed my eyes on Mathur's hirsute face and settled back as he warmed, brewed and slowly poured out the month's achievements into dainty, exquisitely patterned PowerPoint graphs. He served them up slowly and carefully for our appreciation, and I stared distracted at the tangled mess of hair that jumped out from under his collar and cuffs, and from the insides of his ears and nose. He pointed out the subtle improvements and finer points of the manufacturing processes; I doodled pictures of him at waxing salons and saunas. And before I knew it, he was wrapping it up.

For Rana, I could see it had been a moving experience. Chart 1 with its energy savings had apparently touched an erogenous chord, and by Graph 23, which was about higher line efficiencies, he was climaxing. He shuddered after it was all over, and gazed soulfully up at Mathur.

'So in sum it has been another satisfying month with huge strides made in productivity and capacity utilization,' Mathur was concluding. 'As ever, our target next month will be to surpass this month's achievements.'

He paused to stroke the curls at his throat, and turned to Mukesh, who was onto logarithmic functions on the calculator. 'We have eight minutes remaining until coffee break, during which Mukesh will provide a quick update on the next four weeks' production plan.'

Badhwar sat back for a short twelve-second break, cracked his bony knuckles and rotated his ankles. Mukesh slipped his calculator back in his pocket, unfolded his thin, long body and staggered up to the projector.

I watched him closely. Stoned again? Might work in our favour.

With Mukesh, the production programmer, it was a sad case of a good guy going to pot. Or maybe weed; I wasn't exactly sure which. Once a bright, young engineer looking for a quick stamp on his ticket and a posting back to the head office, he had realized after two years at the factory that the company had other plans for him, and as a mark of protest, had fallen into bad company. Erstwhile literary and cultural evenings had taken on a more psychedelic hue, and even more disturbing were the recent rumours about the Chief's daughter having been spotted outside Mukesh's quarters on a number of suspicious occasions. It was probably only a matter of time before the Chief found out.

'Any change in the next month's plan?' Mukesh asked unsteadily when he was done with the plan.

This was the moment.

I took a deep breath, choosing my words with care.

'Yes, we want to include a new unit, a new cake, and we'd like to discuss how soon it can be built into the plan, what would be the cheapest recipe you could work out and how fast we can get it out the system,' Rana erupted, like a burst sewage pipe.

Mathur laughed. 'Ha, ha. But seriously, are we looking at any changes in output?'

Rana turned to me, confused.

'Actually, we are considering the possibility of a new cake and we'd like to discuss the project, get your input at an early stage,' I explained.

Mathur stopped smiling and scratched the tufts at his ear.

'This is highly irregular. The production meeting is not the correct forum for these things. You need to put up a formal note—authorized by the head of Marketing and probably by Finance, Sales and HR too—with all details and estimations, timelines and rationale, and send it to us through the head of manufacturing. We will reply to it after reviewing all the aspects.'

Rana looked defeated. 'I see,' he said. 'Well, in that case, we'll get back to you . . .'

'Wouldn't you like to hear us out?' I persisted. 'It's a highly innovative product, sure to catch the attention of the international R&D centre.'

Mathur hesitated. 'What exactly do you have in mind?'

'An anniversary cake. It's really a makeover of the existing product, with a small adjustment to the shape, new packaging . . .' Rana began again.

'New shape?'

'Actually, we were looking at a heart-shaped cake, with . . .'

'Heart-shaped? Impossible. We only do round ones. We'd have to get new moulds and cartons and, good God, think how inefficient the packaging would be!'

'Couldn't you use the existing round moulds and cut the heart shapes out of them?' Rana complained.

'Aaaaaiiiiieeee! Think of the wastage!' Mathur shrieked, pulling at the locks on his cheeks in agony.

Mukesh giggled and Badhwar put his pen down in wonder.

I almost felt sorry for Rana. Almost.

And then, right in the middle of this highly charged drama, someone stunned the assembly by pushing their six foot four, one hundred and thirty kilos of muscular frame through the door.

'Chief!' Mathur exclaimed and the factory guys all jumped out of their chairs and prostrated themselves on the conference room carpet. I sat back and peered at this messiah of the people that I'd heard so much about.

Our Factory Chief is the king of the IF crazies; even the factory guys agree that he's not all there. In fact, there is a favourite fairytale at the factory (that truly remarkable civilization is rich in myth and lore) about the Chief. They say that one fine day in Y2K, the Chief accidentally pricked his finger on the jagged edge of a crusty old machine part (some say it bore an uncanny resemblance to an ancient spinning wheel) and a marked oddness of behaviour became instantly manifest, transforming tyranny to tolerance and stringency to affection. Thereafter began a long line of oddly philanthropic projects and acts of creative human kindness, each aimed at uplifting the lives of his fellow factory brethren in a multitude of humanitarian ways. I'd heard that the Chief was currently travelling the lands (or rather the IF factories and offices worldwide) to spread his message of hope and good cheer, and his underlings at the factory were desperately seeking ways to make this a permanent, life-long assignment.

The Chief was in a good mood. He smiled around the small room and nodded at his minions. 'Ah, the new cake group,' he beamed, and strode forward as he caught sight of us.

Rana and I introduced ourselves.

'Good morning, good morning!' He leaned across the shrinking table and tested our strength with a hearty twenty-kilo hand squeeze. 'I see Mathur's been taking you through all the productivity improvements.'

He turned to survey the white screen and Mathur's meticulous presentation, and walked slowly up to the projector.

'Very good, very impressive,' he said, running the pointer down the list of improvements. Then he turned suddenly and aimed the pointer at Rana.

'These are all very commendable achievements, but where do you think all this good stuff came from?' he demanded.

'Harder work, more attention to detail, better planning?' Rana ventured, one worried eye on the pointer.

'No, no, no! Look below the surface, dig deeper,' the Chief exhorted, and thrust the pointer into Rana's thin chest.

Rana shrank back and wrapped his arms around himself.

The Chief waited a couple of seconds and then gave up in disgust.

'The heart, young man, the heart!' he boomed. 'It all comes from inside your heart. Everything comes from within, from the steam of goodwill and the electricity of teamwork. The soul is the inspiration, the machines mere instruments.'

Mukesh swallowed, Mathur coughed, Badhwar took notes.

'You see all those big gains and full charts?' the Chief continued. 'None of that would have been possible without worker morale, my friend; without the new blue uniforms, the new jogging trail and sauna, the hybrid double dahlias, the new sprinkler system for the grass, the creation of an entirely unique sylvan environment at the factory. Did you know that this year we've had record sign-ups for the Factory Sports Day and an unprecedented turnout at the annual picnic? It is *this* freshness of approach that is lifting our spirits and driving our business, and it is *this* message that I want you youngsters to carry back to your offices. Think of new ways, good ways, kind ways to bring improvements to your own work, and you too will see the difference.'

There was a moment's awed silence as he switched the projector off.

'Any questions, any suggestions?' he asked, looking round hopefully.

Time to carpe diem.

'Actually we were just discussing plans for a new cake product, a fresh approach,' I said.

'I'm sure Chief was just on his way . . .' Mathur panicked, but the Chief was already lowering his bulk into the chair next to a shrinking Mukesh.

'Not at all,' he said, draping one arm round the chair back and thrusting his torso out happily. 'I have all the time in the world. Tell me about this new cake . . .'

seventeen

Saturday evening I sat on the couch in my favourite jeans and tees and went over the layouts for the anniversary cake ad.

Last night's meeting with the agency had gone on for ever. For once they'd come up with something promising and of course Rana had to seize that rare opportunity and do a 'Devil's advocate' hatchet job on it. If only some considerate virus or bacteria would take a nice little mini-break in his sinuses for a while . . .

Tender Loving Cake . . . the headline read, pencilled in a rare freestyle by some studio wiz who probably made twenty rupees an hour.

I liked it; it reminded me of Elvis.

'Tender Loving Cake', and below it a black-and-white sketch of a heart-shaped cake followed by body copy that continued for another couple of lines.

. . . *because love is a sweet thing. Celebrate your love* . . .

Hmm, too wordy, and gooey besides. We ought to keep it short and flirty, not more than thirty words.

'What do you think of "Tender Loving Cake", Mom?' I called out.

Mom was in the kitchen, bustling about, rearranging everything one last time. She glanced out from behind the cabinet door.

'Too Western,' she said, wrinkling her nose.

Served me right for asking.

'Do you know what your company should really be doing?'

I braced myself.

'Your company should be selling our pickles. They're very good; export quality, in fact. And we're always back-ordered on the red chillies pickle. We could bottle them for you in those brown recycled jars—they come quite cheap—and just think of all the women who'd benefit! Maybe I should talk to that Vik boss of yours?'

'Maybe next time,' I said and ducked behind my layouts. Thank goodness she was leaving today.

She never fails to astound me, though.

In the seven days that she'd been around, she'd completely transformed my apartment. The curtains were darned, the shelves cleaned, the hinges oiled, the floor polished, the cushions fluffed so many times they were in danger of flying away. Every surface in my apartment was now clean enough to eat off; she'd even scrubbed the walls. Where did she get all that energy from? I watched as she sifted and sorted and began stocking the fridge with what looked like a year's supply of spinach, carrots and beans.

'I'm not going to eat all that!' I threatened.

Damn, I'd miss her.

There was a low, long rumble outside. I looked out the window at the dark, agitated sky. It didn't look very encouraging. All morning a cool easterly breeze had been blowing and the birds had been fluttering and chattering with urgency. By the afternoon the clouds had started to assemble and descend in ever-darker layers, and now, at 4 p.m., we were blanketed in a heavy, night-like sky.

'Are you sure you should leave today?' I asked.

'Don't worry, we'll be fine. Sunil is a really careful driver,' Mom called.

She walked over to smooth out the wrinkles in the settee cover.

'By the way, did he call you yesterday?' she asked.

'No.'

He had, and we'd chatted a while, but really, that was none of her business.

'He does have a very busy life, what with all those long shifts and lives he has to save. Maybe you should call him?'

I turned back to my layouts.

A few minutes later the doorbell rang, Mom raced to open the door and I rejoiced. I love my Mom, it's true, but if she'd smoothed one more cushion or scrubbed one more table top . . .

'Hello, Sunil beta,' she said, fawning at the door. 'Thank you so much for driving me home. Would you like some milk or Horlicks?'

'Just some water, Aunty, thanks. We should leave soon; it looks like it could start raining any time.'

'That would be some respite, wouldn't it?' I said, getting up. 'I'll get the water, Mom. You get your things together.'

Sunil had settled down on the couch when I returned from the kitchen.

'What are these?' he asked, pointing to the pile of assorted paper and pencils on the coffee table.

'Oh, just some work I had to carry home.' I handed him his glass. 'We call these layouts; they're skeletal ads, sort of like those skeletons you medics keep around at home. Only friendlier.'

'And more appetizing!'

I pushed the stuff aside and sat down beside him.

'Anyway, thanks for driving Mom back. I really didn't want her rattling on the Roadways bus all the way to Meerut, especially in this weather.'

'There's nothing wrong with the Roadways bus,' Mom called.

'Yes, there is.'

'No, there isn't.'

'Yes, there . . .'

'Don't worry,' Sunil said, 'I'll make sure we get there safe and sound.'

'Thanks.'

Mom picked up her jhola.

'I'll call you once I get home,' she said.

I nodded.

'It's so nice you and Sunil got to meet up,' she continued. 'Sunil beta, maybe you could take Minal out some time? She tends to just sit around at home and mope on weekends.'

'Mom!'

I turned to Sunil, harassed. 'Don't mind her; she . . .'

He was smiling. 'I'd love to do that. In fact, there's a talk on some new research we've been working on, Thursday evening. Would you like to come?'

For a talk on cancer research?

'Doctor Dubey is a great speaker, and I have a short piece too,' he explained. 'It should get over by seven, and then we could carry on for dinner.'

'That sounds nice,' Mom exclaimed. 'Minal, you must go.'

'But I'll be in Mumbai most of the week.'

'You said you'll be back on Wednesday!'

'Only if everything goes okay.'

'Of course it will!'

I found myself shrivelling under Mom's dark glare.

'I guess I should be able to make it.'

'That'll be great,' Sunil said.

'Wonderful,' Mom beamed. 'So, should we leave now?'

The apartment felt empty without Mom's nagging presence; I missed her already. It had been nice to have someone around to argue with over dinner and to kiss goodnight. This singleton thing was no good; I really needed to make a serious push towards finding someone.

Someone who was kind and caring and didn't mind driving two hours through a storm to drop Mom home?

Someone who had a tan back and made my insides float around senseless with just one look?

I pushed aside the futile image and settled back in the balcony with my layouts.

'Celebrate your love . . .' the ad said. I doodled hearts and candles in the margin, searching for a fresh phrase.

A moment later, a magnificent flash split the sky, the roar that followed resonated in the very earth, and the rain came pouring down in the 4.5 billionth season of God's great sound, light and water show. The monsoon had arrived.

I put my papers aside and leaned over the railing of the balcony. People all around were running and ducking, all wet smiles and plastered hair. The newlyweds who lived on the top floor sprinted by, laughing and huddling close together, rushing home to make love.

I wondered what it would be like to make love in the rain. A misty cloak of privacy, transparent sheets of water, all ambient noise drowned out save for the water pounding on the roof and muddy rivulets murmuring softly by. I'd been kissed once in the rain, a long time ago. That exchange student who'd spent one term in college before returning to Iceland. He'd been fair and slight and one good kisser. Or maybe it had been the rain and the surreptitiousness of it all. Cool, crisp droplets tickling cheeks and noses; moist lips and tongues tasting and exploring. That kiss in the rain under the dripping tree had been sweeter than the golden mangoes in the branches above.

I sighed and watched the local urchins playing happily in the muddy ramparts of the crummy old well, slipping and splashing and whooping with delight. I stuck my tongue out to taste the wayward drops that slanted onto my balcony, and I longed to join them. Back when I was a girl, the coming of the monsoon used to be big deal at Nani's house. Nani and her buddies would gather in the veranda under the huge awning, the dholak would be brought out, and folk songs would be sung to greet the first rains till every single voice went hoarse. I remember the earthy voices of the women, especially the newlyweds, and the wet soil that smelled unbearably delicious. Many a time I'd seen one or the other of them, sneak a mouthful of it when no one was looking. I'd always wondered how that wet mud tasted.

Where had time and freedom and romance gone? Why did it all seem such a long time ago; when did I get from nine to twenty-nine? Rain kisser lost to a land of glaciers and geysers, Rajiv from Class 12 to a Beatles classic, Anand . . . oh, what was the point. Yudhishter had his toothy blonde; Aman was going out with that new girl at the ad agency (I'd noted with satisfaction that his portfolio was down forty per cent since); even Rana was engaged.

I sat back in my folding chair and found myself grateful for Sunil and the way he'd resurfaced suddenly and out of nowhere, like an easy leap of faith in a favourite fairytale. Funny how life could just pluck a guy out of Class 5 and re-launch him as a new, improved romantic lead. Was he the one? Back in the '80s he'd hardly seemed like any kind of hero, but now here he was, calling up every day, saving Vik's mom's life, driving my mom home in the rain, giving talks on cancer research like some modern-day Clark Kent.

I wondered what he'd be like to kiss. Would that kiss smell of disinfectant and ammonia, or would it be soft and creamy like Baale's Choco Bars?

And what about Ali, a stupid voice nagged and I swatted it dead. Good thing Mom had been around; I'd managed to stick to my promise of not returning his calls.

I eyed the phone warily when it rang a few minutes later.

'Hello?'

'So, you *are* at home.'

'Who is this?' I asked, pitching my voice at noncommittal-acquaintance level.

'Ali.'

'Ali! What a pleasant surprise!' I trilled, injecting great enthusiasm into my voice.

'What are you doing right now?'

'Oh, nothing much. Just sitting out, watching the rain . . .'

'I'll come over.'

'Actually I'm in the middle of . . .'

The phone went dead.

'Cheerful, pleasant, neighbourly.' I repeated a couple of times to myself, like a mantra. It shouldn't be too difficult; he was just a young boy after all. Minutes later, the doorbell rang, and I walked to the door with a careful smile.

I opened the door and my smile froze. On the doorstep stood the man of my dreams, drenched, running water, heartbreakingly handsome, holding a ridiculous bunch of assorted flowers (the ones that grew all along the boundary wall of the apartment complex).

He held these out with a smile that lit up the darkened room, and a big lump got stuck midway down my throat. I took the bouquet wordlessly and stood watching the tiny droplets of rain water shower down on my wrists.

'What's the matter, don't you like them?' he asked.

'They're lovely.'

'Yes, they are. I almost didn't give them to you.'

He wiped the rain off his face with the back of his hand and sneezed.

'You'd better go straight to the bathroom, you're soaked.'

He sauntered in, trailing drops of rain all over the floor. 'Isn't this wonderful? I love the rain. Someday I'm going to mix a CD of all my favourite rain music.'

I smiled.

'Stop making a mess on the floor. And hurry up and dry off. You'll catch a cold.'

'Not if I could get a cup of coffee.'

I pushed him into the bathroom, arranged the flowers in a jug, and put some water on the stove. Already the flat seemed warm and cosy.

Why couldn't things have been different?

I spooned the coffee into two mugs. Maybe I could just be his nurturing older neighbour. Someone who handed him a towel when he got wet in the rain, someone who fed him midnight snacks when he was hungry, someone who commented with a long-suffering air on his awful taste in women. Maybe we could be just friends. Maybe we could work out some such comfortable space in between.

He walked out, damp and rain-fresh.

I kept my eyes on the cups. I'd be fine if I just kept my eyes on the cups.

He walked up behind me as I poured the water into the mugs, and I felt long, warm fingers on my shoulders.

'Hey!' I said and moved quickly away.

He leaned back against the kitchen counter with a frown.

'So, how was your week?' I asked, stirring the sugar.

'Why didn't you call me?'

'Oh, you know, this and that, work, Mom . . .'

I stirred some more.

'Your Mom was here? I'd have liked to meet her.'

'Maybe another time.'

Maybe not.

'Just why did you leave the party that day?'

'Huh? Oh, that. Just, you know, tired. Old age, I guess.'

With all this stirring it was a wonder the spoon didn't dissolve too.

'Don't be ridiculous.'

'I'm twenty-nine, you know.'

'And?'

'You're twenty-four.'

'That doesn't change the fact that I'm terribly attracted to you.'

For a moment I thought I hadn't heard right, he'd said it so matter-of-factly.

'And I don't know what went wrong at that party; I thought you felt the same way.'

I stopped stirring and turned around. The look in his eyes made me want to wrap myself around him, to run my fingers down that ridge in his back, and across the tan skin that showed through at his collar, to feel those arms around me once again, to kiss him senseless.

Minal, he's twenty-four! My conscience squawked.

I picked up the coffee and handed him his mug. 'Gorgeous weather, isn't it?' I said. 'Let's go out to the balcony.'

On the balcony he flipped over the drawings; the heart-shaped cake and the TLC and the fluffy words below. I studied his shirt buttons, the three that were closed, the two that lay open.

'Did you do these?' he asked.

'No, it's an agency layout. For a new product we're working on.'

'A heart-shaped cake. Ironic. "Because love is a sweet thing. Celebrate your . . ." '

I snatched at the layout; he dodged and held it at arm's length.

I went for it again, and in seconds it was a grand romp all across the balcony. By the time I finally got to the layout, he'd wrestled me to the floor, and pinned me down by my wrists.

'Let me go.'

'Nope.'

'Look Ali, I may like you, but . . .'

'*Like* me?' he challenged, edging closer.

'Attracted then,' I said quickly, 'but it won't work out.'

'Why not? We're both adult and unattached.'

'What about Lara?' I sidetracked.

'What about her?'

'You seemed pretty close.'

'We are,' he laughed. 'We work together and kid around sometimes, that's all. Why? Are you jealous?'

'Of course not. Can I get up now?'

'I kind of like it here.'

'Ali, I'm twenty-nine!'

'You told me that already.'

'You have to understand; you're way too young for me.'

'I don't feel too young right now.'

'I don't mean right now. I mean later. For ever. I mean for a relationship that's good for a lifetime.'

'This feels good enough for a lifetime.'

He moved closer, his thumbs caressing my wrists, his face inches from mine.

'Ali, you can't put attraction above everything else! There are a lot of things that matter; career, marriage, long-term plans. You won't understand; you're still a kid.'

'I'm not a kid, Minal. I think you know *that*.'

His lips were a breath away, teasing, challenging, provoking.

I reached up and put an end to the conversation.

We clung together for ever it seemed, drinking, tasting, exploring.

He tasted of the rain and the wet earth. I held him close, kissing his jaw, his neck, feeling his hands run over me, drawing me closer. I slid my hand inside his shirt and found that ridge down his back, and traced its length with my fingertips, lost in the feel of his skin. And then the wind flung a vigorous burst of rain our way.

He grinned and brushed the water off his hair. 'Let's take this inside.'

'No,' I said, and closed my eyes.

'Okay, whatever you say.'

He bent his head again.

I pushed him away. 'No, I mean let's not take this anywhere. Let's stop right here.'

He sighed and sat up.

'Spoilsport.'

I got up, brushing my jeans.

'Look, Ali, try to understand. I'm almost thirty. I want to get married, I *need* to get married. You're just twenty-four, you don't! Where does that leave us?'

'How about we take it one day at a time, see how things go?'

'I don't think that's a good idea.'

'You think too much.'

'Curse of the old and jaded.'

'Would you stop throwing your age in my face?'

'Maybe you should leave now.'

'You know what? Maybe I should.'

He got up, disgusted, and started back inside.

'Bye, Ali,' I called. It was for the best.

He stopped by the door and turned.

'Minal?'

I walked up, wary.

'We can't pretend this never happened, you know.'

'Let's try.'

'Think about it; give us a chance. That's all I'm asking you to do. I'm going to be in Bangalore till Wednesday. How about I call you when I get back?'

'I'm out all next week.'

'Then you call me. Or better still, just drop by.'

'I don't think . . ..'

'Shhhhh.' He put a hand on my chin and kissed me lightly. 'Just think about it. Think about how good it could be.'

Oh, it would be good. I knew that. But it wouldn't happen. I knew that too. I shut the door behind him and went slowly back to the balcony. I could still taste his lips on mine.

eighteen

The wheels of the plane touched the airstrip with a shudder and a hundred seat belts clicked open. The passengers in the aisle seats shot up as one and lunged for the overhead lockers. The guys in the middle followed; those with window seats stood cramped between their seats and the ones in front, and looked on enviously.

'Ladies and gentlemen, welcome to Mumbai airport,' a voice crackled on the PA system. 'The temperature outside is 30°C. Please remain seated with your seat belts fastened until the plane comes to a complete halt and the seat belt sign is switched off.'

It was as pointless as asking a pack of hungry wolves to say grace before a meal.

It is a proven fact: Indians cannot wait. Not in lines, not in seats, not at traffic lights, not ever. It is genetic. I look forward to the day when some bright young doctoral student finally puts out a research paper correctly identifying the special gene that's at the bottom of it, christens the condition 'Patience Deficiency Disorder' or some such and, with a sympathetic worldwide cluck, we are all upgraded from 'uncouth boors' to 'people with special needs'.

I collected my bags and joined the crowd that pushed its way through the exit, a narrow, sinuous valley of speed-walking laptopped and cellphoned executives. We were flanked on both sides by immovable masses of sign-bearing chauffeurs. 'Mahindra

& Mahindra welcomes Mr Raj Hans', 'IDBI welcomes Mr Kapil Goel', 'Vidarbha Exports welcomes Mr Okinawa'. . . on and on the line snaked and thinned. A short, pot-bellied man was standing a disdainful distance away from the riffraff, flashing a breakfast bar self-consciously every time a female passenger went by. I made my way round to him and held out a hand.

'Mr Shinde? I'm Minal Sharma.'

Subhash Shinde, Area Sales Manager, Mumbai city, shook my hand with relief, adjusted a pair of Ray-Bans and led me across to a waiting cab. He leaped inside the cool interior, fluffed his shirt up round the collar and instructed the driver to crank the air-con up to maximum.

'Bloody hot and humid day,' he offered, by way of ice-breaker.

'You must be used to it.'

'Oh, sure. In Sales, you get used to the tough life. Are you from Delhi?'

'Yes, I've lived there for a while now.'

'Bloody nonsense place; all politicians and babus,' he said. 'So what is this new cake that's got the boss so excited? That reminds me; I need to make a few phone calls, get the boys in on time.'

I nodded. I understood perfectly.

I have been making a quiet study of the peculiarities and distinguishing traits of the 'Sales Manager' species for sometime now, and the findings are truly remarkable. For instance, it is uncanny how all the really big egos, smooth tongues and small brains in the IF world have inexplicably landed up in Sales. The tougher, smarter ones have worked their way up and are leaders to contend with. The lucky ones have worked their way out to other jobs, much chastened and vastly improved by the experience. And the rest, the ones that got left behind to circle endlessly in the rough waters of the trade are the irreparably delusional and chauvinistic lot of current IF sales managers.

This last sub-species is surprisingly homogenous. Fancy black loafers with patterned socks, pot bellies and a suboptimal use of deodorant are key identifying traits. Moustaches occur in most varieties, as do gold watches and cellphones.

There is one important difference, though, between the two distinct strains that are commonly found. It is the look in their eyes. The punier ones have that 'I'm king of my territory, no one messes with me' expression, and the uglier ones the 'I don't see too many women in my job, so don't mind if I mentally undress you' leer. Shinde, I noted gratefully, belonged to the former category.

I watched him punch in a string of numbers on his chunky cellphone. The line went live with a snappy 'Yes, boss?'

'Patil? *Saala*, where have you been? I've been trying to reach you all morning.'

'Boss, here at the distributor's only. The line must have been engaged; lot of phone orders this morning.'

'I know you and your orders. Listen, you better clean up your act, man, or I'll transfer you to Nasik; you'll be an old man before you move from there.'

A sad sputtering emanated from the earpiece.

'What the bloody hell do you mean "sorry, sir"? That shopkeeper Gopal said all kinds of nonsense things about our company in front of me, and I had to listen to him. You should be more careful in future about where you take your senior officers.'

Silence for a minute. The driver weaved through some heavy Bandra traffic.

'Weak words, Patil, weak words. Be a man, Patil, control your area with an iron fist. That bloody distributor Parikh's not buying enough, you need to get tough with him, man, send him thirty lakhs of inventory right away.'

'What, Patil. I don't care where he gets the money from. Let him pull some money out of his brother's hotel business, sell his fancy car, I don't care.'

He scratched his belly and listened to the steady whine at the other end with a deepening frown. Suddenly he exploded, '@#$%&@! You *saala* Patil, always whining, always excuses. Dammit, you have no control over the market. Bloody no one even offers refreshments to your senior officer when he visits. Even that bloody car you were supposed to arrange for me didn't show up. *Saala*, I'll be back next month, surprise visit, you better take charge or pack your bags. And listen. I want you in the office at noon sharp. That product manager from HO is here.'

He closed his phone with a snap.

'Got to keep them on their toes,' he grunted, and dialled again.

'Desai? Be in the office at noon. Some cake briefing. *Bhai*, what's this going on in the Pune market? It's been three months since you took over the area and no improvement?'

The expletives poured forth once again. I smiled out the window.

'*Saala,* don't give me *goli,* I know the Pune market inside out. *Saala,* every shopkeeper's *sayaana,* playing one company against the other. Bloody all cash transactions in the Pune market, never give these fellows credit, you'll never see your money again.'

He listened with a long-suffering air.

'What "Ramanand is very powerful sir"? You just have to know which buttons to push. *Yaar*, that new manager there, Devikaji? Send her some flowers, take her out, show her a good time; be a man, *yaar.*'

Desai whispered something in a tinny voice.

'Desai, brother, don't tell me I have to teach you how to do even that? Hee, hee, hee.' He threw me a sidelong glance, whispered something in Marathi, and both sides of the line erupted in raucous laughter.

I shook my head and went over my notes for the meeting.

The audience Shinde had lined up for the briefing session was impressive. The entire Mumbai sales force was there, assembled together from stretches far, wide and traffic- jammed. They fidgeted through my presentation, skittish as a bunch of school boys on a field trip, and I could see a hundred questions and opinions bubbling behind their sharp eyes and too-eager smiles. They held it in till the last slide, then erupted en masse.

'What is this new cake exactly, ma'am, what is the launch date, what will the ads be like?'

'Ma'am, you need to do something explosive with the ads. Our ads are all very boring, no josh.'

'Yes, ma'am. How come we never use any film stars or cricketers? I swear, if you put Sachin in the ad, the product will be a guaranteed success.'

'No *yaar,* this is a housewife product. Ma'am, why don't we ask that Ekta Kapoor to write an ad for us this time?'

'Ma'am, my uncle's neighbour's son-in-law is an assistant director in Bollywood. He knows all the big producers and all. If you want, I could put you in touch with him.'

'And why don't we ever advertise in films, ma'am? The film stars are always drinking Coke and Pepsi in every movie; why can't they eat IF cakes instead?'

'*Yaar*, there's a new Rajnikant movie coming up. Mega blockbuster. If we want to corner the South market, we must put our product in it.'

'And what will Rajnikant do; decorate cakes or bash up villains with them? No, ma'am, music, that is the key. This time we should have A.R. Rahman compose the music.'

'Ismail Darbar, *yaar.*'

'No *yaar*, Rahman is the best.'

A brilliant bolt of inspiration brought me back from the brink of hopelessness.

'Guys, these are great suggestions, you're really thinking outside the box. I think we should send your ideas straight to the ad agency. In fact, I'll give you Yogi's cellphone number. He's the account director responsible for the development of the ad; you can call him any time.'

I felt a slight pang, just the littlest one, as they all took the number down. The old conscience thing again, you know.

'What about the cake, ma'am; what flavours will we have?'

'Basic sponge and chocolate to start with; this is a test market after all. We can expand into more flavours later on.'

'We should do some Indian flavours, you know. Zafrani Kaju Kishmish, Kulfi, Mango Mazaa . . .'

'What about a food service pack, ma'am, for industrial use?'

'Um, we'll have to see how we can market anniversary cakes for industrial use, but thanks for the suggestion. I'll ask Mr Mathur at the factory to look into it.'

I looked at my watch; it was time to break up the picnic.

'Well, this has really been a very stimulating session,' I said. 'Could we now put some hard numbers down for the initial production run, some firm sales commitments?'

Everyone flinched. I'd said the 'C' word.

Shinde fixed Patil with a glare. 'Patil? How much, man?'

'Sir, I can place it in all A class outlets, six packs each.'

'But that's just a handful of outlets,' I said.

'Ma'am, if you give a five rupees off scheme, I could place it in all B class outlets too. That would take it to about sixty outlets.'

'Five rupees off? But we haven't even decided the price yet!'

'That doesn't matter. Five rupees off always works.'

'And if you can give ten rupees off, then we can even push it into C class outlets,' the guy next to Patil added.

'But then won't the dealers just discount the cakes and sell them? Aren't we talking about discounting something we haven't even introduced yet?'

'Okay, then how about a trade scheme instead—fifty rupees back for every five cases sold or something?'

'Or gold coins? Gold coins are very popular, you know.'

'Guys, this is a test market! We're trying to gauge genuine consumer and trade reaction, not dump our stock in the market!'

Shinde sighed and looked at his watch.

'Minal, do you want this product to succeed or not?'

'Of course I do! But . . .'

'Well, then let me handle it. Boys, here's the deal. I'm going to base your bonuses for the next quarter entirely on the new cake. Minimum sale: ten cakes per outlet. You meet your targets; you get a twenty per cent bonus. Now let's start; how many in the first month, Patil?'

'Sir, seventy cases.'

'Gajju?'

'Forty-five.'

'Joshi?'

'One hundred.'

I watched as he took the numbers down.

'Right,' he said once he had everyone's estimate. 'So let's just multiply that by three and up it by fifty per cent, month on month for the next two months, and that's your target. And anyone who doubles his target gets three times the bonus. There!'

He scribbled a figure and passed it to me with a flourish.

'That's our sales plan. We'll pass it on to the secretary; she'll key it in to the new system. So shall we all head out for a beer now?'

I got up slowly, much impressed. So this was how the much-touted SAP-ed, ERP-ed, highly sophisticated and accurate IF sales planning process really worked. Amazing!

nineteen

A thrill of anticipation shot through me as we followed the maître d' to a quiet table by the heavy oriental drapes. They were pulled back a little, and through the fine lace of the sheer curtains beneath I could see the dark waters of the swimming pool. Tall lanterns made of bamboo circled its shimmering length; their soft, yellow lights reflected in its gentle ripples seeming to set it ablaze. A dense wall of trees cordoned off the private grounds of the hotel and, beyond these, landscaped gardens rolled gently down towards the quiet tree-lined street.

The maître d' pulled a chair out across the smooth carpet, and I sank down into a cloud-soft seat. A white napkin lay folded in an artistic swan shape on the table, almost too perfect to open up and spread on my lap. A waiter glided up and filled our crystal from a frosty bottle of Perrier. I admired the flair with which he poured exact amounts of the sparkling water into each glass. He lit the tiny candle, and a small flame flickered and grew. Slowly, it spread its warm wings in the votive and illuminated the frescoes on the wall above.

'This is fantastic,' I said, smiling brightly across at Sunil.

'It's a nice place. A little smaller than the House of Ming, but the food is good.'

Food is good? I'd dreamed of dining at this famous restaurant for years. Of dancing to the live band, of ordering chilled champagne and Peking Duck, of powdering my nose in the pink and gold ladies' room, of leaving a thousand-rupee tip for the meticulously attentive waiter, and all he could say was 'the food is good'?

A lot of money *could* be a bad thing.

The waiter came back to pour Chinese tea into inch-high porcelain cups.

'What will you have to drink, Madam?' he asked.

I studied the wine menu, even though I had my answer ready.

'A glass of Chardonnay, a drier one, please,' I said. I'd practised it a hundred times.

'May I suggest the 1998 Napa Valley Robert Mondavi? It's a rich Californian wine, with tropical fruit, peat, hazelnut and spice flavours, and a really delightful finish.'

'That sounds very nice.'

'Very good, Madam. And you, sir?'

'I'm okay.'

'We just got a new consignment of some exquisite Riesling from Germany; light and . . .'

'I'll just have the tea, thanks,' Sunil said.

'Very good, sir.'

'You know, I think I'll just have the tea too.'

Perhaps I *was* getting a little carried away.

'No, no; you go ahead,' Sunil said, 'I never drink; I find it impairs my judgement.' He turned to the waiter. 'The Chardonnay for her; tea for me.'

The waiter nodded politely and withdrew.

Well, anyway. Here I was at the Mecca of good taste, fine dining and big money, with a charming escort who just happened to be a brilliant surgeon who'd just finished giving a talk to doctors twice his age on some earth-shattering, paradigm-shifting, new piece of cancer research. From a romantic possibilities' standpoint it couldn't get much better than this. I pushed aside a distracting image of polished teak and leaned forward to smile at Sunil.

'You should have told me you didn't drink.'

'It's nothing,' he shrugged.

'I'm not much of a drinker myself.'

'That's good.' He turned his attention to the menu. 'So, what'll you have to eat? I'm hungry.'

I opened the menu that lay next to my swan napkin and flipped through it; page after page of delectable dishes that went on and on like the pages of a novella.

'What's good here?' I asked finally.

'The spinach. And the eggplant's delicious; it's very delicately spiced.'

Eggplant?

'How about the Peking Duck; have you ever tried it?'

'I'm vegetarian.'

'Oh.'

'Would you like to order the duck?'

'Oh, no. I don't care much for the meaty stuff myself.'

'Yes; we are Brahmins after all, aren't we?'

'Do you believe in all that caste stuff?'

Bapu would not have approved.

'I meant that non-veg is just so alien to our culture.'

I guess Bapu would have approved.

We ordered the spinach and the eggplant and the steamed rice.

'So, what did you think of my talk?' Sunil asked, as we waited for our food.

'You were brilliant.'

'Do you really think so? I was a little nervous; there were quite a few highly respected doctors there.'

'I didn't understand a word of what you said, but I'm sure it was good.'

'You were bored!'

'No, it was interesting. And seriously, all those old fogies were nodding and scribbling furious notes the whole time you were talking. I'd say you did okay.'

'Funny girl! Those old fogies are very, very important and distinguished people.'

'I knew that.'

'Anyway, I'm glad you came. Thanks.' He said it quietly, earnestly, like he really meant it, and I almost felt glad I'd gone too.

I studied the three-member band that was just setting up shop at the far end. They were an interesting ensemble—the lead singer in studded jeans and slithery shirt, the gay drummer with a red bandanna and matching lipstick, the balding, bearded guy in crumpled overalls at the keyboards. They started with a soulful ballad and the neighbouring tables fell silent.

Sunil, meanwhile, did his best to explain his work in lay terms to me. He started with the PMT entrance exam, worked his way through detailed accounts of med and post-med, internship and residency and by the time the food arrived we were deep in the throes of some critical operation with the illustrious Dr Dubey at the scalpels.

I watched the waiter spoon out long strands of runny spinach into our plates and felt incredibly sad. *I know just how you feel,* I told the spinach. *I'd feel the same if all my patients were on chemotherapy and radiation.*

The waiter withdrew to assemble the famous eggplant and I forced a smile. 'All this talk of metastasis, thrombocytopenia and leucopenia! I think I'm ready to cry.'

'You know, you're just like Mom. She never lets me talk about work at the dinner table.'

'How do you cope? I'm surprised you manage to ever smile at all!'

'It's my job. Anyway, let's not talk any more about work. This food looks delicious. *Bon appétit!*'

I poked at the steamed rice with my fork.

'So how was your trip to Mumbai?' Sunil asked, between mouthfuls of spinach.

'Not bad. I got the branch to agree to some good numbers.'

'Excuse me?'

'I mean I got some very encouraging sales commitments for this new product we're launching.'

'That's good.'

'I wonder if they'll really deliver, though.'

'Here, have some more eggplant; it's really good.'

I eyed the evil glop and put my fork down.

'I'm not really that hungry.'

'Really? That's a pity.'

I watched as he reached for seconds, flawlessly manoeuvring the purple pulp with his ivory chopsticks.

'Where did you learn to use those?'

'Chopsticks? At medical school. Mostly to impress the Chinese prof in third year, but it still comes in handy when I want to make a good impression. It's not that hard.'

'Really? Let me try.'

He showed me how to lift the food cleanly off the plate, resting one chopstick lightly on the ridge between thumb and middle finger and cleverly manipulating the food with the forefinger on the other. A few minutes into the practice session and I was hopelessly tangled in the spinach.

'So much for impressions,' I laughed. 'So how many women have you worked your chopstick charm on?'

'None. I've always been a bit awkward around women.'

I noticed he had turned a little pink round the ears and nose and sides of his glasses.

'You could have fooled me,' I smiled. 'I'm *very* impressed.'

'You're different. I feel like I've known you all my life.'

'Uh huh?'

'Mom called this morning, you know. She was asking about you.'

'How is she? And your Dad?'

'They're fine. Dad's busy planning their next holiday. You know how he is.'

I smiled, remembering. 'He's always been so full of life. I still remember that time he drove all us kids down to Agra.'

We reminisced a while about the 'good old times' in Meerut. Sunil mentioned meeting up with a couple of old schoolmates and acquaintances, which reminded me of the Rana situation. He gratifyingly dropped his chopsticks when I told him.

'Rana Bhatia? That's terrible. How do you manage to work with that fellow?'

'Don't ask. Thankfully, there's Vik.'

'I can ask Vik to transfer Rana some place else if you want.'

'I sure wish you could.'

'No, really, let me know if he gets to be too much trouble. I'll talk to Vik. What are contacts for if they can't help out every once in a while?'

I burst out laughing.

For a moment he'd sounded like he could really make it happen.

The dessert arrived at ten, as did the coffee.

'Mmmm!' Sunil said and dug into his ice cream with gusto. I sipped at my coffee, enjoying the music. The band picked up tempo and a few people got up to dance. I watched the young couple in the far corner. They were easily the best dancers, working the floor with style and ease and an enviable lack of self-consciousness. They looked like they were having a blast.

'They look good,' I said.

Sunil turned round to see. After a moment he returned to his dessert.

'I'm not much of a dancer; I've always had two left feet.'

Of course.

'So, no wine, no women, no dance; what vices *do* you have, Dr Pandey, assuming there are one or two?'

'Minal!' A voice shrieked at my elbow.

I jumped.

'Radha! What are you doing here?'

'Just getting away from the pack; you know how it is.'

'Vinod!' I said, as Radha's husband joined us. 'Hi, how are things?'

'Perfect,' he said, looking decidedly frazzled. 'Of course the wedding is tomorrow, everyone's going crazy, and Madam here was craving Chinese food!'

'Oh, come on, Vinod, your aunt was driving me nuts!' Radha complained.

'I know, baba,' he said, with a fond smile. 'Anyway, you are coming tomorrow, aren't you, Minal?'

'I'll try to make it.'

Radha had been busy studying Sunil. She nudged me pointedly as he got to his feet. I sighed and performed the introductions.

'Won't you join us?' Sunil asked.

'I'm sure they're in a terrible hurry.'

'No, we're not,' Radha shot back with a brilliant smile.

She launched into me in the ladies' room ten minutes later. 'You're dating someone and you never told me!'

'Don't get carried away, we're just friends.'

I explained about Aruna Aunty and all.

'Childhood sweethearts. How romantic.'

'Hardly. I just bumped into him two weeks ago.'

'What does he do?'

'He's a surgeon. Cancer specialist.'

'Really, where?'

'At Apollo. In fact he's treating Vik's mum.'

'He's *Dr Pandey*?' she shrieked. 'I must have spoken to him a dozen times over the phone! I always thought he was a lot older.'

'He's thirty-one or -two, I think. He used to be a couple of classes ahead of me.'

'He's obviously doing really well then; Vik thinks the world of him.'

I felt an irrational surge of pride.

'So when's the wedding? We'll have to do another round of shopping, of course. I know just where to go for those . . .'

'Whoa, back up. We're just having dinner.'

She rolled her eyes.

'Really, there's nothing going on!'

'Right. Just candlelight dinner, live music, hand holding. The usual.'

'We weren't holding hands!'

'Don't worry; you soon will. Ooh, I can't wait to tell Vik!'

'*Radha*!'

'After it's official and all. Oh, come off it, Minal, don't give me those coy ones. He's perfect.'

Was he?

'Anyway, let's get back and rescue him. I'm sure Vinod must have drowned him in his long list of aches and pains by now.'

'You carry on; I'll just be a minute.'

I watched her leave, and groaned long and loud into the silence.

When's the wedding, she'd asked, like it might be next month or next week. It would be hard to keep it off the office grapevine now. Tons of speculation, and no substance.

Or was there?

I studied my reflection in the mirror and tried an objective assessment of the way I felt about Sunil. 1. Terribly excited 2. Somewhat excited 3. Marginally excited 4. Not excited 5. Bored to tears.

Hmm . . . 1. Terribly excited.

What? my conscience scolded.

'Okay, okay, 3. Marginally excited, then. It could have been somewhat excited, if it weren't for the eggplant.'

Eggplant? My conscience was truly shocked now.

It was right of course.

For once I'd met a guy who I couldn't find fault with; a serious, good-looking, well-to-do, *normal* guy (*older than me!*), and all I could think about was the eggplant?

I brushed my hair, yanking at the ends angrily.

The door opened and the girl from the dance floor walked in, flushed and perspiring. She joined me at the mirror, splashed her face with cold water and picked a fluffy white towel from the immaculate stack by the counter.

'Man, that feels good, it's so hot out there,' she breathed.

'You were working up quite a sweat on the dance floor,' I smiled. 'You and your friend.'

'He's cute, isn't he? I just met him a couple of weeks ago, but we just . . . clicked.' She snapped her fingers. 'You know?'

'Uh huh.'

She watched as I rummaged around in my purse for some lipstick.

'You look familiar, are you in LSR?' she asked.

I burst out laughing.

'You're off by a whole decade, but thanks!'

'Hey, now I remember, you were at that party last week! With Ali!'

'Oh yes, my neighbour,' I said, hoping to make it sound like he was my son. 'Hardly know him.'

'Really? I could have sworn you were . . .'

I shook my head emphatically.

'Well, guess not,' she said, still doubtful. 'Though you guys did look pretty hot yourselves!'

I waited for her to leave, then bent to the sink to splash some cold water on my own burning cheeks.

We *had* looked hot at the party. I wondered what she'd have thought if she'd seen us on my balcony. What would Sunil think?

What was Ali thinking?

I pulled the crumpled Post-it out from the inner pocket in my purse, the one I'd found pushed under my door when I got back from Mumbai.

Private party, B-406, it murmured. *Let's make some music.*

A vivid image of the earthy rug and the chocolate-brown eyes filled my vision again. And that back with that deep ridge . . .

Stop it! my conscience snarled. Stop, stop . . . STOP!

I looked at the Post-it one last time, then tore it into a million deliberate shreds and dropped them in the waste basket. Several deep breaths and squaring of shoulders later, I strode briskly out to rejoin the group at the Chinese restaurant.

The band was playing again, slower, softer this time.

'Why don't you come with Minal to my brother's wedding?' Vinod was saying to Sunil.

'Yes, we'd love to have you,' Radha was nodding.

'I'd love to come,' Sunil was smiling.

Let's make some music, a voice in my head was whispering.

'Let's dance,' I said to Sunil, and yanked him up on his feet.

twenty

I winced as I clipped the long earrings on to my ears. They pinched, sticking out at the sides like giant clothes pins. Undaunted, I clasped a giant choker round my neck, slipped two dozen glass bangles on my wrists and adjusted the shiny red sticker bindi midway between my brows. It was one of those exclamation mark things that never quite pointed straight up (this one tended to list a little to the left), but it was all I had and it would have to do. I pulled out mascara and liner, eyeshadow and glitter, ruthlessly set them about their business, and a few minutes later I sat blinking at the mannequin in the mirror. I could have been one of those busts in the display windows at the jewellers.

Disgusting, but this was the only way to blend in at Radha's.

I got up from the stool and tested the weight of the sari. It was as I'd expected; I'd need to stick a few dozen safety pins in, for sure. Already the petticoat felt loose around my waist; the sari was already falling out in a couple of places.

The doorbell rang and I hobbled stiffly over, holding the pleats high and away from the ground. Maybe Sunil could help me with the pins?

I opened the door, and Ali dangled across the doorway, hands thrust deep in brown corduroy pockets, shirt carelessly askew, a bottle of something tucked under one arm. He was looking down, studying the tops of his Timberlands. The laces were undone, I noticed, as though he'd just thrust his feet into them and rushed over.

My heart thumped loudly against my ribs. Part of me had been expecting this all day, but now that he was here . . .

He looked up with a smile that widened to a grin as he took in my ensemble.

'Minal? Is that you?'

'Hi, Ali.'

'Fancy dress party?'

'No; wedding.'

'Not yours, I hope!'

'How are you?' I smiled.

'Lonely.'

His voice turned husky, caressing, and despite all my firm resolve, my knees trembled just a little.

'How was Bangalore?' I asked.

'How was Bombay?'

'Oh, hectic. I just got back—'

'—last evening. I know. I was waiting for you. I thought you'd come.'

'Oh.'

He leaned against the door and folded his arms across his chest. I noticed the sleeves were rolled back, revealing the fine hair along the back of the tanned skin. 'I've missed you,' he said softly.

'Yes, well, nice of you to drop by . . .'

'Isn't it? And I brought some wine and music too.' He held out the bottle, and pulled a CD out of his shirt.

'I was just heading out, you know.'

'Don't. Let's stay in.'

'I can't; it's a friend's wedding.'

'Everything around you seems to be about weddings, doesn't it?'

'Bye, Ali.'

'No wait, I was just kidding. I'll swing by later. When will you be back?'

'Very late.'

'I'll wait.'

'I don't think that's a good idea.'

'Tomorrow then?'

'I'm very busy all next week. And the week after.'

He sighed.

'Minal . . .'

'I thought I'd made myself clear, Ali.'

'And I thought you'd have thought this through.'

'I have. And it won't work.'

'It will,' he insisted.

'Ali . . .'

'Look, maybe things just moved too quickly. How about we start over? How about we cycle back to that time we had coffee in my kitchen and take it from there? What do you think should come next—dinner, a movie?'

'Neither.'

'I'll even play Scrabble if you really want to.'

I couldn't help smiling. 'Thanks, but maybe not.'

'Have it your way then. What?'

There was no easy way to say this, but it had to be said.

'Ali, I've met someone.'

'What do you mean?'

'I'm seeing someone else.'

'*In one week*?'

'He's an old friend.'

'I don't believe you; you're just getting cold feet.'

'I wouldn't pull an excuse like that even if I were. But I'm not.'

'I see.'

'Look, we can still be friends, right?'

'You're dumping me without even giving me a chance, and you want to be *friends*?'

'I'm not dumping you.'

'What do you call this then?'

'Ali; you're much too young. Sunil really is more my type.'

He looked like I'd slapped him across his face.

'Last week you have your tongue down *my* throat and now suddenly *Sunil's* more your type?'

'Look, last week was a big mistake.'

'What *is* more your type Minal? Is Sunil more loaded, is he waiting with a wedding ring, is *that* more your type?'

I flinched; the venom in his voice was startling.

'Ali, I've been trying to tell you . . .'

There were footsteps coming up the stairwell.

'Shhhh, I think that's him.'

He wheeled round and watched Sunil emerge on to the landing.

'Look, don't make a scene, okay?' I hissed.

Sunil walked up, dusting drops of rain off his raincoat. 'Hi, Minal, you look very nice.' He wiped his feet carefully on the doormat. 'Don't you just hate this rain? It gets in everywhere.'

'Just your type,' Ali murmured under his breath.

I shot him a warning look. *Behave, please behave,* I prayed silently.

Sunil looked at Ali, a polite smile on his face. 'Hello?'

'Sunil, meet Ali, my neighbour. He lives upstairs.'

They shook hands, the two sets of thin long fingers; the fair ones that saved lives, the brown ones that made music. Sunil stepped back with a friendly nod; Ali receded into a sullen silence.

'Sunil is a cancer surgeon,' I said, turning to Ali, 'He works at Apollo with Dr Dubey. You must know Dr Dubey—he's one of the best oncologists in India. We met quite by chance the other day, at the Blind School. You know Mom and I were there to meet one of the organizers and Sunil's mom was . . .'

I found myself chattering on brightly in newfound moron style, and was grateful to Sunil who helped punctuate the narrative with well-placed nods and smiles. Ali stood quiet, hands deep in pockets, eyes never leaving my face.

'Blind School,' he murmured as I wound down. 'It figures.'

'So Ali, what do you do?' Sunil asked.

'Mostly I keep trying to get it off with Minal.'

'Don't be ridiculous!' I tittered, and gave him a playful, resounding smack on his arm.

'Ali is my wild little neighbour,' I explained. 'He hangs out with all these carefree college types and they have really wild parties and all. In fact he took me to a radio party once; quite reminded me of our own college days. Don't you sometimes wish we were his age?'

I smiled what I hoped was an indulgent smile and linked my arm with Sunil's.

'Are you in radio?' Sunil asked. 'What do you do there?'

'I host a show. On 107.4 FM.'

Sunil looked thoughtful. 'That's owned by the Jatiyas, isn't it? I've met Varun Jatiya a couple of times. He seems like a sound man.'

'I wouldn't know; I'm just a sound employee.'

'It must be interesting, being a radio jockey. Of course I hardly ever listen to radio. I'm afraid I'm not much into music.'

'I can tell,' Ali said. 'I bet you haven't seen the view from Minal's balcony either.'

'I'm sorry?'

'Ali's just kidding. Sunil, maybe we should get going; it's getting late.' I tugged at his sleeve, turning my back on Ali.

'Wait.'

Suddenly he was in front of me, holding my shoulders, blocking my way.

'It's not right,' he said.

He was going to make a scene.

'What are you talking about?' I hissed.

He stared into my eyes for a few angry seconds; and then, thankfully, he began to smile.

'Your bindi, what else?' he said. 'It's crooked.'

He reached up and moved it right, then left, then right again, taking his time, grinning.

This was supposed to be funny?

Finally, after what felt like an eon, he stepped back and turned to Sunil.

'There. Much better, don't you think?'

'Sunil, why don't you come inside? Ali, thanks and all, but we really have to leave now.'

'Nice meeting you, Ali.' Sunil held out his hand.

'See you around,' Ali drawled. 'And Minal . . .'

Now what?

'Watch out for the rain.'

He blew me a kiss and raced up the steps back to his apartment.

I'd kill him, I promised myself, and shut the door.

twenty-one

Nothing besides work and rain dared happen for the next couple of weeks.

This was just as well, since production schedules and packaging proofs took over my waking hours, and missed deadlines and errant suppliers haunted my nights. To recap the fortnight's big and small events:

- It rained heavy and long for most of the week, forcing folks in Subzi Mandi, Shakti Nagar and other low-lying areas to row to work as clogged drains and water jams ran amok in my own neighbourhood.
- The factory completed the final trials on the heart-shaped cake and Mathur went on a month's vacation to recover.
- The final sales forecast that came through from Shinde's team was robust enough to run the Mumbai marathon.
- Yogi at the ad agency got a ten-thousand-rupee mobile phone bill on incoming long-distance and had to get his number changed.

Meanwhile Sunil had to dash off to Chennai for another series of conferences, and the angry Post-it messages I left Ali must have shamed him into disappearing completely and effectively from my life.

On Sunday I awoke at noon with nothing but cups of coffee and four pages of cartoons on the day's agenda. I snoozed and stretched, then floated around the house for a while. I threw open the windows; the skies had finally appeared after a week of showers and rain. The hot, damp sunlight streamed in and fell on the sofa, making it come to life.

Maybe I'd curl up and snooze on it later.

I padded barefoot to the kitchen and put some water on the stove. I opened the new Nescafé Gold jar I'd bought last week, and breathed deeply, closing my eyes as that first heavenly blast of strong, rich coffee hit my nostrils. One day, when I was rich and successful, I'd open up a fresh jar of coffee every day.

I fished a pack of Curly Cookies out of the cupboard, and poured all twenty cookies out onto a china platter. I picked one up and nibbled on it as I waited for the water to heat up. Next weekend, I thought as I licked at the cream that oozed out, I could be eating my own cake!

I stirred the coffee and brought it over to the table, right next to the giant poster positive of the anniversary cake that I'd stuck to the wall. I ran my hand over the poster, outlining the creamy, heart-shaped walls that rose like majestic bluffs, and the ruby-red icing that trickled down the sides like molten lava. In just a few days, this poster would be up all over town, and Mumbai would be abuzz with my new cake; soft and moist and delectable and path-breaking. And I'd be responsible. After all those bleary nights and snafu-ridden mornings, those fights with the agency and showdowns with Rana—finally—after all those weeks of coaxing and cajoling and plans and reviews, something to touch and taste and savour and feel incredibly proud of.

I still couldn't believe it was coming true.

I took a sip of the coffee and opened up my Sunday newspaper. The headlines were the usual shit, and I turned the page.

And then I died.

Or perhaps I didn't die; perhaps I just sank through the floor and the car park and the flower beds and the various layers of the earth's crust and hurtled straight down to its burning core. My heart went dry, my throat wobbled, my knees beat fast and my hair caught fire.

The murder weapon?

A 200-cc full-colour ad on page three that there was no way anyone could ever miss.

TENDER LOVING CAKE™

. . . the headlines read, above a super-sized picture of a not-so-moist, not-so-creamy, heart-shaped cake decorated with sickeningly familiar strawberries and icing.

Presenting SWEET MEMORIES, *an anniversary cake by Gourmet International, for that special moment in your life. Soft, sensuous, incredibly romantic. Because love is a sweet thing . . .*

I sat lifeless in my chair, my cup filled with ashes, my eyes full of despair. There was nothing left to do; it was checkmate and endgame.

They'd even f——g trademarked the f——g brilliant line.

twenty-two

'How did this happen?' Vik asked, and the question buzzed round the dark heads in the room like flies on a muggy summer evening.

Everyone recoiled from the newspaper splayed ad-side up on the gleaming tabletop. Yogi opened his mouth to speak.

Vik held up an impatient hand.

'I hope you're not going to suggest it's a coincidence, Yogi.'

Yogi looked at Tanmay, helpless.

Tanmay, the agency head, spread his manicured hands out in a placating gesture. He had been summoned especially for this meeting from his cosy Bombay office this morning. He'd probably been in his new Honda City when Vik called him, on his way to a five-star brunch with some prospective client, no doubt. An hour later he'd been on the first available flight to Delhi.

'Vik, we appreciate it's too close to be a coincidence,' he agreed in a well-educated, well-modulated voice. 'Though I must assure you that we maintain the highest standards of integrity and confidentiality at our agency . . .'

Rana twisted his thin lips in a sneer.

'Let's cut the crap, Tanmay. It's a leak, and someone at your end is responsible.'

Tanmay blinked, not accustomed to sudden, vicious attacks from the ranks. And although Vik frowned, he let it go.

'Isn't it a little premature to be jumping to conclusions?' Tanmay said, holding on to his careful half-smile. He turned to Vik. 'Like I was saying . . .'

'Who were the people on this project?' Vik asked.

'Just the immediate team,' Tanmay said. 'Yogi?'

'The creatives and servicing, and the studio staff,' Yogi said. 'All these guys have been around for years; I'd trust them with my life.'

'Are you sure? No one new on the team?' Vik asked.

'We always have a new face or two on the creative side for every new campaign we're working on. It helps maintain a freshness of ideas.'

'Freshness of ideas?' Rana snorted. 'You're kidding, right? Some of your ideas are as fresh as a public lavatory.'

Vintage Rana. Didn't merit a reply, even from Yogi.

'Yogi, are these creative people trustworthy?' Vik asked.

'One hundred per cent.'

'Vik you know IF is one of our most valued accounts,' Tanmay added. 'We are your partners; we've been working with you for years. Trust me; we'd never let anything jeopardize this relationship.'

'Then how do you explain the fact that the GI ad is an exact copy of that earlier version you showed us?'

'I'm as foxed as you are, Vik,' Yogi said. 'But if someone at our end had done it, don't you think they'd have disguised the ad, changed it around to prevent suspicion?'

'Oh, so is that what you usually do?' Rana sneered. Yogi was out of his chair in a trice, his neck red above his starched white collar.

'Are you suggesting that—how dare you—I've been here for ten years, never in all this time—' he was gasping and stumbling over his words.

'Calm down, Yogi,' Vik said. 'No one is suggesting it was you.' He waited for Yogi to take his seat.

'This is a serious breach, guys,' he said, after a moment's pause.

'Tanmay, I'd hate to have to review doing business with you, but we cannot work together unless we can trust you completely.'

There was a momentary hush as he waited for the full import of his words to sink in. Tanmay bit his lip and picked up his coffee, taking a slow sip and stalling for time.

'I know some people at Adworks,' Rana whispered loudly in Vik's ear. 'They're dying for a chance to work with IF. And they're a really good agency.'

Tanmay looked at Rana as he might a fly in his coffee. He put his cup down with a snap and leaned across the table towards Vik.

'I'll look into the matter personally, Vik,' he said with a newfound edge to his voice. 'We'll do background checks on all the team members, and . . .' He broke off abruptly, looked at his watch and frowned at Yogi. 'Yogi, where's that new copywriter from?'

I stared at the slim Cartier on Tanmay's wrist with distaste. 3 p.m. He was probably planning to catch the five o'clock flight back to Bombay. And here in Delhi it was pin-the-tail-on-the-donkey time. Find a scapegoat; hold on to lucrative business; make it back home in time for drinks before dinner.

Piece of cake, in the big bad corporate world.

Yogi had a confused furrow between his brows. 'Copywriter?' he said. 'You mean Chandan? He's from that agency, Impressions. Why?'

'Didn't that girl Lara also work there?'

'Lara?' I asked.

'The GI brand manager,' Yogi said.

'What if Chandan showed the ads to Lara?' Tanmay said.

Yogi shook his head. 'No. That's absurd. Chandan is the one who told media to yank advertising from her show after she joined GI.'

'What show?' I asked.

'A radio show, 107.4 FM I think. She still hosts it, weekday mornings.'

'You don't mean the Lara and Ali Show?'

'Yes, that's the one.'

Lara and Ali?

'I think we should sit down and have a chat with Chandan,' Tanmay said.

'There's no need. Chandan wouldn't do it,' Yogi insisted.

'Why, is he related to you?' Rana asked sweetly.

Yogi scowled. 'Chandan is a sound guy. I recruited him myself. He's got a clean reputation.'

'Well, you never really know, with these new recruits.'

'I know my people. I work with them day in and day out. I'm willing to bet anything that he had nothing to do with it.'

How come Ali never told me Lara worked at GI?

'Well, someone somewhere leaked our ad, and we have to get to the bottom of it,' Vik said, sounding impatient.

'Vik, don't take this the wrong way, but have you considered the possibility that it slipped out at *your* end?' Yogi asked.

Oh dear.

'Oh, no, I'm sure it wasn't . . .' Tanmay began.

'Our end? That's impossible. No one except for the three of us saw that ad,' Vik said.

And Ali of course. 'Celebrate your love' he'd mocked.

Tanmay was nodding. 'Don't worry Vik; we'll do a thorough investigation. Yogi, we really shouldn't have let this slip-up happen.'

Maybe it was *Chandan.*

'But there's no evidence; it could have happened in a million different ways!'

What if it was Ali?

'We have to set an example. We must ensure something like this doesn't happen again.'

'Not by ruining someone's career!'

It *would* ruin Chandan's career. He'd lose his job, his reputation, his dreams. He stood to lose a lot.

I stood to lose a lot.

'Yogi, sometimes you have to take hard decisions. And don't forget we have to protect our *clients'* interests, not our own.'

This was said with a patronizing smile and some reproof and, despite the soft tone of Tanmay's voice, it was clear that Yogi was skating on thin ice.

I watched his face; he was trembling with barely contained fury. There was a glint of war in his eyes; his large hands were balled into tight fists.

'Tanmay, we can't . . .' he began and despite all our ongoing quarrels, I had to admire his spunk. He was standing up to everyone, even his boss, sticking up for poor Chandan.

Would anyone stick up for me?

'Let's discuss this back at the agency,' Tanmay was saying, getting up. 'Vik, we'll take your leave now. I'll have a word with this Chandan fellow and get back to you as soon as we've taken some action. Shouldn't take long . . .'

'That won't be necessary.'

'What?' Vik said, looking puzzled. Everyone turned to look at me. I trembled, but stood my ground.

'Ali is my neighbour. From the Lara and Ali Show. He . . . er . . . he drops by sometimes.'

Rana's eyes began to acquire a scandalized gleam; Yogi stared.

'It's possible that he may have seen the layout at my place,' I said.

And memorized it while he was kissing me in the rain on my balcony. And rushed over to tell his girlfriend.

Rana gasped loudly; Tanmay coughed and looked down at his hands. Vik was looking at me steadily, an exceedingly grave expression on his face. Yogi kept staring.

'Vik, I'm sorry. I should have been more careful.'

Vik nodded, expressionless; then turned to Tanmay. 'Thanks for coming in, Tanmay. And you too, Yogi. It looks like we have a little homework of our own to do, so . . .'

He waited for them to leave. Rana sat rooted to his seat, smiling a little. I could almost see the wings that sprouted on his back and the halo that hovered above his head.

'Rana, could you excuse us, please?' Vik said. 'I'd like to talk to Minal. Alone.'

twenty-three

Nothing, I discovered, is quieter than the sound of failure. The carpet bristled indignantly, the walls sighed, the air-con vents threw out accusing fingers of icy cold air and the rest of the office observed a moment of silence as I stepped off the elevator the following morning. A grim motorcade of stillness escorted me down the sixty-step walk to my desk, muffling and knocking dead every single sound in the vicinity. The water cooler chatter, the congregated groups of fours and fives, even the usually rambunctious assembly in Sam's room, all fell into a watchful silence as I walked past. I reached my desk with my back on fire and logged quickly on to the office network.

There was just one e-mail message.

'Please see me in my office at 11 a.m. Vik.'

I blinked and looked out the window.

It was a beautiful day; bright and sunny with clear blue skies and little puffy clouds and birds that chirped and squirrels that darted. It was the kind of day that said 'Come, hit me', like the calm before the storm. Maybe if I stopped right here, if I just ignored that one message and pretended everything was all right, everything *would* be all right. Like that coyote that kept walking off cliffs and strolling along in the air and never falling down until the *moment* he looked down. Maybe he'd really make it across that canyon some day, if only he'd remember to not look down. If only life were a cartoon . . .

I sighed and looked up. The guy who'd been gaping at me from across the hall looked hurriedly away. Great, so now I was a freak circus show.

I noticed Aman heading towards the water cooler and set off in determined pursuit.

'Hi, Aman!'

'Oh, hi, Minal.' He looked like I'd stepped on his toes.

'How's it going, what's up?'

'The usual.'

His eyes darted left and right as he scanned the area for a quick escape route.

'Dull day, huh?'

This was pathetic. I was chatting *Aman* up at the water cooler? I was a female Jon Arbuckle sans orange cat.

'So . . . er. . .' he scratched the back of his neck. 'So when are you moving, Minal?'

'Moving?'

'To the branch? Sam told me you'd be moving to the branch office, in sales promotion?'

A vivid image of endless days spent behind desultory food stalls in tired little stores swam before my eyes. 'Here, Ma'am, try this,' I was saying, shoving cold samples of food down the throats of unsuspecting customers. They were recoiling and the rest of the folks in the store were tiptoeing around behind the aisles, averting their eyes from my food-stained apron, avoiding me at all costs.

No, it couldn't be. Maybe Sam had it wrong?

Aman had been watching my face.

'It's a good move,' he said kindly. 'I believe sales promotion is a major focus area this quarter. Now you *will* work hard to push my breakfast bars, won't you, for old times' sake?'

I summoned up a kind smile of my own.

'Oh sure. And how's it going with your telecom portfolio?'

Ah, the simple moments of relief in this horror movie of a life.

I called Rana as soon as I reached my desk.

'Am I being transferred?' I asked the minute he picked up the phone.

'Minal! How are you?'

He sounded joyous and my blood froze.

'Aman just told me I might be getting transferred,' I said. 'You wouldn't happen to know anything about it, would you?'

Was that a *chuckle?*

'Well, I might as well tell you, since you'll be hearing from Vik anyway. Vik *is* looking at a little reshuffling, now that the anniversary cake plans have fallen through.'

'Reshuffling?'

'He's moving you out.'

Damn. 'What about you?'

'Oh, I'll be here. Someone has to lead the development of the low-cost cake after all.'

'When did Vik approve a low-cost cake?'

'Didn't you hear? The US Cakes' R&D centre has developed a breakthrough technology that cuts cost *and* improves quality! They'll be rolling it out to India in the next couple of months. It's going to be very exciting; too bad you won't be here.'

'Any idea where Vik might be moving me to?'

'They are short on hands down at the branch, I believe.'

So it was true.

'Don't take it too much to heart though. No one thinks you did it on purpose.'

'Bye, Rana.'

I started to put the phone down.

'Wait! So tell me about this neighbour of yours. Is he your boyfriend? Really Minal, a *radio jockey*?'

'Goodb——'

'Anyway, let's look on the positive side. At least he saved us the whole bother of launching a doomed product and then having to withdraw it! Better GI than us!'

I twisted the phone cord round and round between my fingers, pretending it was Rana's neck.

'Come to think of it, your friend has done IF a really good turn! You must remember to thank him and . . .'

I banged the receiver down, hard.

Remember to thank him? How could I forget? I'd love to thank him. I was *dying* to thank him. Except that it had been two whole days since the ad and he was still AWOL.

He'd planned it all along of course; him and that red-nailed moll of his. (What kind of person hangs out conducting music semi-naked at 11 p.m. anyway?) He'd worked that back and those eyes and that smile to the hilt, and they'd been as misleading as an R.K. Films trailer for a Ramsay Bros production. I should have seen through him. They were probably out somewhere right now, living it up, laughing themselves silly. Oh yes, I'd thank him; I'd thank him good and proper . . .

The violent ringing of the phone startled me.

'Hello?'

'Minal, it's Radha. I'm calling to remind you of your meeting with Vik.'

'Right, I'm on my way.'

Best get the head chopping over with; there was no point delaying the inevitable. The pain would throb and linger for a long, long time of course, but why prolong the sting of the needle? I pushed back my chair, threw back an anaesthetizing paper cup of tepid coffee and strode bravely out to slaughter.

Vik was on the phone when I walked in. He waved me to a chair.

'No, sir, we still don't know. Yes, sir,' he said into the mouthpiece.

Great. It looked like the big boss was hyperventilating already.

'Yes, we called off the initial production run in time,' he continued. 'I just got off the line with the factory manager.'

Peace, forbearance, fortitude. Ram, Ram.

I studied the giant map of India and tried to locate all the towns whose names began with Ram. Rampur, Ramgarh, Rameswaram. I'd be visiting them all soon, with little trays of sub-standard Rana cakes in hand.

'Yes, we'll inform the Mumbai office, we'll send a note out today, explaining the matter.' He glanced briefly at me. 'She's here now. Yes, I'll speak to her. Yes sir, I understand.'

He put the phone down and I squared my shoulders to await the pronouncement.

A couple of hours later, I sat alone in the cafeteria, contemplating my bleak future over chalk and cheese sandwiches.

'Two years at the branch,' he'd said, 'they really need good people out there right now.'

'Yes, Vik.'

'There's a lot of work that needs to be done there.'

'I understand, Vik.'

'And it will do you good to spend some time away from brand management; take on more man-management responsibility.'

'Right, Vik.'

'I think Rana and I can handle the cakes business for the time being . . .'

So it was a two-year sentence. Two years of my life, during which everyone else would launch big impressive brands, get double promotions and triple increments, go for important international seminars and conferences, and spend happy days dodging headhunters.

I was tough, I could handle it.

Or I could go to Meerut and bottle pickles.

There was a voice message on the phone when I got back to my desk. I pushed the replay button.

'Hi Minal, Sunil here. I just got back from Chennai, and guess what . . . Mom's here! I'm going to try and take the evening off; would you like to come round for dinner?'

twenty-four

Midway through the evening it occurred to me that I probably ranked in the ninety-ninth percentile of luckiest people in this world, and that Aruna Aunty and Sunil were beings from another, kinder planet.

The casual elegance of Sunil's home was more comforting than a pedicure. (And far more chic!) It was a rich home; I sat in the drawing room surrounded by flower-filled vases, oriental lamps, silver picture frames, glossy coffee-table books. It was also a comfortable home, and the fragrance, the colourful glow, the fine Darjeeling tea, the silken feel of the Kashmiri carpet beneath my toes all reminded me so much of the Pandeys' home in Meerut, that I had to clamp down a violent urge to scour the bathroom for KitKat.

'I'm sorry Sunil got delayed at the hospital, beta,' Aruna aunty said as she poured more Darjeeling tea into my china cup.

'That's okay, Aunty; this way I get to catch up with you.'

'Yes. It's been such a long time,' she smiled.

'And these pakoras are great!'

'Have some more,' she said as Bahadur came by with yet another plate.

I snuggled into the high-backed rocker and dug into the pakoras and found myself falling in love with her once again; with the curve of her smile, the lift of her eyebrows, the sweep of her jet-black hair, the easy way in which she filled the space between us with warm reminiscences and cheerful banter.

'You know I've always loved your name; I'd planned to call my daughter Minal if I ever had one,' she said, and I lapped it up, like a wet kitten in a warm lap.

The evening wore on and the moon came up and the stars began to peek curiously in through the windows, and we talked on and on about work and women and shoes and scarves and music and memories and life and living and the courageous children at her school and the neighbour in Dehradun who'd lost a child and a leg in an accident, and my own frivolous cares and concerns vanished in an embarrassed silence in the face of the pain and courage of those nameless people.

And an hour later (or it could have been two), when Sunil walked in, tired and weary, I looked up at him from my perch on his chair and fell instantly in love with his rain-soaked white coat and the stethoscope that hung round his wilted collar and the little circles round his eyes where his glasses had rested all day.

Suddenly, it all came together and I was sure. This was the scene I could replay over and over again, for the rest of my life, and feel the same love and joy spring up inside me. I watched as he walked over to his mom and sank wearily down on the carpet next to her.

'Sorry I'm late,' he said. 'It was a hard case; the family was inconsolable.'

I leaned over and took his hand, and Aruna Aunty got up quietly to supervise dinner.

A little while later, after Bahadur cleared the plates, Aruna Aunty peeled a shining apple from the silver fruit bowl as Sunil smiled across at me.

'How's it going at work?' he asked.

'Not bad,' I replied, and suddenly it sounded about right.

'What part of the business do you work in?' Aruna Aunty asked as she passed me a slice of the apple.

'I used to be in Marketing, but now I'm moving to Sales Promotion.'

'Really? When did this happen?' Sunil said.

'I just found out today. It's a little sudden, but it's probably for the best. It will give me a chance to understand the business at the grassroots.'

Albeit amidst the weeds of mediocrity.

'You don't sound very enthusiastic.'

'No, really, it's hard work, but in marketing it helps to back and forth between brand management and sales.'

If I said it enough times, I might even begin to believe it.

'I hope this has nothing to do with that Rana fellow?'

'No, it doesn't. Though of course he's overjoyed now that I'm out of his way.'

Annoyingly, my voice chose that moment to wobble and crack.

'Minal?' Aruna Aunty asked, concerned.

'I'm sorry, I'm being silly, but it's just that it all happened a little quickly.'

'You're obviously quite upset. Look, you don't need to hang around at IF, you know,' Sunil said. 'Why don't you look around, contact a few headhunters?'

I shook my head. 'I'll stick it out for a while.'

'Are you sure?'

'Yes, I want to wait a couple of months before I decide.'

'Well, whatever you want. So long as you're happy.'

I smiled, grateful.

'You can even decide to give it up altogether. I earn enough for the both of us anyway.'

'I'm sorry?'

'I mean, um . . . er . . . that is . . .' he stopped uncertainly, his cheeks a deep red.

'Sunil! Surely you can do a better job of proposing than that?' Aruna Aunty said, laughing. 'Now I'll go out to the kitchen and get the dessert, and you try it one more time.'

I watched, stunned, as she got up and left the room.

Sunil cleared his throat in the painful silence.

'Umm . . . sorry about that. The thing is . . .'

I stared down at my fork and spoon.

'I didn't mean for it to come out quite like this, but . . ..'

He walked over to where I sat and took my hand in his.

'Minal, will you marry me?'

One month and ten days later . . .

twenty-five

I braced myself as the sales promoter held out a small bundle of bills attached to an 'expense voucher'.

The creativity in these little yellow slips had the power to take my breath away. Today's masterpiece would have given any old maestro a run for his money.

Petty expense voucher No. 14:
(25 Aug, 2002—Paschim Vihar food stall)

Petrol	Rs 10/-	
Parking	Rs 10/-	(two times)
Lunch	Rs 20/-	
Coke	Rs 36/-	(Rs 6.00×6)
Band-Aid	Rs 15/-	(cut finger while opening box of samples)
Paper napkins	Rs 21/-	(missing in demo kit; verified by supervisor)
Total	Rs 112/-	

'Band-Aid?'

He held up a mummified finger to show me.

'Okay, then just the single,' I said, replacing the Rs 15/- with a Re 1/-.

'And six Cokes!'

'It was a very hot day, Ma'am,'

'No more than two,' I said firmly. 'Besides it's really bad for your health.'

'Well, could you convert it into five bottles of Bisleri then?' he grinned. 'They cost the same; actually more.'

'Bring your own water.'

I totalled up the new set of figures, signed off and, before I could change my mind, he'd whisked it from beneath my fingers.

'Thank you, ma'am,' he said with a twinkle that left me feeling duped.

I should have questioned the paper napkins.

I watched him gather his helmet and bob over to the door.

'Bye, ma'am, have a good weekend!' he called jauntily.

'You look happy.'

He pulled two violent green tickets from his shirt pocket.

'*Ek Chhoti Si Love Story*,' he winked. 'Evening show.'

I shuddered and waved him goodbye.

Lucky bastard, I thought.

At least he had somewhere to go and someone to go with.

I pulled the next voucher from my in-tray.

This one was a mile long and added up to a staggering one hundred and forty-four rupees. What did these guys take me for?! I beeped the promoter on his pager and left a not-so-pleasant message for him to drop by the office and see me on his way back from wherever he was out promoting our wares.

I eyed the tall pile in my in-tray with despair. It was charmed, it was invincible. It was like Ravan's head; no matter how hard I attacked it or how much paper I slashed, it always grew back.

It was useless; I was no Ram. I pushed the pile away, got up and walked wearily round the bare floor and empty work stations outside my cubbyhole of an office.

Today the office was even quieter than usual; the entire sales team (which accounted for ninety per cent of the branch personnel) was out in the market scrambling to make the month's target. I envied them too; with their sense of useless urgency and purpose as they hustled and wheedled their top dealers, only to repeat the exact same process the following month and the next and the next . . . Pathetically futile, but even that would be better than the pile of pending vouchers and estimates and vending machine coffee that were my constant companions in exile.

Oh, the branch coffee. They brew a relentlessly evil potion at the branch office; the kind that gets you right out of your chair and running in the streets in agony. I am not a coffee snob (I hope) but the underbrewed, watery sludge that splatters out of the vending machine makes me want to weep. The concentrated disinfectant smell burns my nose; the shrieking sweetness congeals my tongue. And what lifts this styrofoam devilry to dizzying heights of malevolence is the six sigma-like consistency with which it is implemented.

'Don't worry, you'll get used to it soon,' the maintenance guys said soothingly the very first day when I had called them up distraught; and this chilling prophecy, more than anything else the branch had thrown my way, had frozen the blood in my veins.

If only this were the worst of my problems. The past month at the Northern Region Sales Office had seemed like a free fall without a bungee; I'd plummeted to the very depths of mindlessness. I now knew, first-hand, what poor old Gandalf had gone through in the mines of Moria, and could only hope that I too would eventually emerge, seven hundred days from today, sanity intact, intellect miraculously preserved.

Sales Promotion Manager, that's what they call me at the branch. In actual fact I am chief custodian of the great cabinet that contains file upon file of exhaustive lists of everything under the sun. I have lists of distributors and redistributors, of bakers, chemists and grocers, of restaurants and cooks, of hospitals, doctors, nurses, therapists, nutritionists (and even patients), of printers and copiers, of suppliers, mixers and fixers, of amusements and amusement parks, of events and event managers, of weddings and wedding planners, of zoos and zookeepers. They may just as well have called me 'Keeper of the Lists'; I even have a list of Lists.

The constant consultation and updating of these lists forms the major part of my job. Need to order aprons for a food demonstration? No problem; just look up the list of apron suppliers. Need to get rid of excess stock? Just consult the list of direct marketing agencies. Need dental surgery? Somehow, somewhere, I'm sure I have a list of dentists.

The other part of my job, of course, involves the keeping of accounts (especially the really small ones). I am chief bean counter at the branch; I make the entire accounts division quake with insecurity. *Are we in the food or the first aid business?* I ruthlessly ask, as I strike out a fifteen-rupee claim for Band-Aid.

Why are we being charged five rupees for photocopying? I say bravely as I dispute the Rs 12,454 bill for printed billboards.

It is through these and other such careful economies that I justify the ten lakh rupees (before taxes) salary that I am paid per annum. A handsome price for a deep slash in self-esteem and gradually dwindling IQ?

I trudged back to my office and sat down once again. The sharp sunlight from the window opposite pricked my eyelids and magnified the dust on my desk. I walked over to draw the blinds. It was a nice break in the day, the five-minute friendly tug of war that I performed daily with the blinds. I had been noticing how each day it happened at a slightly later hour as we cruised our way towards the autumn equinox. Today it was at exactly 4 p.m. It occurred to me that I ought to start a list of the different times each day at which the blinds needed to be pulled; it would probably be the only list of real value I'd leave behind for my out-of-luck eventual successor.

I pushed back my chair, sank down and gave myself up to a study of the wall to my left. I looked so hard that little rainbow stars started to dance gently across its smooth surface. Startled, I glanced down and then realized it was the sun prisming off the huge diamond on my hand, catching its brilliant edges through a crack between two missing blinds. I waved my hand around in the thin beam of light and watched the rainbow stars prance and weave on the big blank wall, lengthening, shortening, converging and then flying apart in a pretty firework display, not unlike the one at my engagement party.

My engagement ring. For a while I'd been too scared to wear it, it was so big. I jiggled the heavy stone to check the setting again, still worried about it falling off. I wondered if I'd ever learn to wear it with the graceful nonchalance with which Aruna Aunty wore hers, as though it belonged there, as though it were a proud extension of one's finger.

Minal Sharma, Minal Pandey, Minal Sharma Pandey, I doodled on the back of the expense voucher. Maybe I'd stick with my own name? Sunil would understand it was nothing personal, just that my P's always ended up looking like giant question marks. I wished he were here this weekend, not out to yet another doctors' conference. It would have been nice to have him around for a change, to just take in a movie, or even to just chill in front of the TV.

Come to think of it, where *was* his TV? I couldn't recall seeing one in all the times I'd been to his house. I ran through the layout of his home in my mind—hallway, drawing, dining, lounge, kitchen, main bedroom (which I'd only seen from the outside), guest room, study, terrace.

No TV.

Maybe he kept his in the bathroom?

But what if he didn't have a TV?

We'll just move yours into his place after you're married, silly, the right brain chided.

Married. I must confess I have had misgivings about it. Not *deep* misgivings, just a few, scattered, shallow ones. And not about Sunil, of course, but about the *married* part. Take the engagement ceremony for instance. It had knocked me right out of my socks (or rather sari and blouse), what with the elaborate arrangements and the staggering guest list. Not what I'd expected or wanted, but with Mom so deliriously happy and Aruna Aunty (oops, *Mummy*) so visibly excited, it had been impossible to demur. Still, who'd have imagined that my own engagement would take on the fervent frenzy of a Hindi film extravaganza? And now I'd probably have to sing and dance at the reception.

I sighed and looked up at the wall clock—4.15 p.m. They'd be serving fresh coffee at everyone's desk back at the head office. I wondered who I could call. Maybe Radha would have something interesting to report . . . I leaned across to the phone and picked the dust off the grooves between the number buttons. Or maybe I shouldn't disturb her. Maybe it was time I started letting go?

The phone began to ring. I wiped my finger on the expense voucher in front of me and picked up the receiver eagerly.

'Hello, this is Minal.'

'Madam? Hello, madam. How are you? This is Gupta speaking from UP.'

'Hello, Guptaji. How are you?'

I tried to figure out which one of the Guptajis he was. (Of the four distributors in western UP, three were Gupta.)

'Good, good ji. Madam, I have a small request. Those hanging posters you sent us for the new juice range? Very poor quality. Most of them got torn in transit. Also, we did not get enough shelf-liners and that new item, how do you say, jhoomers?'

'Wobblers.'

'Right, right, bobblers. Please send two hundred more of them. In fact, send two hundred more of everything.'

I made a note. Fifty extra juice danglers and wobblers for w. UP. *But which city?*

'And how are sales?' I asked.

'Not too good, madam. Juice is okay, but breakfast cereals ...' he clicked his tongue, 'very slow movement. We need some new gift item; those plastic bowls did not click in the market.'

Are we in the business of selling food or plastic bowls? I asked myself conscientiously, but this time the answer was more blurry.

'What was wrong with the bowls?'

'Poor quality, madam. I was telling you from the beginning only, that Bansal Enterprises is a crook. Low quotes, lower quality. Now these bowls, all of them off-balance, and the edges so rough my Mrs could slice an apple with them.'

Ah, so he was the Hapur Guptaji. I pulled out my list of plastic gift suppliers and crossed out M/s Bansal Enterprises.

'Why don't you send back the defective bowls and we'll try to replace them.'

'Okay, madam. Madam, maybe next time you should place the order on my brother-in-law. M/s Gupta Traders, madam. He deals in these items for many companies; he is hundred per cent reliable.'

'Ask him to send us a fax getting in touch.'

'Yes, yes, definitely, madam; it will be on your desk tomorrow morning. And how is your health, madam?'

'Fine, thank you. And how is business looking? What's happening in your area?'

A few minutes later, the familiar smell of samosas hit my nostrils. I pushed aside my work and stretched, relieved. (At the branch, the 4.30 p.m. time slot was allotted to anyone who cared, for any reason whatsoever, to clog his colleagues' arteries at his expense. I didn't mind, treating this more in the nature of yet another welcome marker of time.) I got up happily and moved, zombie-like, in the direction of the little pantry, and was shortly joined by the handful of other 'non-sales' denizens of the office from the floor below.

Today the snacks were courtesy the accounts clerk, Mehtaji; a generous man who'd driven his scooter three bumpy miles to the new Agrawal Sweets store, and brought back two greasy paper bags on account of his wife being in the 'family way'. I congratulated him and munched my way through a whole quarter pounder of a samosa. This made me queasy, so I washed it down with a couple of gulab jamuns. Too late, I noticed that the newlywed secretary had sidled up again (third time this week), one eye firmly fixed on my diamond ring.

'So, Minal, did you remember to bring your engagement photos?' she asked coyly.

'Oh, the album is now at Sunil's folks'. Maybe next week,' I lied.

'Very bad!' she accused. 'When I had brought my wedding pictures my very first day back at work!'

This was true. Monday last week had been given over to six thick golden albums. I'd also been amongst the privileged few to whom she'd circulated an unfiled, uncensored pack of honeymoon snaps. There had even been one featuring her husband as Adam, wearing nothing but an upside down James Hadley Chase paperback as a dubious modern update to the good old fig leaf.

Mehtaji crunched through a samosa. 'When is the wedding, Minal?' he asked between mouthfuls.

'Oh, not till November. We still have to set a date.'

'You'd better do it fast, once the navratras are over, all the wedding halls are chock-a-block full.'

'Yes, mine had to be booked a full six months in advance,' the secretary nodded. 'So, this will be your first Karva Chauth?'

'Karva Chauth?'

'The fast, you know. I guess your mother-in-law will expect you to keep it since it's so close to the wedding.'

'What does your fiancé do?' asked Mehtaji.

'He's a surgeon. Specializes in cancer.'

'Very good, very good. My wife's uncle cures cancer too. Though he's not really a doctor.'

I waited for more.

'He's a faith healer, he works on auras. Our neighbour's mother-in-law was in last stages; all the doctors had given up hope, then they took her to my wife's uncle. Three hundred rupees for three sessions, and she's already showing signs of recovery.'

'Well, I'm glad to hear that.'

'So do you and your fiancé have any plans for the weekend? I have extra tickets for that new Salman Khan movie, tomorrow at six. Would you like to go?'

'Er, thanks, but Sunil's busy this weekend.'

'I can go!' the secretary beamed, plucking the tickets from his hand.

I picked up my glass of water and escaped to my desk.

Five p.m., and the daytime guard handed off to the evening guard. The Admin. staff began to file out, calling enthusiastic goodbyes. I wished I could join them, but with nowhere to go and a meeting with Bhaskar (Regional Sales Manager, Uttaranchal) at 6 p.m., there really wasn't much of a choice. I attacked my estimates with a vengeance and punched and stapled and copied and filed and had my in-tray down to half by the time Bhaskar strode in.

He tossed a bundle of papers down on my desk.

'We're off by thirty per cent of our target,' he declared dramatically. 'You'd better start planning some pataka event to get that stock moving before it goes bad!'

'I could transfer the extra stocks to Delhi market,' I offered sweetly. 'In any case the consumers in your hill markets must be halved now that the tourist season is over.'

That put him in his place.

'Yaar, Minal, don't kill me. That won't help me get my incentive, will it? Let's come up with some local promotion, yaar.'

I relented.

'How about a local consumer sampling drive?' I suggested, and soon we were consulting my lists of event organizers and high-potential hill markets and debating the rival merits of a street parade with elephants and bears, or a local daily lottery of IF products.

'And about that economy cake—when is it coming?' he asked in the midst of it all.

'It's still under development as far as I know,' I said coldly.

'Yaar, get me some samples; talk to that new manager, Rana. Isn't he a friend of yours? I want to give some samples to the hill school hostels; they are always on the lookout for cheap stuff.'

I studied his face suspiciously, but could read nothing between the lines.

'I'll give Rana a call,' I said finally, 'but can we wrap up our "Mussoorie Masti" plans first?

It was dark by the time we worked our way through all the details. I waited for him to leave, and then reluctantly dialled Rana's extension.

'Yes?' A curt voice answered.

'Rana? It's Minal.'

'Minal! How are you; still at IF or have you found a job with GI?'

'I'm calling from the branch office.'

'Oh, so you're still there. So how are things at the branch? It must be nice to get out in the market, breathe some hot, humid air. Not like us at the head office, stuck behind our chairs in air-conditioning!'

'Wanna trade?'

'Ah, unfortunately my talents are best employed here.'

'Anyway, how are things going with your cheap cake?'

'*Original* cake,' he corrected. 'Things are great; we should be sending the branch offices an update soon.'

'So it looks like you will be launching it.'

'Oh, you bet. Vik's totally in love with it.'

'Good for you. I guess this will mean a big bonus?'

'Oh, I don't really care about the money. What's a few lakhs one way or another? Of course an early promotion wouldn't be entirely out of line. So what do *you* want?'

Your job.

'I need samples,' I said.

'Oh, I'll be happy to send them. Just as long as you don't pass them along to your friend Ali, of course.'

Ha, ha, ha.

Maybe Sunil was right, maybe it was time to move on.

twenty-six

'Did you hear the one about the nurse and the prostrate patient . . .?' began Dr Srivastava.

'You mean prostate patient,' Sunil corrected.

'No, I mean *prostrate* patient,' Dr S insisted with a grin and a wink, and I tuned out.

God knows I love all doctors, but as far as conversation went this lot was about as sparkling as the pineapple juice in my glass. I took a sip of the awful concoction and wondered how soon we'd be able to escape.

My attention wandered off down the little paths of the farmhouse where we'd all congregated for yet another evening of zombifying boredom. At least this time the place was good. In fact it was more than good, it was magnificent. It was the kind of place that they could have charged admission to and printed brochures and organized tourist buses and shot movies and coronated kings in.

All around us were acres and acres of rolling grass; row upon perfect row of emerald blades that looked like they brushed and flossed every night and lived on an exclusive diet of low-fat fertilizer and Hi-C orange juice. And on a hillock in the distance, a palace of a farmhouse, with towering windows and commanding views, and strong young trees that stood guard around it like proud commandos. Vines and shrubs decorated the lower walls and bordered the brick-paved paths along which liveried waiters scurried, bearing silver platters heavy with hors d'ouevres.

The elements too appeared to have been prearranged for the evening; the crickets sang out joyously in the distance as though their dinners depended on it and the stars in the sky shimmered and glowed on full generator backup.

Even the newly surfaced road that connected this unlikely oasis to the busy highway had seemed to lie down deferentially and eagerly in our path, like Sir G's cloak, shielding the premium car tyres from the evil dirt track beneath.

It was hard to believe that we were a bare half-kilometre from the dust and dirt of NH8.

The doctors were still at it.

'What happened about that case with the newlywed?' Sunil was asking the group.

'She turned out malignant; she'll need a mastectomy,' Dr Batra was saying.

'That's terrible. It must be hard on them,' I said.

Dr Batra heaved an elaborate sigh. 'I'll say. The husband's feeling a bit cheated, and the wife's wondering if the hectic honeymoon had anything to do with it.'

Everyone guffawed; I took another sip of juice.

'It's pathetic; really, all the girl can think about is her looks,' Dr B complained. 'She doesn't want her breasts removed, she doesn't want chemo; I told her she'd die and she's seriously considering it!'

'She's quite a looker, isn't she,' Dr Srivastava reasoned.

'It's always harder with the women,' Dr Khattar said with a shake of his head. 'I have this new patient; serious paan masala junkie. She has an ulcer the size of a lemon in her mouth that needs removing and all she was worried about was plastic surgery. Plastic surgery! As though it would matter how she looked in her funeral pictures.'

He snapped his fingers and beckoned a waiter who'd been

standing to attention a few feet away. He glided up promptly and stood to attention at my elbow.

'Have you tried the fried prawns?' Dr K asked, 'They're delicious!'

'No thanks.' I shook my head as the waiter held out a massive tray of assorted fritters.

Did we marketing types sound this grisly when we talked shop, I wondered.

'That new ketchup brand! Such a disaster, totally runny and way too high on sugar!' or 'Did you see that cheesy new Sachin shampoo commercial, his hair looks like spaghetti!'

Nope, fell far short of the 'ruin your appetite' mark, thank goodness.

I shuddered as Dr Khattar crunched the prawns between his great molars and I tried not to think of the poor woman with the lemon stuck like a poisoned dart somewhere in the roof of her mouth.

'So how's it going at work?' Dr Kumar asked, turning to me.

'Oh, the usual. On the positive side I cleared fifty expense vouchers today.'

'Minal's thinking of giving it up,' Sunil added.

'I'm sorry?'

'I meant you're looking at a change,' he clarified.

'I haven't really decided . . .'

'I know, but you're thinking about it, aren't you? This job at the branch really isn't sustainable, with your hours and mine clashing the way they do.'

'Yes, but . . .'

'And you're always out in the scorching heat and travelling to such awful places! It'll be good for you to move to something more appropriate.'

'Well, it's not bad experience getting to know what's happening in the marketplace.'

'But it's so exhausting! You've been looking so tired lately.'

I knew I shouldn't have worn grey.

'Don't worry, all she needs is some vitamins,' Dr K said gallantly.

Sunil shook his head.

'What she needs is some rest,' Sunil said. 'And a long break before the wedding.'

And another facial? Jolen bleach? Plastic surgery?

'Yes, Renu quit after we got married,' said Dr Kumar. 'She's quite happy now with her teaching job; she has enough time for the home and she's not sitting idle either.'

I refrained from airing my views on Renu Kumar's intellect. 'Where is Renu? I haven't seen her today,' I said instead.

'She's around there somewhere.' He waved his arm in the direction of the several groups of women sprinkled liberally across the lawns. Uncanny, the way they invariably managed to separate themselves from the men at these dos, like wheat from chaff. I scanned the colourful clusters and felt a strong magnetic pull of sisterhood radiate from the group of doctors' wives behind me.

'There they all are,' said Dr Kumar. 'Oy, Renu! Minal's been looking for you.'

Renu Kumar smiled and beckoned, and I was trapped. I made my way over to join the chummy group in their saris and diamonds and braced myself for an invigorating session involving servants, drivers, nannies and mothers-in-law.

'Minal, how are you, didn't see you at the Dubey's party last weekend?' asked Renu.

'Yes, I had some work at the office that I couldn't avoid.'

'Oh, what a bore. You'll have to really sort that work thing out. Mrs Dubey was asking about you.'

'Hi Minal,' said Dr Srivastava's wife. I tried not to stare at her fuchsia lips. 'We're all getting together at my place next Saturday to plan a return party for Mrs Dubey; think you can make it?'

'Actually, Sunil's mom will probably be in town next Saturday . . .'

'Oh, yes, the wedding. How are the preparations coming along?'

'Where are you planning to go for your honeymoon? Phuket? Mauritius? Hawaii?' asked Doctor Batra's wife.

'These doctors are all kanjooses,' said Dr Khattar's wife. 'I'll bet he's trying to sell Shimla to her; that's what mine gypped me with. Minal, don't you settle for anything less than Tahiti!'

'We have this cottage in Goa, if you're interested; it's right by the beach,' Renu offered.

'Thanks. Sunil was mentioning Switzerland, actually. There's a ski-town up in the Alps; one of his patients owns a cabin there.'

'Perfect! How long will you go for?'

'Dunno, we still have to work out leave and all.'

'Doctors and leave!' Renu said pityingly. 'Just keep your fingers crossed.'

Everyone nodded and made sympathetic clucking sounds.

'Won't Switzerland be freezing in November?' Dr Srivastava's wife asked doubtfully.

'So what? They're going on a honeymoon; they'll find ways to keep warm!' Dr Batra's wife winked. Everyone tittered and I tried to look dutifully sheepish.

Keep warm, ha. With room heaters and electric blankets most likely. I hoped I wouldn't have to pack whips and chains and leather stuff along for the honeymoon, just to get things started.

I don't mean to crib, but this bashfulness thing with Sunil was really beginning to worry me. Engaged for over a month now, and there was less going on between us than between two nuns in a convent. And the last time I'd tried to kiss him, he'd mumbled something about Bahadur. *Bahadur?*

'What's up, ladies?' the man of my misgivings said, looming up suddenly behind me.

'Minal was just telling us about your honeymoon plans,' Dr Srivastava's wife grinned, and Sunil turned a predictable pink.

'They're just teasing,' I said. 'Were you looking for me?'

'Yes, I want to introduce you to Mr Khanna, our host.' He pointed to a little man in big shorts near the bar. 'He's finally free; let's go and say hello.'

We strolled across the lawns and I studied Harish Khanna, owner of marvellous farmhouse and gracious host. With his mousy moustache, stick legs and huge belly he looked more insurance agent than promoter, property developer and overall powerful Delhi personality. And the hennaed hair didn't help much either.

He smiled broadly as Sunil introduced me.

'Young lady, you are one lucky girl,' he said, pumping my hand up and down. 'This man,' he threw one hearty arm round Sunil, hugging him close, 'this man is truly talented. He's one of the best doctors around.'

'It's very kind of you to say so, sir,' Sunil said.

Sir?

'I mean it. The way you brought my uncle back from the brink was amazing. You are destined for great things, my friend.'

'Sir, now you're embarrassing me.'

Harish Khanna removed his hand from Sunil's shoulders and took a step back. 'Chalo bhai, hata diya haath. No hera pheri here, believe me,' he guffawed.

'No sir, I meant . . .'

'*Chhodo*,' he dismissed. 'Tell me, how long do you plan to keep killing yourself at Apollo? Now that you're getting married, it's high time you started thinking about yourself, about branching out on your own.'

Sunil laughed. 'It's not easy, sir. I don't have *that* kind of money.'

'Well, then you're talking to the right man!' Harish Khanna exclaimed, throwing his belly out a few inches farther. 'I have lots of money, ha, ha, ha!'

I laughed dutifully.

'In fact, I'm very serious about starting something up in the medical line. The market is very hot for specialty clinics these days; it'll be a good investment.'

'That it will,' Sunil agreed.

'There is this prime property in Gurgaon that I'm developing; it's a great location for a nursing home or a specialized clinic.'

'Really? Where?'

'Right off the highway; just go another five miles down this road . . . you can't miss it.'

'That's wonderful! Congratulations, sir.'

'Arre congratulations chhodo; if you and a couple of other young doctors like you are willing to join, this is the right time for a specialized cancer diagnosis and treatment centre.'

'That's true; we're flooded with patients these days,' Sunil said.

'So what do you say; I put in the money, you handle the business?'

'I'm not sure . . ..'

'I'm talking about partnership, yaar; profit, not salary.'

'You mean . . .'

'I mean a fifty-fifty share.'

Sunil's eyes sharpened with interest.

'And you could get Dr Dubey to consult initially,' Harish added. 'It helps establish a reputation if you have a big name on board.'

'I am quite close to him.'

Harish smiled broadly. 'That's great! Talk to him, talk to some other doctors who you think are good,' he said. 'I'm sure we'll be able to make it worth their while.'

I stared at Sunil. His eyes seemed to have glazed over.

Nursing home? Profit? Equity? What about . . .

'Young lady, your glass is empty!' Harish exclaimed suddenly. He beckoned a waiter who'd been hovering around in the background and plucked a can of Coke from the assortment of long-stemmed glasses and chilled cans on the tray.

'Ladies first!' he beamed as he handed it to me. Then he grabbed two glasses of champagne and held one out to Sunil.

'Thanks sir, but I don't . . .'

'But you must! This is imported!' He thrust the glass into Sunil's hand.

'To our joint venture,' he said, clinking the two glasses loudly. 'Cheers!'

Sunil looked down at the amber liquid in the tall glass, then up at Harish, and then tossed it back in one swift gulp.

'Cheers,' he said.

I stared, amazed. *Champagne? But wouldn't it impair his judgement?*

'Minal?' Sunil nudged.

'Huh? Oh, er . . . cheers,' I said and took a hesitant sip of my Coke.

twenty-seven

At some point in time there comes a pivotal moment in your life, a turning point when you realize that the worst thing that could possibly happen to you has already happened. There is a certain comfort, a perverse thrill almost, in recognizing that moment and knowing that Time hereafter can only take you to better, worthier places. And while there will still be shit along the way, it will never be as deep. For me that moment came at 4.17 p.m. on Wednesday the Twelfth of September, Year Two Thousand and Two.

It was at this fateful moment that the branch office coffee-vending machine finally breathed its last.

Now this should have been a moment of vindication, of good triumphing over evil, of conclusive proof that there was a God in heaven looking after the hapless people down below. I know. Except that I had this terrible cold; the kind where my left brain appeared to be stuffed with cotton wool and my right brain leaked incessantly, and as I sat at my desk wet, snivelling and shoeless (on account of having had to change my car tyre in the rain while I was out on some C-minus errand and breaking my sandal strap while I was at it), my blasphemous insides started wailing instead of rejoicing, and a gnawing hollowness echoed round and round inside me like Mogambo's insane laughter.

I missed that horrible branch coffee.

And this was just rock bottom but two; like when you find you've missed your connecting flight *before* you find out your passport's been stolen and someone's slipped a pound of cocaine in your handbag when you weren't looking. Because at that moment on my desk there was a pile of 5×7 high-res digital photographs capturing for posterity and its great grandchildren the glorious moments of the 'Original Cake' launch, that record-shattering, path-breaking unqualified success; that ticket to limitless growth and exponential profits; that 'revolutionary new product' that was being heralded as the best thing to have happened to packaged foods since pasteurization. And on top of that pile was the piece de resistance, the picture in which the big boss just happened to be embracing Rana Bhatia, the long-lost son, the natural heir, the prince among men and brand managers.

And this was just rock bottom but one.

Because in the background of that picture, blurred but not sufficiently, kneeled Minal Sharma, diligently wiping up pieces of fallen cake and other coagulated masses off the floor. 'Thanks for your help at the launch conference' Rana had scribbled across my promoter's apron and shiny cheeks, and as I studied that picture it occurred to me that nothing else that life ever threw my way could possibly match up.

I felt uplifted. I felt carefree, joyous even. This was the turning point. This was where my life had to bounce off Hell's rocky bottom and start climbing back up again. This was the moment that would liberate me.

I honked into a tissue and shut my hurting eyes.

'Insufferable, isn't he?' a voice spoke up, not two feet away.

I opened my eyes. *Yogi?*

'What are you doing here?' I asked.

'Just passing through. Have a few moments?'

'I'm contagious.'

'I'll survive.'

He pulled out a chair and sat down, leaning far back in the chair. I had sunk lower than I'd imagined; I was actually happy to see him.

'So this is your office, huh?' He looked around the small room; at the samples of danglers, the poster allocation charts, the daily promotion and spot sales reports, the zillions of assorted memos and reminders that stuck out like ugly sores from the brown cork board all along the wall. 'Looks pretty exciting.'

I snorted and rolled my eyes.

'No? I like this place,' he said. 'There's a sense of action in here; like things are really happening.'

'You call sales promotion *happening*?'

'Sure.'

'All I see happening is my cold.' My face contorted in anticipation of a sneeze. 'A-a-a . . .'

He leaned forward to pass me a tissue.

'. . . achchoo!'

He examined the pictures on my desk while I wiped my nose.

'I see you got the launch conference photos,' he said.

'Event of the millennium, you mean.'

'Is Rana in every one of them?'

'Ohhh yeah. I'll bet he's busy posting these pictures on his own personal website too, and marking them to every senior manager at IF.'

'I wouldn't be surprised,' he said. 'It's been three weeks since the conference and he still hasn't stopped strutting.'

'That's our Rana for you.'

'How's the Original Cake doing in the market, though?'

'Rip-roaring success. You'd think we'd invented the masala dosa.'

'You sound bitter,' he said.

'Oh, no, I'm ecstatic. The egg feels great on my face.'

He smiled, summoning all the serenity of the Buddha into his broad features.

'Don't take it so personally, Minal. Rana just got lucky the International R&D team came up with that new technology at just the right time.'

'And I had to be the sucker who worked sixteen hours a day, seven days a week on a dud product.'

'The anniversary cake would have been phenomenal with the new recipe,' he said.

I winced. It still hurt, that anniversary cake. Even after all these weeks.

'I sure blew that one, didn't I?'

'It could still be done.'

'What?'

'The anniversary cake.'

'What are you, delusional or just plain *dumb*?'

'That's what I get for being nice to you?'

'I didn't invite you here. Achchooo!'

'Here, take another tissue.'

'Thanks.'

I blew my streaming nose hard into the tissue and closed my eyes. I needed sleep. Or some coffee.

'Are you sure it was you, though?' Yogi asked suddenly.

'I'm sorry?'

'The leak. Are you *sure* it was that Ali guy?'

'Who else could it have been?'

'You tell me.'

'You don't think it was Chandan, do you?'

'Not *Chandan*!' he snorted. 'D-uh!'

'Then . . . ?'

'Mi–nal!'

'Wha–*at*? And don't make that face of yours.'

'What face?'

'That patient one; the one you use when Spineless Jaggu's being particularly dim. See, there you go again.'

'Mi–*nal*!'

'Wha–*at*?'

He shook his head in pained resignation.

'Anyway, I've been talking to Chandan about the whole thing. Lara told him that Ali had nothing to do with the ad; that it was some management trainee's idea.'

'A management trainee? And you believe that?'

'I believe Chandan.'

'It's too big a coincidence,' I said. 'She's lying. '

'Maybe.'

I rubbed my forehead as I felt another sneeze bubble up. 'Achhoo!'

'God bless,' Yogi said, and passed me another tissue. 'You know the interesting thing though? She also said that Rana is being wooed by GI.'

'*What*? Get out of here. What a liar!

'Why would she lie about that?'

'I don't know. I think I'm going to sneeze again.'

'Bless you. Still, don't you think things have worked out particularly well for Rana?'

'Rana's a living example of how unfair life can be. And can we please stop talking about him?'

This he ignored completely.

'Why do I get the feeling that he's out to get you?'

'Because we've always hated each other's guts—achhoo! It's a—a-achhooo—a childhood thing. Could you pass me another tissue please?'

Yogi watched exasperatedly as I buried my face.

'Will you stop sneezing? It's impossible to conduct a decent conversation with you.'

'The sympathy is overwhelming.'

'Seriously, you should take something. Don't you guys have coffee or anything at the branch?'

'Coffee?' The hysterical laughter threatened to erupt again. 'Yeah, sure there's coffee. At my beck and call, every moment of the day. All I have to do is *this*!' I snapped my fingers in his face.

The door flew open and lo and behold, in the doorway appeared none other than Mehtaji with a huge thermos in his right hand and an oily paper bag in his left.

'Hello, Minal,' he smiled, his face creasing and folding from sideburn to sideburn. 'I thought I saw you come in from the rain. Care for some fresh coffee? And some for your visitor too.'

He poured out two steaming cups and set the bag down next to them.

'Enjoy the pakoras!' he called as he left.

Yogi stared at the door for a few moments. 'That was creepy.'

'I'll say.'

'Tell me how you did that.'

'I don't know. I just did *this*.' I clicked my fingers and the door flew open again.

'Oh, I forgot. There are some gulab jamuns too,' Mehtaji said, and carried a small tray over to the desk. 'I'll just leave them with you.'

The door shut once again and I blinked.

Yogi pulled out his wallet. 'A hundred rupees says you can't get some jalebis too,' he said.

I started laughing and ended up coughing and then Yogi joined in (laughing, not coughing, that is) and we laughed and laughed and laughed, till my sides hurt and the tears streamed down my face.

'Wow,' I said, wiping my cheeks. 'I haven't laughed this much in one whole year.'

'These gulab jamuns look good!' Yogi said.

I picked up a pakora; it was still hot.

'That was one nice man,' Yogi said between mouthfuls of gulab jamun.

'He's sweet.'

'And you said life at the branch sucked?'

'I guess it has its moments.' I took a sip of the heavenly coffee and felt some stirrings of life return all along the periphery of my soggy brain.

'I ought to come down here more often,' Yogi said. 'Takes the pants off that stuffy head office of yours any day.'

Yogi was calling the head office stuffy? I opened my waterlogged eyes more fully.

It was like switching from Cinemascope to IMAX; suddenly the room grew twenty times larger and Yogi's fuzzy features resolved into sharp focus. I stared, struck by the marked oddness about him. What was he doing here anyway? And that too in jeans? I hadn't imagined Mr Starch Points even knew the meaning of the word, let alone possessed a pair! And now he was lounging about in a frayed pair at the branch office, a white shirt carelessly open at the throat, munching away at gulab jamuns and eyeing my pakoras.

'What are you *really* doing here?' I asked.

'Social visit.'

'Yeah, right.'

'These are delicious,' he said, and reached for a third gulab jamun.

'Yogi!'

'Well, since you insist, I'm looking for ideas for special activities that we could do around Original Cake. Now that it's been launched and it's doing so well, we need to keep the excitement going. I'm thinking events, consumer promotions, that kind of stuff. You wouldn't have any suggestions, would you?

'*You're* asking *me*?'

'Sure. You've always had some pretty creative ideas about cakes, you know the research inside out, and now that you're working so close to the consumer, who else?

I realized with a shock that he was right.

I *did* know things about consumers that no one else at the Head Office did. Things like how most people felt our orange juice tasted much better with half a teaspoon of honey added to it, or that more cookies were sold at the checkout counters than from the shelves, or that the reason our breakfast bars would never sell at a nine-rupee price point was that shopkeepers never had one-rupee coins, or the reason no one bought our breakfast cereals was because the competition always had some promotion or other running in the first week of the month, which was when most breakfast cereals were bought. Things like that. Small, peculiar, all-important things. Things I'd learned at the branch in sales promotion of all places!

'Ma'am, do you have a minute?'

The disembodied face of Ramesh, one of my sales promoters, was poking round the door.

'Come in,' I said.

Here was another person who knew things. He just didn't know it. I watched with new respect as he strode in.

'Ma'am, guess what? That stall we've put up in Lajpat Nagar for the juices range? Ma'am, we've done fifteen thousand rupees worth of business already and we're almost sold out!'

'Good work! Who else is with you?'

'Sanjay, ma'am. Ma'am, we needed your clearance to get another few cases from the godown. To restock.'

'But aren't you supposed to close shop at five?'

'Yes, but Sanjay got permission from the authorities to continue till the market shuts, so now we have until nine. I think we can cross twenty-five thousand if we keep going. That would be a record, wouldn't it?'

I had no idea.

'It sure would,' Yogi nodded. 'Here, have a gulab jamun.'

I glared at him.

'No thanks, sir,' Ramesh smiled, 'I need to run. Ma'am, could you just authorize this stock withdrawal slip?'

'Sure.'

I'd barely initialled the sheet before he snatched it up and was dashing to the door.

'Oops,' he grimaced suddenly, and stopped. 'I almost forgot, ma'am. One of the women at the market handed me this. I think it's a consumer complaint.'

'Don't worry,' I sighed. 'I'll take care of it. Good luck!'

'Your team seems pretty charged up,' Yogi said when he'd left.

'They are, aren't they? Of course they'd sell your mom if you let them, but they are a hardworking bunch.'

'I'd take them out for a celebratory beer, if they do indeed do their twenty-five grand.'

Beer?

I tried to imagine Yogi at a bar. *'The strategic imperative of this alcoholic beverage . . .'*

'What?' he said as my lips twitched.

'Nothing. Tell me, do you do a lot of that morale-building stuff at the agency?'

'I try to keep my team motivated.'

'Really?'

'Of course you can't do the beer thing all the time,' he said. 'Sometimes you have to kick their butts and sometimes you have to cover for them and sometimes you have to wade in and get your hands dirty, but mostly its about keeping them motivated, isn't it?'

I'd never noticed it before, but when he wasn't spouting jargon the man actually made a lot of sense.

'Motivate', I scribbled on a little memo pad and tacked it up on my wall.

'So, aren't you going to open this?' he said, indicating the letter the promoter had left on the desk.

'It'll be the usual complaints,' I shrugged, and slit the envelope open.

Dear International Foods,

I am writing to tell you that I am a very loyal customer of your company's products. Every month I buy all your products. Even when there is a promotion on other brands, I still buy your products.

Good God.

I give my son your breakfast cereal every morning and your breakfast bars every afternoon and your orange juice every evening and he is growing up tall and strong, by the grace of God.

Poor kid.

Recently I came across a new product of yours called 'Original Cake'. Naturally I tried it. I must say that it is very good, very spongy and tasty. But I have one complaint—that the packing is not what I'd expect from a company of your stature. I think you should pack the cake in high-quality boxes, not the thin foil that you are currently using. I hope that you will change the poor packing as soon as possible.

Yours sincerely,

Mrs Chandwani

I should send this to Rana. Actually frame it and send it. Maybe mark it to the entire management team at IF?

P.S. I am sending a photo of your cake decorated by my son. He won first prize at his school fete for it. I hope that someone from your office will send him a letter of appreciation.

'Some people!' I said, rolling my eyes.

Yogi was staring mesmerized at the attached photo, brows up in his hair. 'Wow, this kid's a natural! Maybe I could hire him as an art director.'

'Can I see that?'

I gasped as he handed me the photo; he wasn't kidding. Our Original Cake had been sculpted in the picture into a staggering work of art; a pulsating NASCAR fantasy in sponge, cream and chocolate icing, a delectable creation that would have put all the chefs in France to shame. The entire top surface of the cake had been converted into a racetrack, with lanes of chocolate icing, powdered sugar markers, candy cane flags and a peppermint victory stand. In the middle was a pavilion constructed from chocolate wafers and around the edges the grass was made from layer upon layer of green sprinkles. Hot Wheels cars and racecar heroes stood steaming at the start line, waiting for the tiny Jack Stone figure at the side to wave his flag and start the race.

No wonder Mrs C had sent us the picture; she must be proud. I was proud. Heck, even Michelangelo would've been proud!

I stared at the little flames rising from the ten small candles that were arranged at intervals round the track and the seed of an idea flickered to life in my caffeine-powered brain.

'Yogi, this is a fantastic idea for a cake event!'

He looked at me, puzzled.

'The resurrection of the Original Cakewalk! It'll be perfect. Remember how we used to have those cakewalks at school fetes back in the eighties?'

'Cakewalks?' My school fetes used to be all about "House of Horrors" and "Dunk Your Teacher".'

I was momentarily distracted.

'House of Horrors?'

'Never mind that.'

'You used to *dunk your teachers*?'

'Are you going to tell me what you mean by cakewalk?'

'It's just a cake exhibition and sale really.' I'd have to exchange teacher-dunking notes with him later. 'The kids bring cakes to sell at the school fete to raise money for charity. They're all displayed in a hall like an exhibition and the parents bid money to purchase them.'

'So you want kids to sell our Original Cake at their school fetes,' he said. 'What's so fantastic about that?'

'They'll sell our cake but with *their* decorations! Unique and original decorations and themes, just like this one.'

Yogi knitted his brows and peered at the picture once more. 'The kids couldn't do it, Minal,' he said. 'This boy is talented but the others would make a mess of it.'

'They don't have to be professionals! The idea is to be creative and have fun.'

'Decorating a cake is *fun*?'

'Almost as much as eating it.'

'But not as much as slamming someone in the face with it.'

I peered at him closely. 'Are you feeling all right?' I asked.

'Just kidding. Carry on.'

'Well, my sales promotion team could organize the whole event. We'd contact the schools, provide the materials, we could even help the kids out with the decorating. And the proceeds from the sale could go towards books for the school library. And we could give out prizes for the most creative cakes. And just think of the fun the kids will have!'

The ideas were churning at 750 rpm or thereabouts in my head. I jumped out of my chair and started pacing the floor, trying to catch up.

Yogi watched me, a frown between his brows. 'Rana had something more for the housewives in mind,' he said.

'So? Moms come to fetes, don't they?'

'Well yes, but . . . .'

'And kids are an important target audience too.'

'Well, if you . . . .'

'And we'll get tremendous publicity! Think about it. "IF helps raise money for school libraries". The schools would love it! The press would love it! *Vik* would love it!' I stopped and looked at him. 'What do you think?'

'I think you should go easy on that coffee.'

'Don't you like my idea?'

'I might.'

'What do you mean *might*?'

'I mean I *might* like it if you stopped beating me over the head with it.'

'Beating you over the head! You're the one who came here asking for ideas!'

'See, that's your problem,' he scowled. 'It's always your way or no way. You're just so pushy.'

'*What*?' How dare he? 'That's rich, coming from you, Mr Jargon Junkie!'

'What did you just call me?'

'Oh, come on, haven't you ever noticed how you're always spouting jargon? '

'Oh yeah? And what about you? *"I don't think this layout quite communicates the core values of the brand, Yogi"*, and *"Vik, we need to broaden the franchise without destroying the mystique"*. I had a hard time keeping a straight face over that one, I can tell you.'

'I never said that!'

'Yes, you did.'

'No way.'

'Yes way.'

'Did NOT!'

'Did TOO!'

We glared at each other for a while and I would have won, but just then another sneeze popped out and ruined it all.

'Damn,' I said, wiping my nose. 'You know, you have to be the rudest, stuffiest, most conc . . .'

I noticed he was grinning, holding two fingers up in a peace sign. 'Here, have another gulab jamun,' he offered.

'No.'

'They're very good.'

'I don't want one.'

'Okay, suit yourself.' He shrugged and popped it in his own mouth.

'You've had five already, you know?'

'So? There's plenty left for you. Anyway,' he wiped his fingers and straightened in his chair, 'to get back to your cakewalk. I do like the idea . . .'

'I knew it!'

'. . . but we have to think about Rana too.'

I bit back the expletives.

'I know,' Yogi agreed. 'It sucks. I can just imagine Rana's reaction. *How many extra cakes will I sell, Yogi?*' That'll be his first question. He just hates spending money.'

'I think we could sell a fair number of cakes,' I said.

'At a school fete?'

'Why not? They're always crowded.'

'That they are.'

'Besides it would be a great way to show off how versatile the cake is.'

'Versatility is good.'

'And it'll be something totally new; it should create some buzz.'

'You know, you're right!' he exclaimed suddenly. 'It's focussed, it's innovative, it expands usage and it has a lot of synergy with the core values of the brand!'

'Ah, the brand core values,' I grinned. 'I was wondering when you'd bring them up.'

'You *know* they're important!'

I couldn't help smiling. 'Yes, they are. So what are the core values for Original Cake?'

'That's the problem,' he grimaced, 'we don't seem to have any.'

'Vik's left it all to Rana and Rana can't get past "economical".'

'Oh dear.'

'I know. I swear I never thought I'd miss you, but . . .'

'Did you say you *missed me*?'

'Disgusting, isn't it?'

'Probably just a passing bug.'

'I'm hoping. Anyway, I'd better get going.'

'Where to? I thought you had the day off or something.'

'I wish. No, I'm headed back to the agency.'

He got up, pushing one thumb through the frayed belt loop of the worn denims.

'You know, I've never seen you in jeans before.'

'Sorry.'

'What for?'

'I hadn't planned on meeting you today.'

'So?'

'I like to look professional.'

'Well, this looks much better.'

'Now you're embarrassing me. Anyway, thanks for the help with the promo idea.'

'No, thank you. So, are you going to check with Rana?'

'Let me toss the idea around with the creative team first, flesh it out a bit.'

'Meanwhile,' I said, suddenly remembering my Lists, 'somewhere in this colossal cabinet I'm sure I have a list of all the schools and principals in town. I could get started right away!' I began rummaging through the files.

'Hey, back up,' he said. 'We do have to sell the idea to Mr God-Almighty first, remember?'

I sighed and sat back. 'Yeah, you're right. Anyway, let me know how it goes.'

'I'll be in touch.' He turned to go and I turned back to my eternal pile of estimates.

'Minal?' he said suddenly, in a much altered voice.

I looked up.

'You know the real reason I stopped by today?'

'What?'

He paused a moment, shifting from foot to foot. 'Look, I've been meaning to say this for a while . . ..'

I raised my brows.

'Thanks.'

'Huh?'

'For sticking up for Chandan the way you did that day. Thank you.' He thrust out his hand and shook mine emphatically.

'It was nothing,' I said, slightly embarrassed.

'No, it took guts. You're a pal.'

And then to my utter astonishment, he put two fingers to his forehead in a strange, solemn salute, patted me on the shoulder and then walked out the door.

I sat staring at the doorknob, too stunned to move. I was Yogi's *pal?* This was turning out to be the strangest day of my life.

The sun had set with Yogi's departure, leaving the room in a twilight gloom. I turned on the overhead lights, poured another cup of coffee and glanced once again at the Original Cake launch pictures on my desk. Rana's smug face smiled up at me from all of them, mocking.

Was he the one who leaked the ad?

Yogi certainly thought so. But why would he do it? To get at me? Was he that insecure?

And what about Ali? What if Ali was innocent? Good God, I'd made a terrible mistake!

Of course it didn't really matter, I was engaged to Sunil now. But if it really was Rana . . . ..

I needed time to think this whole thing through. And rest. My nose was exhausted from all that running; my eyes burned from having watered all day. I shoved the pictures aside, turned off the lights, and headed out the door.

For the first time in forty days I didn't kick the Jeep's tyres in the parking lot when I got home. Instead, I walked slowly up the stairs, pulled out the collection of Post-its I'd been stowing in my old sneakers the past few weeks and arranged them in chronological order on the table.

Wk 1:

1. I'm sorry, I've been sulking. Call me.
2. I said I'm sorry! Will you call, or should I come over?
3. What did you have to bang the door in my face for?

Wk 2:

4. I can't believe you think I did it.
5. You *do* think I did it.

Wk 3:

6. You know what? I've had enough. Hope you have a good life.

There hadn't been any in wks 4, 5, 6 or 7. Men give up so easily.

twenty-eight

The clock in my car flashed 7.58 a.m. the next morning as I pulled out of the parking lot and moved to join the steady stream of traffic on Ring Road. On an impulse, I turned the radio on. Suhasini was pumping iron on Vividh Bharati, reading requests from Chhotu, Motu, Guddi and Pinchoo from Patparganj and Bahadur, Bunty and Prince in Patiala at supersonic speed. I changed channels to FM.

Yogi thought it was Rana.

A Yoga instructor was taking listeners through the 'seven litres of water to cleanse the stomach' routine on 103.6.

Would he really stoop that low?

On 105.5 Minty Mathur was chattering on about college fests in her thirty-third year on earth.

Of course we had no proof.

A toilet-bowl cleaner ad was playing on 106.2. The tinny jingle was followed by swirling, gushing, bubbly water sounds. That Tyagi was good; I had to say that for him.

Still, I'd need to keep my guard up.

The clock flashed 8 a.m. I hesitated a moment, and then moved channels up to 107.4.

'Good morning, Delhi, welcome to 107.4 FM!' a red-nailed voice chirped; awfully lilting, disgustingly breathy. 'It's eight o'clock and your favourite hosts Lara Lahiri and Ali Imran are back with this Friday's version of Morning Reflections!'

'Hey Delhi, what's up?'

It was the same deep baritone, but with a richer, huskier timbre, and it sent a tremor shuddering right through me, from my head to my toes. I turned the radio off.

What was wrong with me? All this time and all these events, and still the sound of his voice was enough to send my systems crashing like a computer virus. Unrequited sex, I thought bitterly, that's what it was. (Or rather requited but unconsummated sex.) I should just sleep with him and get it over with.

Just kidding, of course. I was engaged to be married. To a doctor who saved lives. And lived in a nice home. With furniture. I liked furniture. I moved my left hand along the steering wheel until I could see the diamond on my finger. I liked my diamond too. And I liked being engaged. I liked the fact that I was going to marry the most eligible man in the world.

They'd stopped the traffic for some VIP movement on S.P. Marg. I slowed down to a halt and turned the engine off; it looked like it would be a long wait. In the rearview mirror, I saw a Jeep slow down to a halt behind me. The guy behind the steering wheel had black hair and brown skin like almost all the other men in Delhi but my heart still skipped a beat.

Dumb, dumb, dumb! Ali was down at the radio station doing his show.

I'd have to have a talk with him, though. I couldn't treat him like a liar and a cheat and then carry on as before after finding out he hadn't really done anything wrong at all. My conscience wouldn't abide such callousness.

I'd call him later tonight. We'd do the 'I'm sorry', 'No, I'm sorry', and 'no hard feelings', and 'let's stay friends', and 'hey, I'm getting married' and 'wow, congrats' thing, and we'd all live happily ever after.

Or maybe I should go over? It was always better to do these things face to face, wasn't it?

Not too late though, I wouldn't want to surprise him conducting music without his shirt. Would he still be wearing those . . .

'Kambakht ishq . . .' My phone rang rather violently and I jumped. I groped around in my purse; it was Sunil.

'Hi Minal, what's up?' he said.

'Oh, nothing, nothing. This is a surprise!'

'Yes, I'll be starting my rounds in a minute; just wanted to let you know that Harish called to invite us for lunch on the twenty-ninth. Hope that's fine?'

'Yeah, sure.'

'Good. Listen, do you mind driving straight to the Dubeys' tonight? I'll be a little late leaving work, I'll join you there.'

'Do we really have to go?' I sighed.

'Why, is there a problem?'

'No, just that it's been ages since we had any time alone. I was thinking that if you came over we could—'

'Minal, can you hold on a minute?'

I sat back and watched the VIP motorcade zip by. Maybe we could go out dinner and dancing. Or dinner and dessert. Or just stay home and watch TV.

'Sorry about that,' Sunil said, coming back on the line.

'That's okay. I was saying—'

'Listen, I really have to run right now, but we'll talk later, okay?'

'But . . .'

'The Dubeys'. At eight. See you!'

The phone clicked as he hung up, and all around me vehicles were stirring to life.

The barrier had been removed, I noticed; the guy to my right revved up his mobike, the car to my left jerked forward, and the Jeep guy behind me honked his horn, reminding me that it was time to move on.

twenty-nine

That and the kick in the rear from Yogi turned out to be just what I'd needed to pull me back from that brink of melancholic yearning that I'd always associated with sighing maids and weeping willows.

The office needed me. The rains were over, power-cut season was drawing to a close and there were barely three months left to make this year's impossible targets. The next week went by in a blur of sales plans, the one after that in a series of stalls across the Yamuna, and before I knew it, I was back to having all three meals at the office and enjoying it.

!!!

'The main nutrient in orange juice is Vitamin C,' I said to my team Sunday afternoon, holding up a carton of our orange juice. 'You'll notice that on the information panel we say that one glass of orange juice a day provides hundred per cent of the daily requirement. That's a strong selling point.'

I looked around at the ring of bent heads. Everyone was busy, furiously taking notes. Good thing we'd finally gotten around to this training seminar.

'Can anyone list the benefits of Vitamin C?' I asked.

'It improves resistance to disease?' Ramesh said.

'Yes, and . . .?'

'It keeps your gums healthy,' tried Sanjay.

'Very good. Any others?'

'Helps allergies?' ventured Ravi.

'Well, that's something they're still not sure about, though indications are that that may be true. It does have natural antihistamine properties, though.'

'So should we mention its anti-allergy benefits if customers ask us?' Ramesh asked.

'No, we should stick to the facts.' I said. 'I know it can be tempting to mention all the probable benefits, but we should be careful not to mislead the consumers, or over-promise. Just tell them the proven advantages, like the ones that are mentioned in the handout. If you could just turn to page thirty-seven . . .'

They all flipped to the end. I read through the fact sheet slowly. It was important they understood all the benefits thoroughly.

VITAMIN C:

- Is an antioxidant and protects your body from free radicals, which may cause heart disease and cancer.
- Is responsible for producing collagen.
- Helps your immune system.
- Helps heal scrapes and bruises.
- Keeps your gums healthy.
- Helps protect the fat-soluble Vitamins A and E as well as fatty acids from oxidation.
- Has natural antihistamine properties

'Now let's move to the next nutrient, one that is especially important for . . .'

The meeting room door swung open. It was the new peon. He came in, grinning widely.

'Excuse me, madam; there is a phone call for you,' he said.

'Who is it?' I frowned.

He grinned again. 'I think it's your fiancé, madam. He said it was urgent.'

'Sorry, guys,' I said to my team. 'I'll be back in a minute.'

Why was he calling me at the office? And that too on a Sunday! I checked my cellphone as I made my way to the reception phone. Five missed calls.

'Hello?' I said, trying not to panic.

'Minal! Where have you been? I've been trying to call you for the past half hour!'

'What's the matter; is everything okay?'

'No! We're supposed to be at Harish Khanna's in ten minutes!'

Damn, I'd forgotten all about the lunch.

'What are you doing in the office on Sunday afternoon anyway? And you've put your cellphone on voice mail! I had to look your office number up in the yellow pages.'

'White.'

'What? Anyway, I just called this number as a last resort. What are you doing there?'

'I was in the middle of a training session for my promoters. Say, you're a doctor; do you know if it's been proven that Vitamin C helps people with allergies?'

'*What*?! Listen, I'll try and get there in ten minutes to pick you up. God, I'll have to think of some excuse for Harish; don't think we can reach his place before one thirty.'

'Why don't you carry on by yourself?'

'What do you mean? Harish specifically invited you.'

'I know. I'd come, but we've still got a lot of territory to cover here.'

'You can't cry off at the last minute, Minal.'

'Why don't you tell him I got caught up at the office? I'm sure he'll understand.'

'His wife's going to be there too, you know. Her uncle is a minister. This is a fantastic opportunity to network, Minal.'

'Yes, but . . .'

'You know this is really important to me, don't you?'

'Of course I know. And I know you can handle it perfectly on your own.'

'Yes, but that's not the point!'

I sighed.

'Look, I'm really sorry, Sunil. I don't know how it slipped my mind, but now I'm committed. My team's been wanting this training session for a long time; I've already had to put it off twice.'

'Well, then you can put it off again.'

'No, that wouldn't be right.'

'Oh, come on, Minal!'

'Sunil, try to under . . .'

'It's not as though it's anything terribly important either,' he said.

'*I* think it's important.'

'Okay, okay, so it's important. So is the lunch.'

'Yes, but you don't have to put *that* off; you can still go!'

'I can't believe . . . I thought you hated your job?'

'I don't hate my job.'

'But it's a lousy job!'

'That's *rude*!'

'I'm sorry; you're right,' he said. 'Look, I don't want to fight. I don't care about your job, whatever makes you happy. You know I love you, don't you?'

'Uh huh.' *Why didn't he care about my job?*

'It's just that this nursing home is really important to me, to *us*. I'm doing this for the *both* of us, for our future.'

'I know.'

'So, why don't you finish your training session next Sunday? It's just your promoters after all; I'm sure they wouldn't mind.'

Sure they wouldn't mind. Except that I knew Sanjay had come all the way from Ghaziabad just for this, and Mohan needed to kick off the juice activity in Haryana in a couple of days.

'No, I need to finish this today,' I said.

There was silence at the other end.

'Sunil?'

'You're really letting me down, you know.'

'Oh, it's not the end of the world,' I teased.

More silence.

'And if you decide to drop by my place later this evening, I promise I'll make it up to you . . .'

There was a click and the line went dead.

I looked up; the peon had been eavesdropping with great interest.

'Next time the phone rings, just take a message,' I snapped, and strode back to the training room.

thirty

'Too expensive!' Rana had sniffed and shot down the school activity idea, right after we'd got everyone at the Bharatram Public School all charged up, and my poor promoters had worked their butts off all week preparing.

Yogi had called with the bad news Saturday morning.

'So what are you going to do?' he'd asked.

Then, I hadn't known.

Now, four hours later, I squeezed my car into a tight spot between a bush and a tree in the park adjacent to the school building, picked up the bags of assorted cake decorations and IF signage I'd carried, and trudged up the street to the wide-open school gates.

What could he do, get me transferred to the branch?

Ha.

I stopped to buy pink cotton candy at the candy stand and a fat yellow balloon at the balloon stand and walked up the path past hordes of screaming, laughing children. I felt instantly energized. Forget solar power, if someone could just find a way to harness all the energy of a school fete, they'd drive the Gulf out of business, clean up the environment, add a decade to life expectancy, and then some.

I followed the signs up and beyond the main school building to the cricket grounds where all the amusements and food stalls were set up. A strong gust of wind wrapped the balloon string around the candy stick and as I tried to untangle the two, a skinny woman dressed all in orange streaked across my path and threw herself upon a hearty lady in magenta two inches from my nose.

'Hell-o Mrs Sahni!' the lady in orange shrieked as she grabbed Magenta by the jowls. 'Don't tell me your son goes here too?'

'Where else?' Magenta smiled. 'He started in nursery this year.'

'How wonderful!' Orange gushed. 'Isn't this a terrific school? Karan and Kartik just love it.'

'Oh, yes. Akshay is very happy too,' said Magenta. 'Thank goodness we knew one of the teachers. It's so hard to get admission these days!'

'Especially at BPS,' agreed Orange. 'It's almost impossible to get in without some connection. They are so choosy about family background and values.'

'Oh yes,' laughed Magenta. 'Hubby and I were up slogging the whole night, reading American books on parenting. In fact Hubby had to cancel his Europe business trip because they insisted on both parents being there for the interview.'

'Oh, don't remind me; I had to coach Karan for three whole months for the nursery interview. We even called in an early childhood specialist for some tips.'

Nursery interview? Early childhood specialist?

I tried to recall life in Meerut at age four. Lots of flags, tons of khadi, no memories of any tutors or early childhood freaks, thank goodness.

'Excuse me,' I said as I pushed past.

'In a way it's good that they are so selective,' I could hear Orange's voice fading away as I moved on. 'It's so important to ensure that all the children are from good families, and that they pick up good values.'

There was a huge enclosure to the left that looked like it might be the venue for the cakewalk. I stepped onto the grass and the next thing I knew I'd landed flat on my back, knocked down by some kind of human hurricane. My balloon sailed up into the sky, the cotton candy hanging on at the base of its string like a parachutist and I lay winded and gasping as the tumble of skinny limbs on the grass beside me sorted itself into two surly boys.

'Owww!' I said, rubbing my grazed elbow.

'Watch where you're going, lady!' called the older boy.

'Give me back my Gameboy,' yelled the smaller one.

'Finder's keepers,' tormented the bigger one.

'You bastard!' called the little one, who didn't look a day older than seven.

'Now wait a minute,' I began severely.

'Who're you? Get out of my way,' he yelled. He shoved me out of his way and grabbed a clump of the bigger kid's hair.

'Boys, boys, break it up!' I called.

The bigger kid gave me the finger and jabbed the younger one roundly in the jaw.

Orange came hurrying up behind me. 'Kartik, Karan, there you are,' she called. 'Come children, ice creams!' She watched as I got up, wiping my shoes, collecting my bags.

'They have so much energy at this age, don't they?' she smiled. 'So playful.'

I shuddered and removed myself from the battlefield as fast as my legs could carry me.

'How pretty!' a sweet-looking woman exclaimed. She stopped by the table as I helped Shivani from Class 4 put the finishing touches to her 'Flower Garden' cake. We sat a tiny sugar fairy down beside a row of red icing roses and then took a step back to admire our handiwork.

'Did you do this all by yourself?' the woman asked the little girl.

'No, this IF aunty helped me,' Shivani replied with a shy smile.

'Well, it's beautiful.'

The woman picked up the pen that lay on the table next to the silent auction slip and wrote 'Anjali Bajaj—Rs 250'.

Shivani swelled and turned to me with an excited smile, and then we both held our breath as another woman walked up and wrote 'Rs 300' below Mrs Bajaj's bid.

'Great job,' I whispered in Shivani's ear. 'Want me to take a picture of you next to your cake?'

A couple of tables down the hall I spotted Ramesh helping a little boy touch up the rocket decorations on his cake. I checked the auction slip; the last bid was for four hundred rupees.

'That's some sculpture!' I said to the little boy behind the table. 'At this rate you'll raise enough money to buy a whole new library for the school!'

I was rewarded with a shy blush and a big smile. 'I'm going to help buy the DK series on astronauts,' he said.

I grinned. 'Need any extra decorations?'

'Do you have any planets?' he answered. 'I couldn't find anything to make planets with.'

I rummaged around in my bags.

'Let me see . . . how about these lollipops? I have them in different sizes, and you could draw orbits with some icing sugar.'

'I'm not sure . . . could I take a look?'

I handed the bag over. 'Take what you need. That's a really cool launching pad, by the way. What did you use?'

'Oh, I got some toy models from home, and some aluminium foil, and Ramesh Uncle helped put it all together.'

I smiled at Ramesh.

'That's great,' I said to the little boy, 'just don't tell the judges!'

'Ramesh Uncle, what do you think of this one . . . do you think it looks like Saturn?' he asked, putting together two tiny plastic saucers he'd pulled out of the bag.

'It's perfect,' Ramesh said.

'Can you help me put some Scotch tape to hold them together?'

I left them to it.

Flower Garden, Rocket Launcher, Hansel and Gretel, Sunflowers, the Indian Flag, Sailboats . . . I slowly wound my way past one cake after another, marvelling at the creativity of the kids. The hall was packed; the parents seemed to love it. I walked on down, right to the end of the hall where a large group was gathered round the last table, ooh-ing and aah-ing. I waited for the crowd to disperse and caught my breath as I spotted the large, round cake on the table.

It was beautiful! Little evergreen trees stood on a bed of white icing, their tiny leaves frosted over with sugar. Meticulous cream peaks towered at one end, while a miniature ski lodge constructed from wafers held sway in the centre. There was even a little campfire burning outside, made of yellow-orange and red sprinkles. And in one corner, a tiny ski figurine was poised to zigzag down one of the frosty slopes.

'Winter Cake' a tiny placard next to the cake read. 'By Aditya and Srinivas, Class 4B'. The bids were already up to eight hundred rupees.

'Good work, guys!' I said to the pair who stood behind the table, and introduced myself. 'How long did this take?'

'We've been here since the morning,' the shorter one said. 'We've already ruined four and Aditya's *still* not happy with this one.'

He glowered at the boy next to him.

'We have to win first prize,' Aditya said.

'I know, but this is fine! Just look . . .'

'Yes, just look at this mountain; it's all crooked!'

'It's great,' I assured Aditya.

'See?' said Srinivas. 'And she should know; she's from the cake company.'

'But what about flags?' Aditya insisted. 'We should have flags to mark the ski slope, don't you think?'

'Easily fixed,' I said and held out my bags. 'Dive in; I'm sure you'll find something you could use.'

They emptied its contents and finally settled on some red cellophane and toothpicks. I helped put them in.

'Thank you,' Aditya said when we were done. He looked tired and worn; I doubted he'd had anything to eat all day.

'Why don't you two take a break?' I said. 'Go and have some fun, get something to eat, check out the competition. I'll hold fort for a while, and you can be back for the judging.'

Srinivas brightened, but Aditya looked doubtful.

'Well . . .' he began.

'Don't worry, I'll be really careful and won't let anyone touch your cake.'

'It's just that . . . don't you think the mountains need smoothing?'

'I'll take care of it.'

'Well, okay, but could you make sure you use the back of the plastic spoon to level out the icing and . . . .'

'Shoo!' I yelled, and chased him out.

I got in behind the table, feeling as exhilarated as the skier who was making his way down the steep, creamy slope. This cakewalk was going way better than I'd ever imagined. The cakes were gorgeous, the hall was packed, the bids were high, and quite a few parents had already asked where they could buy Original Cake.

Too bad no one would ever know. We could have had our banners up all over the school; we could have had them up all over town, in fact; we could have been in the papers. We could have started a fad; we could have sold our cakes by the thousands. If only Rana hadn't put his foot down. If only Vik could be here to see.

I sighed and put my promoter's apron on. At least there was today, that had to count for something. Forty proud and happy kids from Class 4B; new books for the BPS library—look on the bright side, there was always a bright side. At least we'd had this one event, and my team had given it all they had. They really were the best, my promoters.

On an impulse, I picked up the pen and wrote my name and 'Rs 900' on the auction sheet next to the Winter Cake. We could all celebrate later, when it was all over, and what could be more appropriate?

I stood admiring the cake, already tasting the creamy white icing. One of the icy mountains did indeed look like it could do with a little touching up. I dived under the table to look for the plastic spoon.

'Now that's what I call a cake!' a familiar voice boomed from across the hall. Heavy footsteps got closer.

I popped my head up above the table.

It was Max the Axe. And too late to duck; he'd already spotted me.

'Minal!' he said, surprised.

'Max! How are you; what brings you here?'

'I'm just doing the Dad thing; my kids are at BPS.'

'Oh.'

'And what about you? Don't tell me *you* made this cake?'

'Oh no, I'm just standing in for Aditya and Srinivas. They'd been here all day; I thought they could use a break.'

'And those kids are your . . .?'

'Actually, I'm here to supervise. This cakewalk is, er, it's one our events. For Original Cake.'

'You mean our Original Cake has something to do with all this?'

He turned to look slowly down the hall at the rows of tables, all packed with cakes. 'How come I'm not aware of it?'

'Actually the head office hasn't approved it,' I said, nervous. 'I'm sorry, I'd have called it off, but we'd already made a commitment to the principal and . . .'

'But this is amazing!'

I stopped, not quite sure where this was headed.

'And a great turnout too! There must be at least two thousand parents here.' He looked down at the Winter Cake again. 'You know, I really must bid for this cake; it's outstanding. Where's the pen?'

'Oh, but I just bid for it!'

'You did? Why?'

'Actually, it's for the sales promotion team,' I said, feeling sheepish. 'To motivate them.'

'That's a great idea.'

'Actually, they'd been working hard all morning and . . .' I stopped as he scribbled 'Rs 1000' on the auction sheet below my bid.

'Four figures! The kids are going to be pleased.'

'Don't worry,' he said, 'your team still gets to keep the cake.'

'Thanks!'

He straightened up, smiling.

'So how're things?' he asked. 'Are you enjoying yourself at the branch?'

Three weeks ago I would have fallen at his feet, begging to be taken back at the head office. Today, I grinned.

'Well, the targets are impossible, the work killing, and the rewards negligible,' I said, 'but I do believe I'm having fun.'

Max threw back his head and laughed. 'Join the club.'

He looked around again at the crowded tables and the bustling parents, then up at the bare walls and ceiling. 'You know, Minal,' he said, 'this is a fantastic event idea, but there's hardly any brand visibility.'

'I know. It's just that since Rana and Vik hadn't really approved the activity, I wasn't sure . . .'

'I can't see why they didn't approve it. This is a great opportunity. We should have had posters and banners all over, and a sales counter or two at the gate. In fact,' he said, stepping behind the table, 'let's see what we have here and make a few signs right away!'

'But since it's not official . . .'

'Official my right toe! Pass me those markers!'

He rolled up his sleeves and I passed him the markers. 'Minal,' he said, as he scribbled away, 'Why don't you send me a one-pager on this school cakewalk event? I'll circulate it to the other branch offices; they ought to implement it there too.'

'Yes, but Vik . . .'

'Leave Vik to me. There, now what do you think?'

He held up his handmade sign, scribbled over in his thick, heavy hand.

'Pretty good,' I said.

'Now where can we put this up?' he said, looking around.

'How about up over the entrance? Ramesh is there by the rocket cake; he can put it up.'

'Good idea. I'll give it to him. Meanwhile I want you to make as many signs as you can and put them up all around the hall. I want to make sure every single parent knows where these goodies came from. And take lots of pictures.'

'Right.'

'And see if you can't send that note in by Monday morning!'

'Yes, sir!' I grinned, and got down to work.

A few minutes later I noticed a woman scribbling 'Rs 1100' on the auction sheet. *Eleven hundred rupees*! I sat back to check her out.

'This is for my husband,' she said with a little laugh. 'He's crazy about skiing; this will be such a great surprise! And it's his birthday today.'

'In that case, I do hope you get it,' I smiled.

'Oh, I'll make sure I do,' she said. 'I think I'll just stand here and outbid anyone who comes along to raise the stakes. You don't mind, do you?'

'Not at all,' I said and started on another poster.

'You're from IF, aren't you?' she asked. 'I must compliment you; all these cakes are just beautiful.'

'Thanks; they are made from our Original Cake, but the creativity is entirely the children's.'

'I wish the bakeries could be this creative,' she said.

'Or employ these children,' I laughed.

'Really, they ought to have catalogues or something, with a range of designs; something other than the usual black forest and pineapple. Too bad none of these cakes will keep till my birthday!'

'You could make your own,' I suggested. 'It's really easy. And our Original Cake will soon be available in all the leading outlets.'

'Thanks. And would you have an ideas catalogue too?'

Ideas catalogue?

I looked down at all the decorations and icing and materials around me, and the boxes of Original Cake. There were a million ideas in there, just waiting to be discovered. *And made available to consumers.* I rummaged in my purse for my cellphone. If I was lucky I'd be able to catch Yogi.

thirty-one

I switched on the projector and the words from the acetate slide shot up onto the white wall of the branch office conference room.

PROJECT: CREATIVE CAKEWORKS

'Creative cakeworks?' Yogi snorted.

'Can you not comment two words into my presentation?'

'Okay, but what were you *thinking*?'

'We can call it Original Cake Plus if you'd prefer. Or Cake Site. Or Cake Zone?'

'Man, you need help with names.'

'Really? And what did you have in mind—Pearly Twirly Curly Cake?'

'Carry on,' he winced. 'Please.'

'Thank you.'

Concept: An interactive website where customers can create and decorate cakes of their own choice (using Original Cake) and place an order for delivery

'Cakes of their choice?'

'Sure. They could create any kind of cake for any occasion. Or even no occasion at all. They could do it just for fun, like an interactive game.'

'You want to get into the interactive games business?'

'Yogi!'

'I'll take that to mean no,' he said leaning back in his chair. 'So what are you getting at?'

'It's simple. We provide a website with a wide menu of options. Say five different shapes, ten different flavours, icing, cream, cookies, fruits, candy, chocolates, sprinkles . . . dozens of choices for the toppings. Plus hundreds of ornaments and decorations. A person goes on the site, clicks on the menu options and simultaneously, a cake starts forming in the graphics window. Click on 'chocolate flavour', the cake turns brown. Click on 'add green grass', it gets covered with a layer of green sprinkles. And we can have drag and drop options too, just like Dress-Up Barbie or Mr Potato Head.'

'Sounds extremely childish.'

'So? It'll cater to kids. They're the biggest existing market anyway. And we could do adult themes too, like a cricket theme for whenever India wins, complete with pitch, stumps and players; or even waltzing on a moonlit night for the more romantic ones.'

'And what happens once a person's created the cake?'

'He or she orders it.'

'The picture?'

'*No-o*! The cake.'

'You mean you're talking about a *real* cake?'

'Of course I'm talking about a real cake. What did you think?'

'But how is that possible? We've just launched a basic sponge cake; we're miles from decorations and toppings, let alone . . .'

'But *we* don't decorate the cake; the *customer* does.'

'Yes, but how?'

'Online!'

'And the cake pops out like magic from the computer screen.'

'Very funny. The order goes to a bakery that decorates and delivers the cake. We'll tie up with a well-established bakery, a chain preferably. They'd use our cake as a base and decorate as per the order.'

'Aah, so you're talking about offline tie-ups,' he said. 'You could have mentioned it earlier, considering we've been here nearly a half hour.'

'And you could have let me get on with my presentation, considering it's all there on page three.'

He grinned and leaned farther back, arms hanging loosely from the armrest, big hands crossed in his lap.

'Okay, so go ahead; I'm all ears.'

'Like I was saying . . ..'

'You know the trouble with franchisees though?' he said, sitting up suddenly. 'No control. What if the actual cake they deliver ends up looking nothing like the virtual one? You're talking about very specialized decorations.'

'The guys at bakeries are very skilled; they do decorations every day. And we could get a pro to train them if we need to.'

'And the delivery?'

'They'll deliver. Think pizza delivery. Choose toppings, or rather decorations—place an order—add transit time—and voila! Fresh, beautiful cake delivered with a smile at your doorstep!'

He leaned his elbows on the table top and cupped his face between his knuckles, squinting at the PowerPoint slide on the wall.

'So what you're saying is I can go online, create a cake any way I please, press enter and someone will deliver the exact same cake to me?'

'Oui.'

He removed one hand from his face and drummed his fingers on the table top. 'You know what,' he said finally, 'maybe you *should* take me through your presentation.'

A half hour later, his elbows were back on the table, his chin cupped between his palms, his knuckles stretching and flattening his broad cheeks. I switched off the projector and waited. He continued to stare at the blank wall.

'So what do you think?' I asked.

Now that I'd put it all down in words, laid it out in front of another person for comments, I wasn't so sure any more. 'Will it work?'

'Will it work?' he repeated, coming slowly to life.

'No? Too far-fetched?'

He sat up and crossed his arms, regarding me with a glazed look.

'Minal, this is the idea of a lifetime! It's brilliant! It's revolutionary! What did Vik have to say?'

The idea of a lifetime?

'Vik doesn't know yet,' I said. 'I thought I'd bounce it off you first, see how you felt.'

'You mean I'm the first person you've shown this to? I'm . . . I'm honoured.'

'It's only just an idea.'

'Vik's going to love it.'

'You really think so?'

'One hundred per cent.'

'But what about Rana? You thought the school fete idea was a real winner and look what he did to that one.'

'But this is different. This is much bigger; it'll have more impact.'

'And it will require major funding.'

'But you'll make money on it. It's a business idea, not just a promotional one.'

'And there's a whole lot of work I still need to do in terms of figuring out all the details; the logistics, the financials . . .'

'I'm sure you can crack that in a few days.'

'Yes, but . . .'

He raised his brows, exasperated. 'But what?'

'Yogi, it *is* my idea.'

'So?'

'Rana's never going to let it get through.'

He sat back, shrugging. 'No, I don't think he will,' he said.

'I mean, see what happened with the anniversary cake.'

'Yep.'

'He really does hate me.'

'I believe you.'

He reached in his pocket, pulled out a mint and began to unwrap it.

'You're being a lot of help!'

'What do you want me to say?'

I sighed. 'There's no point, I know. Anyway, thanks for coming down; maybe you can use some of the . . .'

'What? Don't tell me you're just going to give up?' He looked at me, incredulous, the mint lying forgotten on the table.

'It *is* a great idea, isn't it?'

'The best.'

'Yogi, you present the idea.'

'You're kidding.'

'I mean it. You present it as an agency idea; maybe then it'll go through.'

'You must be crazy.'

'No; I just want the idea to go through. It doesn't matter who gets the credit.'

'Rubbish!'

'Yogi.'

'I'm not going to do it.'

'You're a bully, you know.'

'Got it from you.'

'Okay, okay, I'll give it a shot. Just don't say I didn't warn you when it doesn't work out.'

'But it will, if you present it directly to Vik.'

Directly to Vik?

'Wouldn't that be really sneaky?' I said.

'No, what Rana did was sneaky. And you know I'm not talking about cakewalks here.' He paused, looking me straight in the eye. 'Look Minal, I don't trust Rana; it's best to keep him out of it.'

'It'll be really difficult to get Vik alone,' I said.

'It's still your best bet.'

'I guess.'

'Anyway, about your presentation,' Yogi said. 'I think you should set up a demonstration of what the website will look like, a dummy site, you know. It'll be a lot more convincing if you can actually show Vik how it will work.'

'I know; but how? I'm not very good with technology.'

'I could put you in touch with our in-house web-design team. Those guys are good.'

'But we can't pay for their time unless the idea gets approved.'

'Don't worry about it. Deepak, the guy who usually does this kind of stuff, is a good friend.'

'Are you sure?'

'Absolutely. And you should also put in some visuals of a few of the cakes you have in mind. If you could line up a chef or two to prepare the cakes, I could set up a photo shoot for next weekend.'

'Won't that be expensive?'

'I said don't worry, didn't I?'

'But . . .'

'You'd have to provide the materials though; the cakes and those fancy decorations you were talking about,' he said.

'That I can do. In fact I've got a couple of toy importers coming in this afternoon, and then I'm meeting up with the pastry chef at the Oberoi and some potential bakers whom we could consider tying up with for delivery.'

'And all this on a Saturday?' he whistled.

'I know. I have no idea how I'll ever make it to that Ram Leela thing on time'

'*Ram Leela?*'

'Hey, don't knock it; it's supposed to be a very refined Ram Leela. Two thousand rupees a ticket and black tie and all.'

'You're kidding!' He sounded appalled. 'Who'd pay that kind of money?

'Apparently everyone; the show's all sold out. Of course it helps that it's an Apollo Hospital fund-raiser.'

'Ahhh. That explains it.'

'Gotta keep the doctors happy.'

'So why do *you* have to go?'

'For Sunil. This is "very important" to him.'

'Sunil?'

'My fiancé. He works at Apollo.'

'Fiancé? I didn't know you were engaged.'

'I thought everyone knew.'

He shook his head. 'I should have guessed from the size of that ring, though.'

'It's really big, isn't it?' I twisted it inwards, hiding the big stone.

'I'd insure my finger if I were you. Anyway, congrats. You must be very excited.'

'Uh huh.'

'When is the wedding?'

'Fifteenth November.'

'That's soon!'

'I know.'

'And then you'll be Mrs . . .?'

'I'll keep my name.'

'I'm glad,' he smiled.

This struck me as an odd thing to say. Before I could ask, the office intercom on the side of the small conference table beeped. I picked it up.

'This is Minal.'

It was the peon.

'Madam, there is a Mr O.P. Kalra waiting to see you. It tried calling your room but . . .'

'I'll be there in a couple of minutes. Send him in.'

Yogi was already at the door as I put the phone down. He pushed it open and followed me out.

'So I guess you'll really have to hurry on this website thing,' he said. 'Before you know it you'll be off on your honeymoon.'

'I know. That's why I'm kind of going crazy right now.'

'Well, I'll get going,' he said. 'I'll try and catch Deepak as soon as I get back to the office, and then I'll give you a call.'

'Great,' I nodded. And thanks for all the help, and for coming by on a Saturday.'

'Any time,' he smiled, and raced down the steps two at a time.

I'd barely reached my chair before there was a loud knock on the door.

'Come in,' I called.

A man who I presumed was Mr Kalra poked his balding head round the door, wiped his patent leather maroon shoes on an imaginary mat, and walked in with a self-effacing stoop and a fawning smile.

'Miss Sharma? Good afternoon, Madam, so nice of you to see me. Beta!' he turned and called out loudly, apparently addressing the empty doorway.

I looked up, confused, just as a highly arresting piece of walking art staggered and swayed its way into the room.

I gaped. Was it a carnival? Was it a toy shop? Was it a *man*?

It was, except that hundreds of toys stuck out all over the

creature, like those balloon and toy vendors of the eighties, cycling down the streets with their colourful wares displayed on elaborate wooden structures that towered above their heads. '*Taaay-wallaaaah, Bell-oooon-wallaaaaaaaah*!' they'd call, in their high-pitched nasal voices and all the kids in Gandhinagar, Meerut, would stop playing and run after them like all the mice of Hamelin.

The toywallah in my office, however, had neither the luxury of the cycle nor the support of the wooden frame. Instead, he carried the gigantic load all on his back; the toys crammed into dozens of plastic bags that billowed out around him like peacock feathers, and were suspended from strings that looked like they were digging sharp trenches into his thin shoulders. And on his face in place of a smile he wore an expression of extreme surliness that was contorted with pain as he grappled with the bulk and the weight.

'Oh, please put that down,' I said and jumped as he instantly let go the entire inventory with one loud crash.

'Shabash, Beta,' Mr Kalra beamed.

Beta straightened up slowly, elaborately, and began to pick pieces of food from between his teeth.

Mr Kalra widened his cheeks to a smile the size of a pizza and turned to me. 'Madam, so nice of you. I know I'm a little early for our meeting, but there were so many items, I couldn't wait to show them to you.'

'Yes, I can see that,' I said, eyeing the mess on the floor. 'Please sit down. You too.'

I smiled at Beta, encouraging him to sit down.

'Oh no, that's all right,' Mr Kalra said quickly. 'He has to get the rest of the stuff. Beta, go and get the other samples from the car. And lock the door carefully.'

'No, really, please don't bother. These are just fine.'

'No, bother at all, Madam. I have new samples in the car that are fresh off the plane. I haven't shown those to anyone yet!'

'But really . . .'

It was no use; Beta was already out the door.

I took the business card Mr Kalra was holding out to me and turned it over. It was one of those thin indestructible plastic ones.

'Heh, heh, Goldie Enterprises, Madam,' Mr Kalra said. 'It's my son's name.'

'Very nice,' I said.

'So, Madam, you had expressed an interest in "small plastic toys" when we talked on the phone?'

'Yes.'

'How small did you mean?'

'An inch high,' I shrugged. 'Two inches at most.'

'Yes, yes!' I was rewarded with another cheek-splitting smile. 'There is a lot of variety available in that range, Madam, especially in action figures and cars.'

'What about things like miniature furniture, ballerinas, sports figures?'

'Anything you want, Madam! We are importing all kinds of toys. If you could give me some idea of what exactly you have in mind?'

I wasn't about to tell him I needed decorations for cakes. 'I was hoping you'd bring a catalogue, actually,' I said, glancing once again at the huge pile on the carpet.

'Catalogue!' he dismissed with a massive expulsion of air through his nostrils. 'Anybody can show you catalogues. But I show you the samples, madam, the actual quality. I swear nobody can get better quality than us. We've been in this line for centuries.'

Centuries?

'I go straight to the manufacturer, Madam, no middlemen. I have a man sitting in China right now; his job is to find the latest ideas and the best quality and the cheapest suppliers. Shabash, Beta.'

I looked up; Beta was back again, staggering in with yet another impossible load. This he dumped in the other corner of the room.

'What kind of lead times do you work on?' I asked, trying hard to ignore the alarm clock that had sprung into action from somewhere inside the pile.

'*Arre, bandh karo, Beta,*' Mr Kalra snapped before turning to me. 'Sorry, Madam. Madam, many items we have in stock already, like dinosaurs and action figures, cars, aeroplanes, dolls. We could supply you five hundred of each this afternoon.'

'And for the others?'

'Four to six weeks, which is twice as fast as any other supplier. Of course custom-ordered items will require a little longer and will be more expensive. But still cheaper and faster than any . . .'

'Than any other supplier, I know.'

'Madam, let me show you some of the latest samples. Action figures, for instance are very popular these days. Beta, take out those GI Joes.'

'What about dinosaurs?' I asked. I'd been toying with the idea of a Jurassic cake. 'Do you have any really small ones?'

Beta dipped expertly into the pile of toys and began slapping Stegos, Brontos, T-Rexes on the table. I picked one up.

'See, we have about twenty different ones, and these are the smallest size,' Mr Kalra explained. 'If you want slightly bigger . . .'

'No, these are fine.' I turned the miniature mammoths over. They were of pretty remarkable quality.

'What about for a beach party. Would you have any toys for that?' I asked.

'We have inch-high umbrellas and deck chairs. We could also do plastic palm trees, beach balls, lifesavers. And we could custom order any other that you want.'

'And you can get anything?'

'Anything. Madam, today anything is possible, you just have to tell us what and how many.'

This was turning out way better than I'd expected. I could just imagine the Jurassic cream park and the Hawaiian luau. I wondered what we'd use for foliage, though. Plastic?

'Is everything you have made of plastic?' I asked.

'It is by far the cheapest material, Madam. But we could source items in any material. Umbrellas could be made of bamboo, straw, fabric, or paper. Paper is also very popular nowadays and very economical too.'

'What price range are we talking about?' I asked.

'Anything between twenty rupees and fifty rupees.'

'What?'

Mr Kalra leaned forward in his seat and flashed his teeth. 'Come, come Madam, what is cost for a big company like yours?'

'The prices you're talking about are completely out of range,' I said.

'But Madam, these are the lowest possible! For other . . .'

'I'm sorry, but it looks like I've wasted your time,' I stood up and held out my hand. 'Thank you for coming by.'

'Of course it is all negotiable,' Mr Kalra said quickly, 'depending on the order quantity and the type of items.'

I crossed my arms and shook my head.

'How about these race cars? Porsche, Corvette, Audi? Look at the detail, the quality. I normally quote twelve rupees per piece for a minimum order of one thousand, but for you I'll quote eight rupees. What do you say?'

It was a good price. He must really want our business.

'That's twice as much as I'm willing to pay,' I said.

He looked stricken.

I regarded him silently.

'Maybe for the initial order I'll just do it at cost; no profit margin, okay?'

'I'm sorry, but given the potentially large quantities we may need, we really need to watch the unit cost,' I said.

I waited for him to grasp my meaning. It took him less than a second.

'Madam,' he said, his face breaking once again into a wide smile, 'I'm sure we can work something out.'

The auto-rickshaw I took later that evening came to a halt at the impossible spot where Ajmal Khan Road meets Gurdwara Road and then both disappear under a deluge of fanatic shoppers and a sisterhood of implacable cows. I got down and began counting out my money amidst a cacophony of horn-blowing and idling engines that enveloped the blocked intersection. The driver spat a stream of red paan juice expertly to his left and swore as a scooter knocked past on the right. I paid my fare and weaved through the maze of vehicles to the narrow pavement across the road.

Karol Bagh at 5 p.m. on Saturday was what I imagined an ant-hill would look like on a busy day. Teeming, scurrying denizens, some skipping, others tripping, many labouring under the weight of the stuff they'd been out gathering. There were those that went round in circles, others that collided and routinely fell over each other, and several who darted and stopped and changed paths every few steps as they wound their way through countless alleys and byways.

My stomach heaved as I made my way down Ajmal Khan Road, reminding me that I hadn't eaten all day. It was a long, narrow walk punctuated every few steps by food smells and salwar shops. Pakoras, Lucknowi kurtas, *chhole bhature,* zardosi embroidery, chaat, clearance sales, samosas, latest bridal fashions. Two girls in matching pink tops and low-rise jeans walked past, sharing a plate of *shakarkandi chaat* and college gossip. I shook my head, remembering, and quickened my pace.

'Hankies, didi? Fifty rupees a dozen,' a vendor said, thrusting a tray of plastic combs under my chin.

'No thanks.'

'Forty-five.'

I shook my head.

'Take them, didi, very good quality.'

'No.'

'Didi, *boni karado!* You are my first customer. Forty rupees, and these safety pins for free.'

'*Boni* at six in the evening?'

I shook my head at him and turned down the next alley.

A few minutes later, I stepped through the narrow doorway of Jindal Bakers, with its customary seven green chillies and lemon that dangled from the roof by a string. A delicious fresh-baked aroma enveloped me as I entered and made me weak in the knees. 'Business first,' I steeled myself, and walked resolutely past the desserts display.

'Yes, ma'am, what can I get you?' the thin young fellow behind the counter asked politely.

'I'd like to speak with the proprietor. Could you please tell him Minal Sharma from International Foods is here? I have a meeting with him.'

He walked over to stand a few deferential feet away from a safari-suit-clad gentleman behind the cash register, who I presumed was Mr Jindal.

I studied this gentleman's profile carefully. It was hard to guess his age, but from the way he was flipping expert fingers through a thick wad of notes and conducting a warm and friendly conversation with a customer at the same time, it looked as though he knew his business well. And had the blessings of his ancestors. A solemn, yellowed portrait of one Hari Prasad Jindal, 1912–1975 stood directly above the cash register. (Not unlike the GGF's portrait on my own wall except while the GGF seemed forever ready to preach, this venerable old gentleman appeared to be double-checking each transaction conducted under his impressive bushy brows.)

In a hollowed space on the wall behind the counter stood a beautifully detailed silver statue of Lakshmi, surrounded by a cloud of smoke from a ring of agarbattis at her feet. I glanced round the store, noting the new wood panelling, the clean marble flooring and the quiet Carrier air-conditioners. Established business, strong customer relationships—just the profile we needed.

Mr Jindal's customer finally waved goodbye. The thin assistant whispered something in his ear, and Mr Jindal smiled across at me. He put the money away safely in the cash register, handed off to a grey-haired assistant and motioned me into a small office at the back of the store.

'Hello, Miss Sharma, please sit down,' he said, settling comfortably back in a high-backed leather chair.

'Thank you.' I sat down, noting the Sachin Tendulkar screen saver on the computer monitor on his desk.

So this was a computerized outfit. That would help.

'I'm a hopeless cricket enthusiast,' he shrugged.

'Who isn't?' I smiled.

'So, Miss Sharma, what can I do for you?'

'I wanted to discuss the possibility of a tie-up for cake distribution between you and IF,' I began tentatively.

I'd heard the Jindals were a very conservative group, and highly suspicious of multinationals. And he could view us as competition after all.

'Tie-up?'

'We're looking at a new product line for cakes, and we're looking for partners to manage the decoration and delivery. And since Jindal Bakers has both the experience and a good name, I wanted to see if there'd be any interest in a partnership at your end.'

'Absolutely not.'

Uh oh.

'No interest whatsoever?'

'Not until you tell me what you'll have to drink, that is. Watermelon juice, chocolate milkshake, almond sherbet? And don't say no.'

I grinned. 'Not have one of your famous milk shakes? You must be kidding. And I'll also have one of those brownies. I've heard they're steeped in sin.'

'You've obviously done your homework,' he said, gesturing to a young boy who stood behind the counter.

'That, plus I love food. Especially desserts.'

This nudged a little smile from him. 'You like brownies?' he asked.

'If they're anywhere near half as good as I've heard yours are . . .'

I stopped as the boy came in with a tall shake and a plate of brownies and set them down on the desk. Talk about service!

Mr Jindal pushed the plate towards me with a smile.

'Miss Sharma, your brownies. And I have a feeling we *can* do business together.'

thirty-two

Lord Ram walked up to the mighty bow, flexed his bony shoulders and heaved with all his might. Silence enveloped the auditorium and then, in one smooth, swift flourish, he pulled taut the invisible string and strung the giant gilded bow. The audience erupted in wholesome applause and the unseen gods above supported the proceedings by raining down on the cast and audience a spectacular display of rose petals.

Off in one corner, Sita simpered and Lakshman smiled cockily from behind Ram's shoulder.

I nudged Sunil.

'Do you think there's something going on between those two?'

'Huh?'

'Sita and Lakshman. Offstage. Doesn't she look like she's giving Laks the come-on; one of those 'How about you buy me a drink later' ones?'

'Really, Minal!'

I picked a few stray rose petals from my hair. 'Anyway, I sure hope our wedding is nothing like this. I'm allergic to rose petals.'

Sunil turned to me, worried. 'Really? That sounds serious; you'd better have it checked out. I'll set up an appointment for you with Dr Bhatnagar first thing tomorrow.'

'Don't be silly! I'm fine. I just meant I hope our wedding is nothing too lavish. The way our engagement party went, I'm really scared.'

'It was just an ordinary function.'

'With two hundred people? My folks couldn't put together more than a hundred for the wedding!'

'Well *I've* got a big network of friends and contacts.'

'But it's our *wedding*. A once-in-a-lifetime, personal kind of thing. Don't you think it should be more *private*?'

'You're such a romantic,' Sunil smiled.

I turned back to the Ram Leela. Sita and Ram were garlanding each other. More rose petals, hugs, fireworks and cheers. They plainly weren't skimping on the production budget.

'Minal, a wedding is a big deal socially,' Sunil said. 'You have to follow tradition; you need to maintain a certain standard. It's always been this way.'

'That's ridiculous. A lot of weddings these days are small and more personal.'

'Anyway, it's just a question of a few days.'

'A few *days*?'

'In fact just three; cocktails, wedding, reception and then it will all be over.'

'You never mentioned a reception before!'

'Don't worry; *my* parents are organizing the reception. They've already booked the Hyatt.'

'At least tell me I don't need to be there for your cocktails!'

He shrugged. 'Normally you wouldn't have to, but it's just that when I mentioned cocktails to Harish, he insisted that he was going to host it. Now that we'll be doing business together and all. So I think you'd better be there.'

Great.

'You know, Minal, I've never met a man with a bigger heart.'

Or a bigger wallet.

How uncharitable, my conscience rebuked.

'So your partnership plans are going well?' I asked.

'Knock on wood. I've spoken to Dr Dubey; he said he'd think about it. I know he'll say yes; he owes me one.'

'It must be good to have friends in high places.'

'Hey, I work hard!'

He was right. I was being churlish.

'I'm sorry. I didn't mean that. I'm really glad things are working out.'

'I know.'

I reached out and took his hand. 'And I'm sorry I couldn't make it for that lunch.'

'I know you are.'

'And?' I prompted, snuggling closer.

'And let's watch the show.'

I sighed and leaned back in my chair. At least the auditorium had comfy seats.

'Minal, are you asleep!?'

I woke with a start and noticed that the curtains were down and the lights were on. And all around me, people were getting up from their seats and heading for the door.

'Is it over yet?' I squinted at my watch.

'No, this is just the first interval.'

Shoot.

'I can't believe you nodded off!'

'It's just been a really long day.' I tried to stifle a yawn.

'I can't understand why you're working so hard.'

'The same reason you work hard.'

'Minal, I'm a surgeon. I work with some very unfortunate people who have a deadly disease. My work saves lives.'

'And my work improves them.'

He laughed. 'Good one.'

'But I wasn't . . ..'

'Care to share the joke?' a female voice asked directly behind us. I turned quickly around. The First Lady of the Oncology Department, Apollo Hospital, was standing in the row of seats behind us, all floating silk and wafting graciousness, a ridiculous red organizer's badge pinned to her silk blouse. Sunil immediately jumped to his feet.

'Mrs Dubey! Looking beautiful as always, ma'am. Can I get you anything?'

'Oh, no, just saw you two lovebirds together and came by to say hello. It's been such a long time since I saw you, Minal!' She leaned over and kissed the air round my cheeks. 'Where have you been?'

'She's been working really hard,' Sunil said.

'Oh, you mustn't work too hard dear; you should leave all that to the men!' Mrs Dubey scolded.

I shuffled my feet feeling like a student pulled into the principal's office for poor attendance.

'You just focus on the wedding and what you're going to wear,' she smiled. 'By the way, didn't you just love Sita's lehnga?'

'Oh, yes. Very nice.'

'The play is excellent. Such a fresh interpretation,' Sunil added.

'Isn't it? The director, Abhiram, is my friend's son. You youngsters! I keep telling Dr Dubey how talented you all are these days! Look at you, so handsome and dashing, and already such a fine doctor.'

'I could never be as good as Doctor Saab, ma'am,' Sunil said. 'Where is he; I hope he's enjoying the performance?'

'Oh, he be must somewhere, chatting with someone.' She waved an arm vaguely in the air. 'You know how it is; you doctors are always so busy. Never any time for your better halves. I hope things work out better in your case, Minal.'

'Actually here they're the reverse,' Sunil said with an elaborate sigh.

'Oh, stop exaggerating,' I said.

The lights began to dim again; people were settling back in their seats.

'Ah, a lover's tiff! How sweet,' Mrs Dubey beamed. 'Well, you two kiss and make up. I'd better be getting back to my seat. Oh, and Minal, you must keep an evening free before the wedding; Doctor Saab and I would like to have you over for dinner.'

'Er, actually I'm...'

'Any time, ma'am; we'd love to come by,' Sunil said.

I scowled at him when she was gone.

'What?' he said. 'You weren't going to refuse, were you? Dr Dubey's the HOD! In any case, once we're married, everyone will want us over for dinner.'

'But how will I ever get any work done?'

'Why don't you quit? You were planning to, anyway.'

'I've changed my mind.'

Sunil was silent as the curtain began its slow ascent again.

'I'm making some real progress with my website idea, Sunil. Yogi thinks it's the idea of a lifetime. Have I told you about Yogi? He's this really . . ..'

'Shhh . . . we'll talk later. They're starting again.'

I slumped back in my chair as the orchestra struck a mournful tune. The lights on stage revealed a deserted, gloomy Ayodhya. Inside a mock palace someone, presumably Dashrath, was wailing.

After an agonizing few minutes Ram and Sita and Lakshman came mincing out of the right wings, ready at last to head out to exile.

And then '*Kambakht ishq*' rang out loudly. Sunil sat with lips thinned as I fumbled in my purse. I grabbed at the phone. It was Yogi.

'Hi, what is it?' I whispered.

'Remember I was telling you about Deepak? I managed to catch him just now, and he's pretty excited about the website; he wants to go through your presentation as soon as possible.'

'That's great!'

'Shhh,' Sunil hissed.

'Yogi, could you hang on a minute?' I ducked my way out of the row of seats and headed for the exit.

'So when does Deepak want to meet?' I asked, once I was in the lobby.

'*Now.* Is that a problem?'

'I'm at that Ram Leela I was telling you about.'

'Oh, right. I forgot. So just tell me where you've kept the presentation and I'll pick it up from your office myself.'

'Actually I brought it home with me.'

'Oh. It's just that Deepak's going to be out most of next week. If he could get some idea of what's required, he could work on it while he's away, maybe even come up with something by the time he's back.'

Ayodhya was still wailing. Even through the thick auditorium doors I could hear the anguished howls.

'I really shouldn't have called you,' Yogi said. 'Don't worry, I'll try to brief him as best as I can.'

'No, wait. Why don't you meet me at my apartment in half an hour and I could give it to you?'

'But your Ram Leela?'

'I'll never make it through the whole thing anyway.'

'Are you sure?'

'Yeah, it's fine. Got a pen? I'll give you directions.'

A few minutes later, I slid quietly back in my seat. 'Sorry about that,' I murmured as I sat down. 'It was Yogi.'

Sunil's profile nodded in the dark.

'Would you mind if we left a little early?' I asked.

'What do you mean?'

'Actually, something's come up. I need to go home.'

'We're in the middle of a play!'

'I know. I tried to avoid it but this guy Deepak's going out of town and I . . .'

'Minal, I know you're not enjoying the show, but this is a fund-raiser.'

'I know. I just need to give Yogi a presentation for this guy Deepak, and then we can come right back. Or better still, we could go straight on to dinner.'

'But there are still another couple of hours to go!'

'I'll even buy you dessert. Two.'

'Don't be childish.'

'Sunil, I wouldn't ask, but it'll actually save time. You know how important it is to . . .'

'You go.'

'Sorry?'

'Why don't you go? You have your car here, don't you?'

'Yes, but . . .'

'Minal, I can't leave; it won't look nice. You go, do what you need to and try and come back in time for dinner. Otherwise I'll see you Thursday.'

'You're kidding, right?'

'Not at all. Listen,' he lowered his voice and leaned closer. 'I think we're disturbing the people behind us. You carry on.'

'But . . .'

'Shhh.' He sat back and tucked his legs under his seat to allow me to go by. 'Go on; I'll call you once the show's over.'

thirty-three

Charred thoughts swept through my head like gusts in a wind tunnel as I pulled out of the theatre parking lot. To drag (Sunil out by his hair) or dismember (him slowly and painfully), that was the question.

How could he just abandon me like that?

I circled the theatre block in a seething orbit, too angry to just drive away. I neared the main gates for the fourth time and the security guard peered closely at my car license plates.

'Lost your way, madam?'

Good question.

'If you go left from that traffic signal, you'll hit Tilak Marg. That will take you to India Gate,' he offered.

'Thanks.'

I rolled up the window and set off on the ten-kilometre drive back home.

Why was I marrying this guy? He was colder than an ice pack.

He's a good man, a virtuous inner voice reassured, *you've just got the wedding jitters.*

Oh yeah? What if I said I hated him?

Why?

What do you mean why? He just sent me off into the cold, dark night alone!

Don't be so melodramatic. It's a lovely night. Just look around!

It was true. A week before Dussehra, and Delhi was aglow. Exhibitions, street fests, melas, parties, weddings; everywhere around me people were celebrating. Some of the buildings had already donned their Diwali decor, as though they couldn't wait to show off their newest jewellery. Ashok Road was a parade of dancing trees, preening and waving in the soft breeze and ablaze with thousands of flickering lights. I almost smiled and waved back. Sunil would have disapproved, no doubt.

Don't you think he should have come along? I reasoned with The Voice.

Not at all. You're a team now. This way you get to do both things: attend the fund-raiser and hand over the presentation.

And what about spending time together?

What's the rest of your life for?

You always have an answer for everything, don't you?

Technically, that was a question.

Was it just me or did everyone have a smartass prick for a conscience?

The overhead light on the second-floor landing was still out. I stood fumbling around in the dark and had just managed to fit the key in the lock when a thunderous crash shook the roof directly above my head and something big and heavy came thumping down the steps. I looked up to see a battered old suitcase take an ominous six-step leap down to the landing and send its contents gushing forth in a colourful fountain of clothes and sundries. A bottle of perfume smashed inches from my foot and immediately set about emanating a frantic, fragrant SOS.

'Freakin' bloody suitcase!' a voice came hurtling down the stairs.

I yanked the door open and jumped inside my apartment. Just in the nick of time—loud footsteps raced down the stairs and stopped right outside my door.

'Damn, damn, *damn*,' the voice swore.

I got down on my knees to peer through the slit under the door.

It was Ali of course; I didn't need the Timberlands to tell me that. They stood planted, despairing, amongst a mess of candy and CDs, books and toys, tees and pyjamas and the lacy pink strap. As I watched, they moved gingerly round the puddle of perfume, then denim-clad knees and a fine pair of hands hit the floor, and half a head swung into view. A left eyeball glared into my right one.

'Are you planning to help or are you just going to watch?' he asked.

I opened the door and stepped outside. I'm sure I could have come up with a logical reason why I'd been hiding behind the door, watching him from under it, but at that moment it sort of eluded me.

'How are you?' I said instead.

'How do you think I am? It's a bloody mess and I'm late. Do you think you could help?'

He crouched down next to the suitcase; I handed him some CDs and books. He kicked at the broken glass; I dusted off the stuffed toys. We worked efficiently for a bit, and it occurred to me that most of our relationship seemed to involve the creating and cleaning up of messes. Two, no three times we'd ended up doing the whole janitor bit, counting that time we'd cleaned his Jeep. Two cups of coffee. Five, no twelve Post-its. One music lesson. Two non-arguments. Four months since we'd first met. Two months and twenty days since we'd last talked. One rainy kiss.

'Minal, are you planning to pass that to me or keep it?'

I handed him the hardback Harry Potter and reached for a gift-wrapped package to my right. A burly GI Joe crouched defensively behind the large slit where the gift-wrap had ripped open. A Barbie peeked out from the slim package next to it.

'I thought you were young, not retarded,' I said, holding out the doll. 'What's with all the toys?'

'That's for my niece. And those are for my nephew.'

'I thought you were an only child?'

'They're my best friend's kids.'

'Really? And this must be your best friend's, no doubt.' I held up the bra.

'Nope. It's mine.' He took it with a fond smile.

'*What?*'

'Don't tell anyone, but it's the last thing I ever shoplifted.'

'I don't want to know.'

'Hey, I told you I was a little wild in college!'

'And you still carry it around?'

'More as a good-luck charm.'

'You couldn't have settled for a horseshoe or a bamboo plant, could you?'

He sat back and laughed out loud.

'I'm glad we ran into each other,' he grinned. 'I've missed you.'

My heart skipped a beat.

'And things have been so crazy lately; I've hardly been around.'

'Yes, I know. I've wanted to come over and . . .'

'Anyway, my site's going live in a week!'

'That's great.'

I sat on the suitcase as he snapped it shut.

'I've been working on a website too,' I said.

'You left IF?' He sounded surprised.

'No, it's going to be a site for our cakes.'

He straightened up slowly, testing the weight of the suitcase. Satisfied, he put it down and turned to me.

'And you're telling me because . . .?'

I took a deep breath.

'I'm sorry about that misunderstanding earlier,' I said. 'I don't think you were the one responsible for the ad.'

'I'm glad,' he said. 'And I'm sorry I behaved like a jerk. About that guy. You know?' He punched my arm lightly.

I punched his back. 'I know,' I said.

'Now we can be friends,' he grinned. 'I've missed that.'

Was that all he'd missed?

'So, is that an engagement ring?'

'Yes.'

'Congrats. I'm glad things worked out for you.'

I looked at him, searching his face.

'Don't worry,' he smiled. 'I've moved past it too.'

Moved past it? He wasn't *supposed* to move past it! He was supposed to be languishing in my love, losing weight, growing dark circles and a scraggly beard!

'So who's the lucky guy—that doctor?' he asked.

I nodded.

'When's the wedding?'

'The fifteenth of next month.'

'That's soon!'

'Listen, I wanted to invite you . . .'

'I'd come, but I'm not sure I'll be here.'

'Oh.'

'Well, I'd better get going,' he said and held out his hand. 'Thanks for all your help.'

I followed him down the steps.

'Where are you going?' I asked.

'Bombay.'

'Work?'

'Sort of.'

'What do you mean?'

'It's a secret.'

'Here we go again.'

'No, it's not that.'

He put the suitcase down and hesitated.

'Promise not to tell anyone?'

'Sure.'

'Promise.'

'Cross my heart.'

'Okay.' He took a deep breath. 'There's this MTV VJ contest in Bombay, and I'm one of the finalists!'

'*What?*'

He nodded, his eyes shining.

'Ali!' I slapped his arm.

'What?'

'You mean, you're *serious?*'

'Of course.'

My lips began to twitch.

'Right. Go ahead and laugh.'

'I'm not laughing; it's just . . . did you say *MTV*?'

'You think it's ridiculous?'

'No.' *Yes!* 'But what about your website?'

'They'll find someone to run it,' he shrugged. 'Setting it up was fun, but now . . .' he made a face. 'Anyway, this is a once-in-a-lifetime opportunity, you know.'

'But isn't this MTV VJ thing just for, you know, teenagers?'

'Yeah, the cut-off age is twenty-six; but I'm hoping my experience will work to my advantage. Do you think I'm too old?'

'I don't think you're too *old*.'

'You really think so?'

I stepped back and took a long, hard look. Handsome young face, loose denim shirt, ragged brown jeans. Open Timberlands that shifted uncomfortably under my scrutiny. Eyes that were bright with hope and excitement and dreams and earnestness. And for the first time, it felt like I was really seeing him.

'I really think so,' I said and kissed him lightly on the lips. 'You're great MTV material; you're gonna knock 'em dead.'

'Minal?'

'C'mon, let's hurry; you don't want to miss your flight, do you?'

'No, I don't.'

'Well, then let's go!'

I walked him to a waiting taxi and waved him bye.

'Break a leg!' I yelled as it revved up and zoomed off. 'And don't forget to send me an autograph!'

I waved till the taxi rounded the corner and disappeared, and then walked slowly back up the steps. He *was* just a kid after all.

My phone rang lustily inside my purse as I pushed open the door.

'Yogi?'

'Minal! Thank God. Listen, I'm stuck somewhere near Sarojini Nagar Market. The damn car refuses to move; I think I may have run out of petrol. Do you think you could come get me?'

'Yo-*gi*!'

'I thought I'd filled the tank last month . . .'

I sighed.

'I'm on my way,' I said and picked up my car keys.

Guys, I thought wearily, as I reversed out of my spot.

See? Aren't you glad Sunil's so mature? the conscience cheeped up. *Now* he'd *never run out of* . . .

'. . . gas?' I snapped. 'I don't believe he would.'

thirty-four

'Is it your birthday?' the receptionist asked Monday afternoon when I got back from lunch.

'No, why?'

She handed me a bouquet and card.

'This came for you while you were away.'

I couldn't believe it. *Flowers? Card?*

I looked at the note stapled to one side of the cellophane. It was one of those 'Best wishes' floral things, with 'I LOVE YOU, SUNIL' printed neatly below.

'It's from my fiancé,' I said.

'Oh, how romantic!'

I slit the envelope open.

Dear Minal,

Printed flowers

Miles of printed flowery language

Sunil

Hallmark logo.

'You're so lucky,' the receptionist said.

Signed. As in literally; as in chequebook or credit card signature. Or medical prescription.

'I wish I were getting married!' she gushed.

'Wanna trade?'

She looked oddly at me as I started up the steps.

I didn't blame her; I'd look oddly at me too if I were her. Or better still, I'd sock me one in the head. He had sent me flowers and a card and all I could bubble over with was sarcasm. He *was* the man I'd agreed to marry, wasn't he? And I wanted him to be the man I'd wanted to be with; not the man I wanted him to be.

Say what?

I stopped outside my room, trying to figure that last bit out.

You really need to spend less time talking to yourself, Minal, the old inner voice sighed.

I pushed the door open and stood rooted to the spot. Rana lounged in the visitor's chair, flipping with interest through the papers on my desk.

'What are you doing here?' I said.

'And a very good afternoon to you too, Minal,' he drawled.

I snatched the papers away from him and shoved them in the drawer.

'What do you want?'

'I have a meeting with the branch manager,' he shrugged. 'Thought I'd come by and see how the other half lived. Quite a tacky room, this.'

I sat down and turned on my computer, ignoring him.

He picked up the bouquet of flowers and smelled them. 'Aaah, roses. Are these for me?'

'Go away; I'm busy.'

'I can see that. Flowers, cards, long lunches. No wonder no work ever gets done at the branch office.'

1, 2, 3, 4 . . . .

'I heard you got engaged. It's that fat boy from Meerut, isn't it?'

5, 6, 7, 8 . . .

'Well, congrats.'

'Thanks. Was that all?'

He looked at me for a few moments. 'You're living dangerously,' he said.

How much did he know? How long had he been here? He hadn't seen the Creative Cakeworks presentation in the bottom right drawer, had he?

'What do you mean?' I asked.

'You went ahead with that school activity behind my back.'

'Oh, the school activity. It was too late to cancel,' I said, relieved.

'I don't care. I'm the one who calls the shots on cakes now.'

'If you say so.'

'I mean it. Any more fetes and you'll be in serious trouble.'

'Maybe you didn't hear. Max has already given the go-ahead for the rest of the year.'

'You think you're so cute, don't you, sucking up to Max? Maybe someone forgot to tell you that all remaining budgets have been frozen.'

'Oh?'

'Yep.' He smiled nastily. 'No spending till Vik gets back. They decided that today. You'll get the memo soon; your pal Radha's typing it up.'

Vik was going somewhere? When would he be back? What about the website?

'And after that I'll make damn sure all school fetes are out.'

'What? Oh, right. Fetes are out.'

The branch manager's secretary appeared in the doorway. 'Mr Bhatia?' she said. 'The manager will see you now.'

'This isn't over,' Rana said as he got up. 'I know you're up to something. Well, it won't work. You don't outsmart me and get away with it, just remember that.'

'Bye Rana.'

I called Radha as soon as the door swung shut behind him.

'Hi Radha, it's Minal.'

'Hi sweetie, long time no hear. How are you?'

'Not bad. Listen, is Vik going somewhere?'

'Yes, he has a conference in the US next week and then he's off on vacation.'

'For how long?'

'About three weeks.'

No! 'When's he leaving?'

'Friday evening. Why?'

'I needed to meet him,' I said. 'When is he back?'

'Twelfth November. Er, Minal, I'm getting another call. I'll call you back, okay?'

Twelfth November. I'd be in Switzerland, signing 'Thank you' cards for wedding presents. I slumped back in my chair and held my head. There had to be a way.

I called up Yogi. 'How's the presentation coming along?' I asked.

'Not bad. Deepak wanted to know if you're free Friday. He may have something to show you then.'

'I need to present to Vik on Friday.'

'What? That's impossible! We haven't even shot the pictures yet.'

'Yogi, Vik's leaving for the US on Friday night. He'll be out for nearly four whole weeks, and then I'll be out for the next three.'

'Where are you going?'

'I'm getting married, remember?'

'Oh. Right. Well, you'll just have to postpone the wedding.'

Could I?

'Hey, just kidding,' he said. 'I guess the site will just have to wait till you're back.'

'No, Vik's already announced a budget freeze. He'll probably review and allocate the remainder of the year's budget to the most important activities when he's back. I have to make sure Creative Cakeworks is one of them.'

'Creative *Cake*works?' Rana asked behind my shoulder.

I almost dropped the receiver.

'Er, Yogi, hang on a minute,' I said.

'You're talking to Yogi from the *agency*?'

'What do you want now, Rana?'

He picked up a briefcase from the side of the table. 'Forgot this in here,' he said.

I waited for him to leave. He stayed put.

'I'm on the phone,' I prompted.

'I know. What are you and Yogi talking about?'

'None of your business.'

'I love it when you say that.'

He pulled out a chair and sat down.

I turned back to the phone. 'Yogi . . .' I began wearily.

'I heard. Listen, don't worry. I'll try and do what I can. Let me speak to Deepak and I'll call you back.'

I put the phone down.

'What's Creative Cakeworks?' Rana asked.

The phone rang again.

'Hello?'

'Minal, Radha here. You wanted to meet Vik?'

'Yes.'

'The week he's back?'

'No, on Friday.'

Rana was sitting still, eyes fixed, ears twitching. I wondered if he could recognize the voice at the other end. I squeezed the headphone into my temples.

'He's very busy on Friday,' Radha said. 'You could meet him tomorrow.'

'I won't be ready tomorrow.'

'What's the meeting about?' she asked.

I shot a look at Rana. He was leaning so far ahead that he seemed to be in real danger of falling off his chair and into the phone receiver.

'I'll call you back,' I said to Radha and put the phone down.

I remembered to call Sunil before I went to bed.

'Thanks for the flowers,' I said.

'You liked them? I ordered them from the Hyatt flower shop. They're supposed to have the best roses.'

'They were very nice. And the card too.'

'Good.'

'So how was your day?'

'Not bad. I met the Home Secretary's son today; he'd come by to visit one of my patients. Decent fellow.'

'That's nice.'

'Yes, I mentioned the clinic to him; he was very encouraging. Asked me to get in touch if I needed anything.'

'That's nice.'

'And how was your day?'

'The usual.'

'I'll take that to mean really busy. I hope you remember that lehnga fitting tomorrow? I can take you there at lunchtime if you want.'

'Thanks. I'll manage.'

'Are you sure?'

'I'm sure. In any case, it's out of your way.'

'That's not a problem.'

'No, I'll be fine, really.'

'Well, okay then.'

'Okay. Goodnight.'

'Goodnight.'

thirty-five

Thursday evening I hurried into the noisy, crowded bar and looked around for Yogi and Deepak.

'It'll be a half-hour wait, ma'am,' the guy at the reception said. 'Could I have your name?'

'I'm looking for my friends,' I said. 'They might be here.'

'You're Minal, right?' he asked, looking me up and down with interest.

I turned to him, astonished.

'Yogi's told me about you.'

???

'They're over there,' he said, pointing to the smoking section in the far left side of the bar. 'The last booth to your left.'

I almost didn't recognize the guy who sat in jeans, flannel shirt and rolled-up sleeves, doubled up with laughter over something the guy opposite him was saying.

They both hastily stubbed out their cigarettes as I approached. 'Minal, meet Deepak,' Yogi said, getting to his feet.

Deepak looked a lot younger than I'd expected.

'How do you do?' I said politely, as I shook hands. *I hope you've done a decent job.*

'Shall we sit down or would you like to move to the non-smoking?' Yogi asked.

'This is fine,' I shrugged and sank down on the leather upholstery next to him. 'I like booths. I didn't know you smoked.'

'Just once in a while,' he grimaced, turning bright red.

'Like when he's nervous,' Deepak said.

Yogi made a face. 'Don't mind him, he tends to talk a lot,' he said. 'I ordered for you. Hope beer's okay?'

'Beer rocks,' I declared firmly. 'You will not believe the day I've had.'

'Join the club,' Deepak grinned.

A server staggered up with a tray the size of America. He slapped down coasters and then six fat drinks, two big bowls of peanuts and one basket of mirchi chips.

'Are we expecting company?' I asked.

'Thursday evening specials,' Yogi said. 'You get two of everything and unlimited munchies.'

'And 10 per cent off if you're a regular,' Deepak added with a wink. 'Cheers!'

We lifted our mugs. I took a long, thirsty swig.

'Do you guys spend a lot of time here?' I asked.

'You could call it a second home,' Deepak smiled. 'Actually, more like Yogi's first home.'

Yogi kicked him under the table. 'Shut up, Deeps; you'll have her thinking we're a couple of drunken bozos!'

'Oh, no, do tell,' I encouraged. This was turning out to be fun.

'Did he ever tell you what he was called in college?' Deepak began.

'Why don't we show Minal what we've got?' Yogi interrupted.

'Spoilsport,' Deepak winked, but he pushed his mug aside and pulled out a laptop.

Well, this was it, no point delaying the moment any further. My heart beat faster as I watched him start the programme. *Hope it's good, hope it's good, hope it's good,* I prayed.

It wasn't good; it was mind-blowing.

Through some sleight of digital technology and Pentium-powered creative genius, my sketchy PowerPoint presentation had been lifted to motion picture tautness and clarity, and the dummy website that followed was fiendishly perfect.

'Go ahead, try it,' Deepak urged as I stared at the home page.

I pulled the laptop towards me and roamed around the home page. Everywhere the mouse passed, little dialogue boxes opened up with menus and options. Two clicks and I had created a 'Sea World' out of Original Cake, complete with whales and dolphins and even sea horses; ten clicks and I'd put together a whole musical orchestra atop the golden yellow sponge. I browsed and clicked and exclaimed as one delectable cake after another came to life before my eyes.

'What do you think?' Yogi asked.

'It's fantastic!'

'See?' Deepak grinned. 'Yogi's been having hives thinking you'd hate it.'

'What's not to like?'

I turned to Yogi, puzzled.

'Well, I'm not totally satisfied with the way some of the ornaments have turned out, and I think the graphics could be brighter. Also . . .'

'Whoa, back up, man; whose side are you on?' Deepak said.

'Sorry.' Yogi pretended to zip his lips and sat back with a wounded expression.

I started to laugh.

'Anyway,' Deepak continued, 'there *are* a few small changes that I want to make, but nothing fundamental. In fact, I can have it sent around first thing tomorrow. Is that okay?'

I nodded.

'When's the presentation, Minal?' Yogi asked.

'Soon, I hope.'

'You haven't set it up yet? I thought Vik was leaving tomorrow night?'

'Don't remind me. I've been calling Radha every hour, but she just hasn't been able to confirm a time. Apparently he doesn't have a moment free.'

'So what are you going to do?'

'I'm counting on Radha to slip me in. She won't let me down.'

'I hope so,' Yogi said. 'Or we can just say goodbye to the whole thing till next year.'

'If that.'

Deepak looked confused. 'What do you mean?'

'It's a pretty tricky situation,' I said. 'If we don't get it through now, chances are we never will. As it is Rana's been asking all kinds of questions.'

'Isn't that a good thing? I thought Rana was the brand manager.'

I looked at Yogi, who shook his head slightly.

'It's just that I'd like to keep it a surprise,' I said. 'It'll have more impact that way.'

Deepak looked doubtful. 'If you say so,' he shrugged and reached for some peanuts.

'You think it isn't appropriate? Does it seem slimy?' I asked.

'Not at all,' Yogi said quickly. 'You're just presenting an idea with maximum impact. It's not like you've already implemented it or spent any money.'

'But I *have* spent money.'

'Says who? We're not billing you unless the idea gets approved, and then I don't think anyone will care.'

'But what if it doesn't get approved? Who's going to pay for all the work you've done?'

'Whoever buys it,' Yogi shrugged. 'At the agency if an idea's good, we try and develop it to its full potential. Then we worry about who pays. If IF doesn't buy the idea, we'll take it to GI.'

I stared at him aghast.

Deepak took one look at my face and burst out laughing. 'Don't worry, he's just pulling your leg,' he said.

Yogi grinned. 'Gotcha,' he said softly.

I breathed.

'If you ever pull a stunt like that again . . .' I began.

'I know, I know. You'll kill me. Here, have another beer.'

He pushed the mug towards me.

'You should have seen your face, though,' he grinned.

I smiled and reached for some mirchi chips. 'You guys are the best,' I said.

I raised my mug. 'To the best agency in the whole world.'

'To friends,' Yogi said.

'To real friends,' I corrected.

'Ugh, this is getting too senti for me,' Deepak complained. He picked up his mug. 'Bottoms up, anyone?'

Yogi instantly reached for a fresh beer. I eyed the tall mug; my brain was already beginning to cloud over. Yogi raised his brows as I hesitated.

'What the heck,' I figured and raised the mug to my lips.

thirty-six

'Radha, any news?'

I knew this bordered on harassment, but these were frantic times.

'Minal! You just called ten minutes ago!'

'I know, I'm sorry. Got anything yet?'

'I'm sorry, Minal; Vik's really busy. In fact he's running a bit late, and the big boss just called him in for another meeting. Are you sure you can't wait till he gets back?'

'Radha, you promised!'

'Okay, okay, just checking.'

'Why don't you just bump off one of his meetings?'

'You'll get me fired one of these days. I just know it,' she groaned.

'Half an hour, that's all I ask.'

'I know, I know. Just hang in there. I'll try and catch him as soon as he's done with the boss.'

I looked at the clock on my desk. 1.40 p.m. Less than four hours to go before Vik left for the US and still no sign of any meeting. I couldn't handle this much longer; I'd just have to shoot myself at sundown.

I shoved the clock into the drawer and ran through my presentation again.

Perhaps we should have used a darker blue for the background? Or maybe yellow?

I pulled the clock out. 1.42 p.m.

Concept, USP, market size, estimation, financials . . . Damn. There was a typo on slide twenty. Thirteen thousand instead of 1.3 lakhs. Bad, bad luck. I called Deepak.

'Deepak? It's Minal. We're in deep trouble.'

'What happened?'

'The profit estimation slide. Slide 20. There's a typo, line five, column two.'

'1.3 lakhs? Isn't that the correct figure?'

'Oh. Right, it *is* 1.3 lakhs. I don't know, for a minute it looked like thirteen thousand.'

'That's okay. Was there anything else?'

'Well, I *was* wondering about the background colour. Don't you think yellow would stand out better?'

'No. Light blue is good.'

'What about some shadow to the font? A little bit of shadow might make it more dynamic, don't you think?'

'It won't make the slightest difference.'

'I guess you're right.'

'Minal, relax. We've been through the presentation with a microscope. It's fine.'

'Yes, but . . .'

'Besides your idea's sure to go through anyway.'

'How do you know that?'

'Well, I know you wanted it to be a surprise, but Rana had stopped by the office last night when I was making the final changes.'

'*What?!*'

'Well, he did seem to know about the website already; in fact he walked right up to me and asked for the Creative Cakeworks presentation.'

'You didn't give it to him, did you?'

'Sure. And he was really excited about it. Anyway, don't worry, he won't tell Vik anything; I told him you wanted it to be a surprise.'

Rana had my presentation.

'I didn't do anything wrong, did I? I mean you both are from the same company and all. Right?'

Rana had my presentation.

'Minal? You there?'

I dialled Radha with trembling fingers.

'Radha?'

'Sorry, sweetie, he's still with the boss.'

'No, it's not that. Just . . . do you know if Rana's had a meeting with Vik today?'

'Rana? I haven't seen him all day. Why?'

'Oh, nothing special.'

'I'll call you as soon as I have something, okay?'

'Okay.'

What was Rana doing with my goddamn presentation?

There was a light tap on the door. I jumped.

'Surprise!' Sunil called.

'Sunil, hi!' I made a superhuman effort and smiled.

'Guess what?' he said.

You shot Rana?

'What?'

'Today I performed the most challenging surgery of my career! And it was successful! I saved his life; I mean it was almost a miracle! The patient had checked in last week; he was really critical, a matter of days, in fact. And then he had a seizure and I got called in early this morning to operate, and we tried this new procedure, and *I pulled him through*!'

I got up and hugged Sunil close. Someone had pulled through.

Someone would live. Someone was getting better. Screw Rana, there were bigger, better things in the world. And my fiancé was one of them.

'I knew you'd be thrilled,' he chuckled. 'I couldn't wait to tell you. Can you believe it? *I* saved him. Single-handedly!'

'Congrats.'

'Dr Dubey was out of town, but even he called up to congratulate me.'

'Wow.'

'Come on,' he said, pulling me out of my chair. 'Let's go out and celebrate.'

'Huh?'

'Anywhere you like. The sky's the limit. I have the whole day free!'

'Sunil, it's a working day for me. And there's this really critical . . .'

'I know, I know,' he sighed. 'Let's just do lunch then. I'll drop you back, and then you can carry on with your work.'

My stomach growled as I hesitated. Lunch wouldn't hurt, would it?

'Just give me a minute,' I said and headed for the ladies' room.

The wall clock in the loo showed 2 p.m. Radha *still* hadn't called. Maybe I should call her one last time. Or maybe not; she had my cell number anyway. We could make it a really quick lunch too.

Sunil was waiting by my desk when I got back. 'Are you ready?' he smiled, handing me my purse. 'Where shall we go?'

'How about that new coffee shop next door?' I said. 'Everyone's been raving about the pasta.'

And the quick service.

Lunch was lovely. It took one hour and eight minutes, end to end. The restaurant was elegant, the pasta al dente, the salad crisp, the fruit fresh, the coffee strong, the music easy. Sunil was charming. We could have shaved off the last twenty minutes, but he insisted on ice cream. Hot chocolate fudge, with extra cherries, extra fudge and extra nuts. It was wonderful. It almost took my mind off the fact that the clock was ticking and somewhere out there Rana was running loose with my presentation. It was excruciating.

My watch showed 3.05 p.m. as he finally signed the bill. 'Could you drop me off at the head office?' I smiled, getting up. I'd make sure I saw Vik today, even if I had to barge into his room and fall at his feet.

Ten minutes later, I was hurrying up the steps of the head office. I raced past reception and nearly collided with Radha.

'Minal? Where have you been? I called and called . . .'

'But I didn't . . ..'

'And I just kept getting your voice mail. I thought you'd be with Vik.'

'But I just got here.'

'Well, you're late. I told Vik you'd be here at three.'

'But . . .'

'You'd better hurry; you only have until 3.30 you know. He's in the fourth-floor conference room.'

I tore down the corridor, pushed the conference room door open and immediately turned to stone.

Vik was there all right.

So was Rana.

And a laptop and projector that stood poised dramatically at one end of the table.

A presentation seemed to be in progress.

I was too late. It was all over.

At least he hadn't taken my idea to GI.

'So you think it won't work?' Vik was asking.

'I don't think there will be too many takers,' Rana was saying.

'I think it's a refreshing idea.'

'We could spend the money in better ways.'

'May be I should ask a few people around the office?'

'You could, but I don't think they'd be willing to cough up the money.'

'They would, they would!' I yelled and charged into the room. Two sets of dark heads whipped round to look at me.

'You're not even giving the idea a chance,' I said. 'It could be wonderful. We could be writing history, starting a new era. All I'm asking is that we give it a shot before we toss it out the window!'

Vik looked overwhelmed. 'I didn't think you'd feel so passionately about it,' he said.

'Oh, but I do, in fact I'm willing to . . ..'

'Er, Minal,' Rana interrupted, 'we were discussing plans for the office party.'

'Huh?'

'Vik thinks that if everyone contributed part of the cost, we could convert the regular party into a Christmas weekend out of town.'

'Oh,' I said. 'Well, that's a good idea too.'

'Anyway, now that you're both here, can we start the meeting?' Vik said. 'It had better be good, Minal, considering you've made me wait for nearly half an hour.'

They hadn't started?

'Don't worry, it's great,' Rana said. 'Minal, why don't you start at the beginning? I've cued the presentation to the first slide.'

I walked in a daze to the laptop and pushed the Enter button. The first slide of my presentation shot across the carpet and onto the huge white screen behind me.

Project: Creative Cakeworks

Concept: An interactive website where customers can create and decorate cakes of their own choice (using Original Cake) and place an order for delivery

'Creative Cakeworks?' Vik said, furrowing his brows and I felt a smile slide up my spine. They hadn't started.

'Let me explain,' I said, and picked up the pointer.

Half an hour later I sat alone in the conference room, numb and shaking. My head was still ringing with the sound of Vik's voice.

'But this is fantastic!' he had said.

'When can we start?'

'Forget test market, let's roll it out pan-India.'

'Have you briefed the agency?'

'Minal, this is BIG.'

'Rana, what's your budget for the December five rupees off promotion—three million? Just pull that promo and we'll put the money behind Minal's website instead.'

Minal's website.

'Minal, can you set up meetings with all the potential franchisees the moment I'm back?'

'And we should contact Disney for a tie-up for decorations.'

'And Sony, too.'

'Guys, I don't care how you do it; I want the site up before Christmas.'

'God guys; this is HUGE!'

Vik had been amazing, of course, but it was Rana who had knocked me dead.

He had *liked* my idea. *He* had liked *my* idea! He hadn't presented it to Vik, he had waited for me. He hadn't tried to hog the credit;

he was even going to put his precious brand budget behind it.

I confronted him as soon as he came back from the bogs.

'You stole my presentation.'

'I got a copy from Deepak. That's not stealing.'

'You weren't supposed to know.'

'It's an idea for cakes! You should have told me.'

'I thought you'd sell it to GI.'

'What? Are you crazy?'

'But I'd heard . . .'

'What had you heard?'

'Nothing,' I shrugged. 'So now you're going to put your brand budget behind my website?'

'It had better work, or I swear I'll shake you down for every single paisa,' he glared and started collecting his papers. 'And nothing's going to happen if you just keep sitting there,' he added. 'Why don't you meet me in my room in five minutes? We need to run through the details and establish a flow chart and timelines and all. And you'd better hurry; I'd like to show Vik something before he leaves.'

I stuck my tongue out at him. 'I don't work for you, remember?'

'Thank goodness!' he said, and stormed out of the room.

I found myself laughing as the door banged shut. I hated him, and he hated me, but he hadn't stolen my idea. Or sold it to GI. It wasn't him. It had never been him.

But then who'd done it?

Let it go. It doesn't matter, said the serene, enlightened inner voice, and for once I agreed. Maybe it *had* been some management trainee's idea. Stranger things had been known to happen. After all, hadn't Vik and Rana approved my idea?

thirty-seven

Diwali, like everything else, came easy and elegant and early to Sunil's home. Two weeks to go, and the decorations were already up; clean, simple rows of translucent white lights that glowed on the roof, designer diyas that lined the brick-paved path, a perfect rangoli that brightened the front door.

I ran up the path, narrowly avoiding the rangoli and leaned on the doorbell.

Bahadur opened the door. 'Bhabhiji!' he exclaimed. 'Namaste, namaste. I'll tell Doctor Saab you're here; he's sleeping.'

I followed him into the baithak, amused, as he scurried about cleaning up. 'Sorry about the mess, bhabhiji,' he said, clearing a space for me on the wicker chair.

'You've made an early start on Diwali,' I said.

'What to do; Doctor Saab's patients!' he said. 'The bell keeps ringing, the gifts keep coming. I haven't even had time to put them away.'

I poked around the stuff as I waited for him to wake Sunil up. Fruit baskets, Eagle flasks, casseroles, tea set, dinner set, crystal, chocolate gift-packs, silver trays, dozens of gift hampers and enough shiny boxes of dry fruits and sweets to start a shop.

What did he do with it all?

Sunil padded into the room, bleary-eyed and stifling a yawn. 'Minal! I thought you'd be coming over tomorrow.'

I grabbed his hands. 'Yes, but guess what, Vik approved my idea!'

'What idea?'

'The one I've been working on all this while! My website idea.'

'Oh.' He scratched his jaw, pushed aside some boxes and sat down on the sofa. 'Well, that's good, isn't it?'

'Good? It's wonderful. Now I know exactly how you felt after saving that poor man's life.'

'Really?' he smiled. 'Who's life did *you* save?'

'My own.'

'Well, that's something.'

'Believe me, there were some pretty tense moments there.'

'I'm glad it worked out.'

'It almost didn't. In fact, everything seemed to be going wrong. First Rana got hold of my presentation, and then Radha couldn't get through to me and the meeting started and we were out for lunch and . . .'

I noticed he was staring into nothingness.

'Doesn't this mean anything to you?' I asked.

'Of course it does!' He sat up and rubbed his eyes. 'I'm very happy for you. It's just that I've been up since 2 a.m.'

Of course. He was exhausted.

'I know. We'll talk later.' I patted his hand.

'No, I'm awake now,' he said. 'So what does this mean for you? Are you getting a raise, a promotion?'

I shrugged. 'Not for now.'

'I see. But you still won't be quitting your job?'

'When things are finally looking up? Not in a million years.'

His lips twisted in a semblance of a smile. 'Well, at least you'll have more time, now that the pressure is off.'

I cleared my throat. 'Actually, they're keen on implementing the site right away,' I said.

'What do you mean?'

'Vik wants it to be ready before Christmas.'

'That sounds ambitious! Who'll be working on it—Rana?'

'Of course not—me.'

'But you're getting married!'

'I know. That's what I wanted to talk about.'

He raised his brows.

'I was wondering . . . could we postpone the wedding? Just till January?'

'Very funny.'

'I know it's a little late and it'll mean some reorganizing, but it *is* possible, isn't it?'

'Oh sure. We've only just sent out a thousand invites, and booked the venues and the caterers and the Switzerland tickets and the . . .'

'It means a lot to me,' I said quietly.

'And getting married doesn't?'

'I'm just asking for two months.'

'And then it'll be two more and then another six and . . .'

'You know that's not true.'

'Minal, do you or don't you want to marry me?'

'Of course I do.'

'Well, then why are we having this conversation?'

'I'm just trying . . .'

I stopped mid-sentence as the faint digitized strains of '*Kambakht ishq*' tickled my ears. I groped around in my purse, and then remembered my cellphone was missing. This was strange; the music seemed to be coming from inside Sunil's home. And I thought he disapproved . . .?

The ring tone became louder and louder and burst into the drawing room. Bahadur thrust the phone in Sunil's hands. 'Doctor Saab, you left this in your room,' he said.

Sunil switched off the phone and tossed it aside.

He had my phone?

I snatched it away. Four missed calls. From Radha.

'Why do you have *my* phone?' I asked.

'Oh, it's your phone. I was wondering; it did look familiar.'

'Familiar? You've seen it a thousand times!'

'I found it in the restaurant,' he shrugged. 'It must have fallen out of your purse or something.'

'Why didn't you give it back to me?'

'Probably slipped my mind. Anyway, no big deal, at least it's not lost.'

'*It slipped your mind*?'

'Well okay, I may have taken it. Just for a little while.'

I stared at him.

'You *may* have taken it? I missed some really important calls!'

'Minal, you're always on the phone. At Harish's, at the theatre, at the restaurant, everywhere. Always distracted, always working. I can't stand it.'

'So you took my phone?'

'I work too you know. And I'm a doctor!'

'So you took my phone?'

'I just wanted us to have one quiet meal together.'

'So you took my phone!?'

'Yes, I goddamn took your phone,' he snapped. 'It's not the end of the world, is it?'

I stared at him, taken aback. Somewhere outside, someone was ringing the doorbell.

'I work too you know,' he said, getting up. 'And I'm a *doctor*, not some salesgirl pretending the world depends on me.'

'*Salesgirl*?'

The doorbell rang again.

'Minal, you're my fiancée,' Sunil said. 'The future Mrs Sunil Pande. We're supposed to be getting married, setting up home together. You're supposed to make time for me damn it!'

'Oh yeah? Well, not anymore.'

I tugged at my ring.

'Oh, for God's sake . . ..'

'Doctor Saab?' Bahadur was clearing his throat in the doorway. 'Saab, there's someone to see you.'

'Show them in,' he snapped.

'I'll be right back,' he said, turning to me. 'We can sort this out.'

'Go to hell.'

The damn ring was stuck. I pulled and pulled. *I* was supposed to make time for him; like he was some God and I was his slave. I glared at all the Diwali gifts around me. Him and his fawning patients and his super-sized ego. I bet he kept all the gifts too, he would. The Eagle flasks, the casseroles, the kaju kishmish, even the freakin' Gourmet International hamper. Who'd sent him that crap anyway?

I walked over and peered at the business card attached to it.

Dear Sunil,

Thanks for all your help.

Happy Diwali.

Dhruv Dubey.

Marketing Assistant, Gourmet International

Marketing Assistant?

'Thanks for all your help?'

'It was some management trainee's idea.'

'Dr Dubey owes me one.'

'What are these drawings?'

'We call these layouts; they're skeletal ads, sort of like those skeletons you medics keep around at home.'

Dhruv Dubey.

The skeleton in his cupboard.

Finally, the ring came off. I looked at the brilliant, harsh diamond for a second, and then walked over to the bathroom and flushed it down the toilet.

thirty-eight

December 22. I raced up the circular, sweeping steps to the Hyatt ballroom and was instantly sucked up into the light and revelry that blazed within. A huge cloud of red and gold confetti sprung up and showered down around my ears as I entered, and a flushed management trainee beamed 'Merry Christmas!' and thrust a tiny box of chocolates in my hands. I looked down at the signature gold box and whistled; it was imported. So Vik hadn't skimped after all.

I pressed through the throng, searching. They hadn't been kidding when they said they had a theme this year; there was red and gold everywhere: shooting down the walls, racing up the doorways, twisting round and round the branches of the huge Christmas tree, adorning the hundreds of people gathered within. Or perhaps thousands; they were all over—clustered like grapes round the bar, scattered like apples round the tables, packed and shimmering like confetti on the dance floor. Everywhere I looked, people in red and gold, and faces, familiar, smiling faces, and more that streamed in behind me.

I looked around, wondering if he was here already, and saw Jaggu bearing down on me.

'Minal, there you are. Quite some party, huh?'

I eyed his red cummerbund.

'I'll say. You're in fancy dress?'

'Why not,' he shrugged, and I marvelled at this new, wilder side. 'I notice you didn't go to any great lengths?' he said.

'I rushed here straight from the office.'

'Working hard, that's good. So when are you rolling it out to Bombay?'

'It's Bombay, Pune, Bangalore, Hyderabad, Chennai, Calcutta, and Ahmedabad now. Vik wants them all up by end Jan.'

'Well done!'

'I'm not so sure. I haven't slept in weeks; I don't know if I'll make it through alive.'

'You'll be fine.' He turned to observe Sam pushing his way towards us. 'Didn't I tell you she'd go far, Sam? People who work with me always do.'

Sam plucked a couple of flutes from an orbiting waiter and trotted over.

'Minal, great to see you! Here you are.' He presented the glass to me with a flourish and clinked it with his own.

'To a great launch of a great website,' he said.

'Thanks, though it's far from great. There must be a million improvements we still need to make.'

'Trust me, it's terrific. In fact, I'm thinking of making it the theme for next year's calendar.'

'But you just came out with this year's calendar!'

'Forward planning never hurt.'

'Sounds good,' I said, 'as long as you don't put swimsuits on every page.'

'No, I was thinking more like every other page.'

Jaggu looked puzzled as I burst out laughing.

'Cake site—swimsuits? I don't get it.'

I left Sam to explain his version of Advertising 101, and moved on down the hall, looking this way and that.

Where was he?

Up in the distance, in a corner by the window, I spotted Rana talking to Aman, or rather, if I knew him, Rana mocking Aman.

'Hi guys, is this men only or can I join in?' I called.

'Minal! Long time no see,' Aman smiled, looking relieved.

'So are you going to have Bombay up by New Year?' Rana said by way of greeting.

'In your dreams.'

'It does seem a bit unrealistic,' Aman agreed.

'Not at all. Your problem is you don't set your sights high enough. Now if it were me . . .'

'If it were you, you'd shut up, since you don't have enough stock to sell till February anyway,' I said.

'But if I did . . .'

I turned pointedly towards Aman.

'What's the latest on your cereal bar figures?'

'Not good. I think we'll have to rationalize some of the products next year.'

'You should keep the banana flavour; it has potential,' Rana said.

'You really think so?'

'Though your advertising could use a facelift.'

'Like what?'

'A Caribbean beach with banana trees,' Rana suggested.

'Hmmm . . . I don't know if we'll have enough in the budget for an overseas shoot . . .'

He stopped as Rana began to snicker.

'He was just kidding,' I explained.

'Man, you're *dumb*,' Rana chortled. 'I think it's the product manager that needs rationalizing.'

Aman smiled sheepishly and waved to a group of trainees by the bar.

'Er, well, see you guys around then,' he said and made good his escape.

I rounded on Rana.

'You're pathetic,' I said.

'He's a moron.'

'How's your wife?'

'Mom was wondering if you'd found anyone yet.'

'She'll be the first to know, I'm sure.'

'I hear that neighbour of yours is now a famous VJ?'

'He's doing okay,' I said, thinking back to the last Post-it I'd received in the mail. 'We did it!' it had said simply, with a recklessness and enthusiasm that still made me smile.

'You should have hooked up with him instead of Fat Boy,' Rana said.

'I'll make sure I check with you next time,' I smiled sweetly.

'Oho. Methinks you've got someone up your sleeve.'

'Several.'

It wasn't entirely untrue; I'd just received a fresh letter from Mom with a whole new short-list of tall suitors.

'Who?'

'None of your business.'

'I'm not so sure about that,' he drawled.

'What do you mean?'

'Nothing. So where's your agency?'

'I just got here. And they're *your* agency too.'

'Unfortunately.'

I stole a quick look around the room.

'Don't worry,' Rana drawled. 'They'll be here.'

'See you, Rana,' I said, and hurried over to join Max, who stood at one end of the room, ringing his bell and adjusting his beard.

'I didn't know Santa drank,' I said, as he grabbed a glass from a passing waiter and took a long swig.

'This one does.'

'How long are you planning to keep that outfit on anyway?'

'Just till the cake is wheeled in, thank God. I hope you're planning to make it for the branch party tomorrow?'

'I wouldn't miss it for the world.'

He shook his beard sadly. 'I never should have let you go.'

'And what about the website?' I laughed.

'You'd better start turning in some profits soon, young lady!'

'I'm trying my best. You wouldn't have happened to see the ad agency here, would you?'

'Don't know, I think I saw that crazy woman somewhere . . .' Max said, looking around.

I noticed the laughter around us had died down to a murmur, and the music was dying down. Somewhere in the distance the crowd thinned and drew back and, in the middle, Vik was clinking a spoon on a glass, looking extremely dashing in a black suit and gold tie.

'Sorry to break up the festivities, folks, but I promise this will only take a moment!' he said.

I moved forward to listen.

'First of all, I'd like to thank everyone for being here tonight. Radha, I still can't believe how you managed to get everyone in on time and in costume too! And the tree and the gifts and the punch . . . everyone, let's hear it for Radha and the rest of the organizers!'

Everyone clapped heartily. Vik waited for the applause to die down before he continued with a grin, 'of course the prize for the most creative costume goes, as it should, to the creative head of our agency, Ms Lolita De!'

I turned quickly, following his gaze, and goggled as Lolita pranced demurely forward, with antlers on her head, a red bulb on her nose and red fur-lined boots on her feet.

'Lolita, Tanmay, a big thanks to you both and your team for all the hard work you put in around the year,' Vik said. 'You're a great team, and there's no way we could have made this year happen without you!'

This time the applause lasted a full two minutes, and I looked carefully round the cluster of beaming, glowing agency faces in the far right corner.

Where *was* he?

'Speaking of this year's achievements . . .' Vik continued.

'Hi Minal,' a voice right behind my shoulder made me jump.

'So there you are,' I hissed.

'Got stuck in traffic.'

'You're late.'

'And that's my fault? I'm coming straight from the office, and I'm heading right back after this is over.'

'I hope you don't expect me to feel sorry for you?'

'God forbid,' he grinned. 'Anyway, I wanted to show you this . . .'

'Shhh,' I hissed. 'Pay attention.'

'But . . .'

'Yogi!'

He turned to face Vik who was running through the year's achievements.

'. . . It's been a great year . . . two new juice launches . . . looking into the feasibility of a new line of frozen products . . . higher profitability in the snacks business . . . in cakes, we've picked up five market-share points, and for the first time in five years, we've dislodged Gourmet International from the number one position!' he boomed.

A loud cheer went round the room.

Rana swelled and bowed a few feet away.

'Could anything be more disgusting?' Yogi grimaced.

'I've seen worse.'

'*You* should be getting the credit.'

'Hush.'

Vik was continuing, '. . . successful launch of a new, path-breaking website . . .'

'Satisfied?'

Yogi raised his glass in quiet salute.

I eyed the pink liquid suspiciously.

'What's that stuff you're drinking?"

'Dunno. But the barman assured me everything was strictly alcoholic.'

I shook my head and turned back to Vik and his speech.

He progressed through the new products and milestones, weaving in anecdotes and humour and numerous toasts, and I could see why he was jubilant. It had been a fantastic year.

He brought his speech to a rousing end, and as the last of the applause died down he plucked a bottle of champagne from a nearby waiter, shook it like a rattle, and popped it recklessly open.

The cork shot across the room like a comet and millions of bubbles gurgled out from the depths of the green and gold bottle, twinkling and frothing ecstatically to the floor after years of confinement. A loud cheer went up, and Vik poured the golden liquid into tall, slender glasses.

'To the best marketing team in the world!' he announced and glugged down half his glass.

'To the best Christmas party ever!' he proclaimed and finished the rest.

'He's drunk,' Yogi said.

'No, he's just happy. And you're one to talk!'

'But I'm on my best behaviour!'

Except his arm was creeping round my waist.

'Hey,' I squirmed.

'What, scared?'

I saw Radha moving up to occupy centre stage now, resplendent in a red and gold Kanjeevaram that I was sure had been procured just for the occasion.

'Shhh,' I said. 'Listen.'

'Gather around everyone, it's cake time!' Radha called.

The overhead lights faded out completely, leaving the room dark and glowing. As I watched, a blaze of candlelight began to move out from the far left corner of the room, its reflection streaking across the dark roof like a fireworks display. Everyone gasped and, as it got nearer and nearer, I saw through a gap in the row of dark heads in front of me what must have been the most beautiful Christmas cake in the world.

A few feet long and a couple of feet across, it was a multi-kilo sculpture in chocolate and dreams. At one end stood a miniature replica of the IF office, proud and precise as an architect's model, constructed completely from chocolate wafers and icing. A path of chocolate bricks led all the way up the length of the cake to the office building, and was flanked on both sides by candy-studded Christmas trees, grass of green icing, flowerbeds of sprinkles and hundreds of fiery red candles. And in the middle of the chocolate brick road, pulled by chocolate reindeer, a six-inch-high porcelain sleigh, overflowing with miniature gifts and a grinning porcelain Santa.

'Minal! Yogi! That new franchisee of yours has outdone himself,' Vik called, walking up to join us.

'This was done by Jindal Enterprises?' I asked, astonished.

'Well, I *was* the one who designed it. I'm thinking of copyrighting it and putting it out as Vik's Christmas Cake next year,' Vik said.

'As long as you remember our fifteen per cent agency commission,' Yogi grinned.

'You never forget your commission, do you,' Vik laughed. 'But seriously Yogi, we couldn't have done all this without you. Great job.'

He raised his glass, and I joined in. Yogi coloured and mumbled something about teamwork.

'So, are we all just going to stand around admiring the cake, or is someone going to cut it?' someone complained. It was Max.

'Minal will cut it,' Vik announced grandly.

He *was* drunk. I laughed, embarrassed, as everyone clapped.

'Go ahead.' He held out a massive knife with a big red bow at one end.

'You have to be kidding, Vik.'

'No, I'm serious. After all, it *is* your cake.'

'But you said it was yours?'

I looked helplessly at Yogi.

'It *is* your website,' Yogi winked, totally uncooperative.

'Here,' Vik thrust the knife into my hand and propelled me forward.

'I'm not really sure about this . . .' I began.

'Come on, Minal,' Radha called from the table, and everyone stood back to make way for me.

'I'm not very good at this sort of thing.'

'That's okay, you'll do fine.'

I surveyed the glowing chocolate path and the beautiful flower beds. They were even more breathtaking up close.

'It's so beautiful; I don't think I can bring myself to . . .'

'*Cut-the-God-damn-cake*!' Max roared.

I closed my eyes, took a deep breath, and drove the knife clean through the soft, spongy layers. A drop of hot wax fell on my hand.

'Oh no, the candles! I forgot the candles!'

Max groaned.

'Will someone please help her out?' he called. 'A one and a two and a . . . *threeeee*!'

Everyone gathered round the table and released one big collective whoosh. The flames went out, the lights came on and before I knew it, everyone was clapping and cheering and rubbing cake into each other's faces.

'Don't you just love the food business?' Yogi said, as I wiped bits of cake off my eyes and licked my fingers.

I laughed and pushed a fat slice in his mouth.

The psychedelic lights and smoke machine came on across the hall on the dance floor, and the DJ cued the opening bars of Pink's party album.

'Shall we?' Yogi grinned, a reckless gleam in his eye.

'I don't know; it's the office crowd . . .' I looked around self-consciously.

'They're all family,' he said.

Family? Out of the corner of my eye, I could see Rana watching us with great interest.

Off in the corner I thought I saw Jaggu give me two thumbs up. I caught Vik's eye; he was grinning, raising his glass.

Family.

'Let's get this party started,' I laughed, and swung Yogi out onto the dance floor.

ALSO IN PENGUIN BY SWATI KAUSHAL

A GIRL LIKE ME

'Ani. I say the name over in my head. Funny, how I've resisted it all these years, how I like it now . . . My abbreviated Indian name, for my abbreviated Indian self.'

Recently transplanted from the quiet, green suburbs of Minnesota to the bustling concrete jungle that is Gurgaon, sixteen-year-old Anisha Rai is determined *not* to take to the new place she must call home. While her irrepressible mom, Isha, thrives on the crazy juggling between a hotshot job and their new home, Annie—desperately clutching on to memories of her father whom she lost three years ago—plods through each day with as little enthusiasm as she can.

But it's not going to work, is it? Not when she's discovered that her goofy childhood friend Keds has transformed into quite a dude and still remembers their first kiss; that she's been severely infected by her quirky classmates' zest for everything fun despite utmost resistance; that the H-O-T-T college-going theatre enthusiast Kunal wants to teach her a *lot* more than drama . . . And when her deceptively unassuming neighbours reveal hidden agendas, Annie's life suddenly becomes hotter to handle than she could ever have imagined.

Deftly weaving through home and school and the secret places in Annie's world, *A Girl Like Me* is an unforgettable story, crackling at every turn with the heartbreak and promise—and the breathless exuberance—of teenage life.

Fiction
Rs 250
www.penguinbooksindia.com

READ MORE IN PENGUIN

YOU ARE HERE

Meenakshi Reddy Madhavan

'The trouble with my life is that it's like a bra strap when you put your bra on wrong . . .'

At twenty-five, life's innumerable entanglements are getting to Arshi.

Her blonde American step-mom's trying too hard (she's taken to welcoming guests with a traditional aarti). The gorgeous guy who has Arshi all flushed and dreamy doesn't seem to be trying at all (he's the Ice Prince who thaws at his own convenience). Her best friend Deeksha's going to be *married* in a few months (Arshi's still in the process of finding the correct labels for the men in her life). And, her otherwise unruffled, cocktail-concocting flatmate Topsy's getting testier by the day because her conservative family will never approve of the darling guy she's in love with. What's more, there's a cheating ex-boyfriend, a weepy neighbour *and* a heinous boss who need to be told where to get off.

Her head spinning wildly with the sheer gravity of her life's quandaries, Arshi realizes what she needs most now (besides a barrelful of alcohol and some serious postcoital cuddling) are just a few epiphanies of the right kind . . .

Saucy, wise and audaciously candid, *You Are Here* introduces a bold and irresistible new voice.

READ MORE IN PENGUIN

BABYJI

Abha Dawesar

A sexy, subversive novel about a schoolgirl and her quest to conquer love and life

'Anamika Sharma is the kind of girl you always hated: she gets perfect grades and, as head prefect of her school in Delhi, has vast authority over her classmates. But Anamika's extracurricular activities are far from exemplary: she is at the center of a love triangle between a lower-caste house servant and an educated, older divorcee. On top of that, she begins serious flirtations with the most popular girl in school, the father of her best friend and the local bad boy. Anamika's amorous indiscretions provide a colorful backdrop to her questions about morality, gender roles and social rank in modern India, resulting in a tantalizing and sophisticated coming-of-age story'

—*Newsweek*

'What you'll love: Fervid scenes of sexual discovery and the fevered vagaries of Anamika's adolescent mind shimmer in unabashed detail'

—*The Washington Post*

'An impressive balance between moral inquiry and decadent pleasure'

—*Publishers Weekly*

READ MORE IN PENGUIN

WHAT WOULD YOU DO TO SAVE THE WORLD?

CONFESSIONS OF A WOULD-HAVE-BEEN-BEAUTY QUEEN

Ira Trivedi

Riya has always had a secret ambition—winning the coveted Miss Indian Beauty crown.

It's Riya's chance to turn fantasy into reality. The Miss Indian Beauty contest could well be her ticket to instant fame and success. After all, she's good-looking, intelligent, confident and, most importantly, tall—how difficult could it be? But Riya is in for a dose of reality, as she soon finds herself in the company of twenty-two gorgeous girls, under house arrest in a five-star hotel in Mumbai for a rigorous training session that will test them all to their limits.

With each girl's eyes set on the crown, the mood is emotionally charged and the atmosphere intense, exhilarating, vicious and explosive all at once. *What Would You Do to Save the World?* is a delightfully entertaining first novel which reveals the dust behind the diamonds, the tears behind the plastic smiles, and dishes the dirt on what really goes on behind the scenes of a beauty pageant.